I0610080

Franz Ahn, Peter Henn

Ahn's Manual of Latin Prose Composition

Franz Ahn, Peter Henn

Ahn's Manual of Latin Prose Composition

ISBN/EAN: 9783337371180

Printed in Europe, USA, Canada, Australia, Japan

Cover: Foto ©Andreas Hilbeck / pixelio.de

More available books at **www.hansebooks.com**

Steiger's Latin Series

AHN'S

MANUAL OF LATIN PROSE COMPOSITION.

With References to

AHN'S COMPLETE LATIN SYNTAX.

BY

Dr. P. HENN.

NEW YORK:

E. STEIGER & CO.

1883.

PREFACE.

In preparing the present volume it has been the author's aim to furnish a **Complete Course of Exercises** illustrative of all the important rules and principles of Latin Syntax. In order to make the pupil acquainted with the purest classical language, the words and sentences are taken chiefly from the writings of CAESAR and CICERO, the written exercises being introduced by model sentences *to be learned by heart*, and accompanied with references to AHN-HENN'S ***Complete Latin Syntax.*** The **Vocabulary** will be found to contain every word and idiom in the text.

TABLE OF CONTENTS.

PART I. — SYNTAXIS CONVENIENTIAE.

1. *Subject and Predicate* .... Page 1
2. *Copulative Verbs* 1
3. *Two or more Subjects* 2
4. *Attribute and Apposition* 3
5. *Appositive and Attributive Adjectives* 3
6. *Agreement of Pronouns* 4

PART II. — CONSTRUCTION OF CASES.

7. *Subjective and Objective Genitive* 5
8. 9. *Genitive of Quality* 5
10. 11. *Partitive Genitive* 6
12. *Genitive with Adjectives and Participles* 8
13. *Genitive with Verbs of Reminding* 8
14. *Genitive with Verbs of Valuing* 9
15. *Genitive with Verbs of Accusing* 10
16. *Genitive with* esse & fiĕrī 10
17. *Genitive with Impersonals* 11
18. *Genitive with* intĕrest 12
19. *Accusative with Transitives, Intransitives and Compounds* 12
20. *Accusative with Impersonals; in Exclamations* 13
21. *Accusative with Verbs of Naming* 14
22. *Accusative with Verbs of Teaching* 14
23. *Accusative with Verbs of Asking* 15
24. *Dative. Indirect Object. With Intransitives* 16
25. *Dative with Adjectives* 16
26. *Ethical Dative. Dative of Advantage* 17
27. *Dative or Accusative. With Compounds* 18
28. *Dative of Possession. With Verbs of Giving and Putting* 18
29. *Dative with Gerund. Two Datives* 19
30. 31. *Ablative of Cause* 20
32. *Ablative of Means or Instrument* 21
33. *Ablative of Limitation* 22

34. *Ablative of Manner* .... Page 22
35. *Ablative of Measure and Comparison* 23
36. *Ablative of Price* 24
37. *Ablative of Separation* 24
38. *Ablative of Plenty and Want* 25
39. *Ablative with* opus est 26
40. *Ablative with Adjectives and Deponents* 27
41–43. *Uses of Prepositions. — Accusative* 27
44. 45. *Prepositions with the Ablative* 29
46. 47. *Prepositions with the Accusative and Ablative* 31
48. *Place. Names of Towns* 32
49. *Apposition with Names of Towns.* domus *and* rus ... 33
50. *Ablative and Accusative of Place* 33
51. *Extent of Space* 34
52. *Time when? how long?* 35
53. *Distance of Time* 35
54. *Special Uses of Adjectives* 36
55. *Special Uses of Personal and Demonstrative Pronouns* 37
56. *Special Uses of Determinative Pronouns* 37
57. *Special Uses of Relative Pronouns* 38
58. *Special Uses of Interrogative and Indefinite Pronouns* 39

PART III. — SYNTAX OF THE VERB.

59. *Tenses. Present and Perfect* 40
60. *Imperfect, Pluperfect, Future. Periphrastic Conjugation* 40
61. *Tenses of the Indicative* 41
62. *Sequence of Tenses* 42
63. *Indicative Mood* 43
64. *Subjunctive Mood* 44
65. *Consecutive Conjunctions* 44
66. *Final Conjunctions* 45
67. *Verbs of Hindering and Fearing* 46
68. *Subjunctive after* quō, quīn 47
69. *Temporal Conjunctions* 47
70. *Causal Conjunctions* 48
71. *Conditional Sentences* 49
72. *Concessive Conjunctions* 50
73. *Comparative Conjunctions* 50
74. 75. *Relative Clauses with the Subjunctive* 51
76. *Imperative* 53
77. *Infinitive* 53

78. 79. *Accusative with the Infinitive (Subject)* .... Page 54
80. *Accusative with the Infinitive (Object)* 56
81. *Infinitives after Verbs of Declaring and Perceiving* .. 56
82. *Accusative with the Infinitive after Verbs of Will and Desire* 57
83. *Nominative with Infinitive* 58
84. *Interrogative Sentences (Simple Questions)* 59
85. *Interrogative Sentences (Disjunctive Questions)* 60
86. 87. *Indirect Questions* 60
88. 89. Oratĭo recta 62
90. Oratĭo oblīqua 63
91. Oratĭo oblīqua *into* Oratĭo recta 64
92. Oratĭo recta *into* Oratĭo oblīqua 65
93. *Reflexive and Reciprocal Pronouns* 67
94–96. *Participial Sentences* 67
97. 98. *Ablative Absolute* 70
99. *Ablative Absolute with Nouns* 71
100. *Genitive of Gerunds and Gerundives* 72
101. *Dative and Accusative of Gerunds and Gerundives* .. 73
102. 103. *Ablative of Gerunds and Gerundives* 74
104. *Passive Periphrastic Conjugation. Gerundive as Predicate Accusative* 76
105. *Supines* 76
106. *Copulative Conjunctions* 77
107. *Disjunctive Conjunctions* 78
108. *Adversative Conjunctions* 79
109. *Causal and Illative Conjunctions* 79
110. *Copulative Correspondents* 80
111. *Disjunctive Correspondents* 81

Vocabulary: *English and Latin* 83

LATIN PROSE COMPOSITION.

PART I. — SYNTAXIS CONVENIENTIAE.

Subject. Predicate.

SYNTAX *1—9**).

Ego valĕo, si vos valētis. Columbae sunt timĭdae. Vita rustĭca parsimonĭae magistra est. Athēnae omnĭum artĭum domicilĭum fŭērunt. Paupertas mihi onus visum est.

1. Time past never returns. Familiar[1] things easily slip[2] from[3] memory. I am nearest to myself. Sleep is the image of death. True friendships are eternal. Men neither wonder at, nor inquire into[4], the reasons of those things which they always see. Conscience is the most severe judge of our actions. Laws are the best protectors[5] of citizens. Rome was the conqueror[6] of all the nations of Italy. Experience is the best teacher; time, too, is the teacher of many things. Fear is a bad protector[7]. The moon is a constant[8] attendant[9] of our earth. The lion is the king of quadrupeds, the eagle is the king of birds. Want[10] is the bitterest[11] enemy[12] of virtue. The elephant is the largest of land animals.

[1]ūsĭtātŭs, -ă, -ŭm [2]ēlābŏr, -ī [3]ē, ex [4]rĕquīrŏ, -ĕrĕ [5]patrōnŭs, -ī; patrōnă, -ae [6]victŏr, -ōrĭs; victrix, -īcĭs [7]custōs, -ōdĭs [8]perpĕtŭŭs, -ă, -ŭm [9]sătellĕs, -ĭtĭs [10]ĭnŏpĭă, -ae [11]ācĕr, -rĭs, -rĕ [12]adversārĭŭs, -ī; adversārĭă, -ae

Copulative Verbs.

SYNTAX *10.*

Piĕtas erga parentes jure summa virtus habētur. Doctus nemo sine littĕris exsistit. Nemo mortālis usque ad mortem beātus mansit. Homĭnes cupiditāte et avaritĭa caeci fiunt. Vetĕres Romāni latrōnes et semibarbāri putabantur.

2. The planet Venus[1] is called the morning star when it precedes[2] the sun, but the evening star when it follows[3] the

*) These references are to paragraphs of ***AHN-HENN'S Complete Latin Syntax.***

sun[4]. The motions[5] of the stars are wonderful, especially of those which are called wandering stars[4]. Not in the same way[6] do all become good and wise. The sun seems smaller to us than it is. Some dreams turn out true. Charles the Fifth was crowned emperor on his birthday[7]. Comets were formerly believed to be[4] the precursors[8] of great calamities. Camillus who had delivered Rome from[9] the Gauls, was called a second[10] Romulus. Dareus, son of Hystaspes, was made king of the Persians by the neighing[6] of (his) horse. The camel is rightly considered[11] the most useful animal of the East. No one is born rich, and no one dies so[12] poor as[12] he was born. Those are regarded[13] as good citizens who for the safety of their country avoid no danger.

[1]stella Venĕris [2]antĕgrĕdĭŏr, -ī [3]subsĕquŏr, -ī [4]not to be translated [5]mōtŭs, -ūs [6]Abl. without Prepos. [7]dies natālis, Abl. [8]praenuntĭŭs, -ī [9]ā, ăb [10]altĕr [11]jūdĭcō, -ārĕ [12]tăm..quăm [13]existĭmō, -ārĕ

Two or more Subjects.

SYNTAX *11—16.*

Beneficĭum et gratĭa homĭnes inter se conjungunt. Senātus popŭlusque Romānus intellĕgit bello opus esse. Cingetorĭgi principātus atque imperĭum tradĭtum est. Corinthus et Carthāgo a Romānis dirŭtae sunt. Tu et pater in convīvis erātis.

3. Without government[1] neither any house nor state nor nation nor the human race[2] at large[3] can stand. The wall and the gate of the city had been struck[4] by lightning[5]. Prosperity, honors, victories are accidental things[6]. You and your brother wrote letters to me. My father, my brother and I have borne arms for our country. Pride and folly are often united[7]. If you and your brother shall be at home, my father and I will also[8] come. The beginning and the end are often very different. Pain, fear, labor, old age are troublesome to most[9] men. Neither my father nor I have read this book. But[10] if you and your father have not read it[6], who has read it[6]? The walls and gates of the captured city were destroyed by the enemies. My friend's father and mother died within[11] a few days.

[1]impĕrĭŭm, -ī [2]homĭnum gĕnŭs, -ĕrĭs [3]ūnĭversŭs, -ă, -ŭm [4]tangō, -ĕrĕ [5]Abl. without Prepos. [6]not to be translated [7]conjungō, -ĕrĕ [8]ĕ.jăm [9]plērīquĕ [10]ăt [11]intrā

Attribute and Apposition.

Syntax *17—20.*

Christiāni colunt verum Deum, omnipotentem creatōrem caeli et terrae. Romāni cum Tigrāne, Armeniōrum rege, grave bellum gessĕrunt. Aegyptĭi canem et felem ut deos colunt. Tullĭae moriendum fuit, quia homo nata erat. Hercŭles juvĕnis leōnem interfĕcit.

4. Manlius slew[1] his own son, although victorious, because he had fought contrary to[2] orders[3]. Pythagoras recommended to all frugality, the mother[4] of all virtues. Entire[5] dominion[6] over the sea[7] was given to Neptune, one of the two brothers of Jupiter. Ennius endured[8] two burdens which are considered the greatest, poverty and old age. Two very powerful cities, Carthage and Numantia, were destroyed by the same Scipio. Mummius, a Roman general, destroyed Corinth, the wealthiest city of Greece. The augur Attius Navius, when a boy, on account of[9] poverty was a keeper[10] of swine. In our boyhood we read the lives of Nepos. The use of gold and silver as[11] the material[12] of all crimes was abolished[13] by Lycurgus.

[1]occīdō, -ĕrĕ [2]contrā [3]impĕrĭŭm, -ī [4]gĕnĕtrix, -īcĭs [5]omnĭs, -ĕ [6]regnŭm, -ī [7]mărĭtĭmŭs, -ă, -ŭm [8]fĕrō, ferrĕ [9]propter [10]pascō, -ĕrĕ, *to be a keeper of* [11]tanquăm [12]mătĕrĭēs, -ēī [13]tollō, -ĕrĕ

Appositive and Attributive Adjectives.

Syntax *21. 22.*

Themistŏcles totum se dedĭdit reipublĭcae. Argonautae primi in Pontum Euxīnum intravĕrunt. Invĭdi virtūtem et bonum aliēnum odĕrunt. Camillus absens dictātor dictus est. Augustus senatōrum numĕrum ad modum pristĭnum et splendōrem redēgit.

5. The elephant has a big head, long ears, thick legs, two long tusks[1], a thin tail. His whole body is huge[2], but his eyes are small and his throat[3] is narrow; he is a very sagacious[4] animal. Achilles slew Hector[5], the son of king Priam (and) the bravest of the Trojans. Aeneas was the only one that escaped[6] the dangers of war. Few receive death in cheerful mood[7]. Spain was the last of the provinces that was subjugated[8]. Prudence is not to be expected[9] from a man who is never sober[10]. Death is shameful in flight, glorious in victory. I received many letters from my brother all written with great care. All lands and all seas submit[11] to the service[12] of men.

[1]dens, -tĭs [2]ingens, -tĭs [3]faucēs, -ĭŭm [4]prūdens, -tĭs [5]Hectŏr, -ŏrĭs, Acc. Hectŏra [6]effŭgĭō, -ĕrĕ [7]hĭlărĭs, -ĕ, *in cheerful mood* [8]perdŏmō, -ārĕ [9]postŭlandŭs, -ă, -ŭm [10]sobrĭŭs, -ă, -ŭm, *who is*, not to be translated [11]pārĕō, -ērĕ [12]ūtĭlĭtās, -ātĭs

Agreement of Pronouns.

SYNTAX *23—25.*

Est Deus, qui omnem hunc mundum regit. Arbŏres serit agricŏla, quarum fructus ipse numquam adspiciet. Diligentĭa in omnĭbus rebus plurĭmum valet: hanc praecipŭe colămus, hanc semper adhibeămus. Hoc illis narro, qui me non intellĕgunt. Lacedaemonĭi Agin regem, quod numquam antĕa apud eos accidĕrat, necavĕrunt.

6. We do not call him rich whose fortunes are increasing[1], but him whose mind is satisfied with little[2]. Firm and steady friends ought to be chosen[3], of which kind there is a great scarcity. No animal which has blood can be without a heart. There is great power[4] in virtues; arouse[5] them, if perchance they sleep. Socrates, whose wisdom we admire, was unjustly condemned to death[6] by the Athenians. Cornelia, mother of the Gracchi, showing her children, said: These are my jewels. There is a river in Germany which is called the Rhine. All boys and girls who had been taken prisoners[7] by the Romans in Spain were restored[8] to their families[9] by the goodness[10] of Scipio. Near[11] the village which is called Cannae both consuls were defeated by Hannibal. All ancient nations formerly[12] obeyed[13] kings, a kind of government[14] which was at first conferred[15] on[16] the justest and wisest men.

[1]augĕŏr, -ērī [2]paucae res; Abl. without Prep. [3]ēlĭgendŭs, -ă, -ŭm, *ought to be chosen* [4]vīs [5]excĭtō, -ārĕ [6]căpĭtĭs damnārĕ, *to condemn to death* [7]căpĭō, -ĕrĕ, *to take prisoner* [8]restĭtŭō, -ĕrĕ [9]sŭī, -ōrŭm, *their families* [10]sanctĭtās, -ātĭs [11]ăpŭd [12]quondăm [13]pārĕō, -ērĕ (with Dat.) [14]impĕrĭŭm, -ī [15]dēfĕrō, -rĕ [16]ăd

PART II. — CONSTRUCTION OF CASES.

Subjective and Objective Genitive.

SYNTAX *26—29.*

Cupidĭtas illa honōris quam dura est domĭna! Jucunda est memorĭa praeteritōrum malōrum. Vestra magis hoc causa volēbam quam mea. Bestĭae homĭnum gratĭa generātae sunt. Instar montis equus.

7. The better part of us is immortal. Men have[1] a great desire for those things which are forbidden. The best remedy for anger is delay. True virtue desires no recompense for labors and dangers. Not the fear of punishment but the love of virtue ought[2] to restrain[3] us from[4] doing wrong[5]. How many has the fear of divine punishment[6] recalled from crime! Follow virtue for its own sake! Rewards are usually offered not for gain's[7] but for honor's sake. The morals[8] of the good become worse[9] by the intercourse[10] with the bad. Do for the sake of your friends the same[11] that you are accustomed[12] to do for your own sake. Love of country is born[13] in man. My[14] mind is part of me. Sleep is a refuge from all toils and cares[15]. The universe[16] was made for the sake of men. Some Romans had houses like cities.

[1]Translate: *to men is* [2]dēbĕō, -ērĕ [3]prŏhĭbĕō, -ērĕ [4]ā, ăb [5]injūrĭă, -ae *(doing wrong)* [6]supplĭcĭŭm, -ī [7]lucrŭm, -ī [8]mōrēs, -ŭm [9]dētĕrĭŏr, -ŭs [10]consuētūdŏ, -ĭnĭs (Abl. without Prep.) [11]ĕădĕm (Neut. Plur.) [12]sŏlĕō, -ērĕ [13]innātŭs, -ă, -ŭm [14]not to be translated [15]sollĭcĭtūdŏ, -ĭnĭs [16]mundŭs, -ī

Genitive of Quality.

SYNTAX *30.*

Tarquinius fratrem habŭit Aruntem, mitis ingenĭi juvĕnem. Claudĭus somni brevissĭmi erat. Hamilcar secum in Hispanĭam duxit filĭum Hannibălem, novem annōrum.

8. The sea produces animals of extraordinary size. Nobody who is of sound mind will deny that[1] there is a God. Titus was a man of such[2] easy access[3] and liberality that[4] he never[5] denied a thing[6] to any one[6]. The Latins carried into the Capitol a golden crown of small weight. The fleet of the enemy[7] consisted[8] of 89 ships. Julius Cæsar adjusted the year according[9] to the sun so that it should consist[8] of 365 days. A general of the greatest valor does not always lead his army to victory. Cingetorix who had been called king and friend by the Romans, was (a man) of the highest authority among the Gauls. The Romans sent Fabricius, a man of approved integrity, to Pyrrhus. Hannibal, (when) a boy of nine years, promised his father eternal hatred against the Romans. The Athenians had a fleet of 300 sail[10].

[1]Acc. w. Infin. say: *to be a God* [2]tantŭs, -ă, -ŭm [3]făcĭlĭtās, -ātĭs, *easy access* [4]ŭt, with Subjunct. [5]*never..to anyone*, nullus [6]quidquam [7]Plur. [8]Say: *was of* [9]ăd [10]nāvĭs, -

Iphicrātes fuit bonus civis fidēque magna. Alcibiădes erat ea sagacitāte, ut decĭpi non posset. Athenienses Phociōnem, virum insigni probitāte, capĭtis damnavērunt.

9. The name of Hannibal was in[1] great honor among[2] all. Cæsar was of lofty stature, fair complexion, black eyes and good[3] health. Cæsar sent to Ariovistus Valerius, a young man of the highest[4] valor and of amiable manners[5]. Ibises are tall birds with stiff legs, with horny and projecting bills; they kill and devour a great quantity[6] of snakes. The ancient Germans were of immense size of body and of incredible bravery and exercise in arms. Those who have a good conscience are usually[7] of a tranquil mind. We willingly keep company with those who are of a cheerful mind. Not all pupils have[8] great talent. In California there are trees of enormous size and of very great age.

[1]*of great honor* [2]ăpŭd [3]prospĕr, -ă, -ŭm [4]summŭs, -ă, -ŭm [5]hūmānĭtās, -ātĭs, *amiable manners* [6]vīs [7]*are usually*, say: *use to be* (sŏlĕō, -ērĕ) [8]*are of*

Partitive Genitive.

Syntax *31—34.*

Magna vis auri Romam allāta est. Quis vestrum hoc intellexit? Trajānus solus omnĭum intra urbem sepultus est. Alexander seniōres milĭtum in patrĭam remĭsit. Catilīna ingentem numĕrum perditōrum homĭnum collegĕrat.

10. Of the Greek orators the most distinguished[1] are those who were at Athens[2], but of these Demosthenes was unquestionably[3] the chief. In the army of Alexander there were 32,000 foot-soldiers, 4000 horse and 182 ships. The most excellent kings of the Persians were Cyrus and Dareus, the son of Hystaspes; of these the former[4] fell in battle in the land[5] of the Massagetae, Dareus died[6] of old age[7]. In the provinces of the Roman empire there was a great number of Roman citizens. The greatest of benefits are those[8] which we receive from our parents. The city (of) Syracuse is the largest and most beautiful of the Greek cities. Of all the Greeks the bravest were the Lacedaemonians. Rome was taken by the Gauls, and the conquered paid[9] a great amount[10] of gold and silver. Only a few of the scholars are lazy.

[1]praestans, -tĭs [2]Abl. without Prep. [3]făcĭlĕ [4]prĭŏr [5]ăpŭd, *in the land of* [6]diem suprēmum obīre [7]Abl. without Prep. [8]not to be translated [9]pendō, -ĕrĕ [10]vīs

SYNTAX *35—38.*

Unus ex multis incolŭmis in patrĭam redĭit. Pythagŏras, cum in geometrĭa quiddam novi invenisset, Musis bovem immolasse dicĭtur. Armōrum erat affătim captōrum Carthagĭne.

11. There are many pleasures to which more or less[1] of trouble is commingled[2]. The change of sky and land gives much enjoyment[3]. There is this badness[4] in anger; it does not want[5] to be governed. There are[6] plenty of men who have nothing to do[7]. Among the greatest vices none is more frequent than that[8] of an ungrateful mind. Where in the world are we? Ships on[9] rivers bear less burden than on the sea. Sulla lost 124 of his men[10]. Which of all the orators was more eloquent than Demosthenes? Of the Persian kings the most prominent[11] have been Cyrus and Dareus, the son of Hystaspes, each of whom obtained[12] the throne[13] by merit[14]. Tarquin had two sons one of whom was like his father[15], the other was of a milder disposition[16]. In the minds of men there is something heavenly and divine.

[1]alĭquid, *more or less* [2]admiscĕō, -ērĕ [3]jŭcundĭtās, -ātĭs [4]mălŭm, -ī (say: *this of badness*) [5]vŏlō, vellĕ [6]Singular [7]nĕgōtĭŭm, -ī, *to do* [8]not to be translated [9]ĭn [10]sŭī, -ōrŭm [11]excellens, -tĭs [12]ădĭpiscŏr, -ī [13]regnŭm, -ī [14]virtūs, -ūtĭs, Abl. without Prep. [15]Dative [16]ingĕnĭŭm, -ī

Genitive with Adjectives and Participles.

SYNTAX *39. 40.*

Medicamĭnum salutarĭum plenissĭma est terra. Semper acceptōrum beneficiōrum memōres estōte. Omnis est natūra dilĭgens sui. Themistŏcles peritissĭmos belli navālis fecit Athenienses.

12. Human life is full of dangers. Men are often more desirous of riches than wisdom. Often a man, although he is endowed[1] with reason, seems powerless to control[2] his anger. Camels are very capable of enduring[3] thirst. Socrates feigned[4] himself ignorant of all things. Farmers are commonly ignorant of city[5] manners. Boys are not always fond enough of truth. The ancient Romans were very eager for glory. The eyes of owls are incapable of enduring[6] light. The soldiers of Sulla, mindful of former[7] plunder[8] and victory, longed for[9] civil war. Those who sail[10] in the same ship, share[11] the same risk. Men's mind is ignorant of destiny and future lot. Alexander was eager for glory and capable of enduring labor, but unable to control[2] his anger. Man alone (out) of so many kinds of living beings[12] is a partaker[13] of reason. Alexander, covered[14] with dust and perspiration, plunged[15] into the river.

[1]partĭceps, -ĭpis [2]impŏtens, -tis [3]pătiens, -tis [4]assĭmŭlō, -ārĕ [5]urbānŭs, -ă, -ŭm [6]impătiens, -tis [7]vĕtŭs, -ĕris [8]răpīnae, -ārŭm [9]exoptō, -ārĕ [10]Say: *are* [11]partĭceps [12]ănĭmans, -tis [13]partĭceps [14]plēnŭs, -ă, -ŭm [15]se prōjĭcĕrĕ (-iō)

Genitive with Verbs of *Reminding*.

SYNTAX *41.*

Vetĕris te amicitiae commonefacĭo. Non omnes possunt esse Scipiōnes, ut triumphos recordentur. Anĭmus memĭnit praeteritōrum, cernit praesentĭa, futūra praevĭdet. Alcibiădes lacrĭmans benevolentĭam civĭum suōrum accipiēbat, reminiscens pristĭni tempŏris acerbitātem.

13. Men sometimes forget things the most renowned[1]. I remember, nor shall I ever forget that night when[2] our house was destroyed[3] by fire[4]. Tiberius reminded the judges of the laws and their oath[5]. Men usually[6] forget benefits more readily[7] than insults. So strong[8] was the memory of

Hortensius, the orator, that he recollected all the words of his opponents[9]. Good citizens remember the benefits of their country. The leader of the Helvetii exhorted Cæsar to remember[10] both the former[11] disaster of the Roman people, and the ancient[12] valor of the Helvetii. The father reminded his son of his duty. That is a happy memory which forgets nothing but an injury received. Every day a slave reminded Dareus not to[13] forget the Greeks.

[1]praeclārŭs, -ă, -ŭm [2]cŭm [3]absūmō, -ĕrĕ [4]Abl. without Prep. [5]rĕlĭgĭō, -ōnis [6]Say: *are wont to*, sŏlĕō, -ēre [7]făcĭlĭŭs [8]tantŭs, -ă, -ŭm [9]adversārĭŭs, -ī [10]Say: *that he should remember;* ŭt with Subj. [11]vĕtŭs, -ĕris [12]pristĭnŭs, -ă, -ŭm [13]*not to forget;* say: *that he should not forget; that not*, nē, with Subj.

Genitive with Verbs of *Valuing*.

Syntax 49.

Commĭi regis auctorĭtas in Britannĭa magni habebātur. Divitĭae a me minĭmi putantur. Quanti ista civĭtas aestimanda est, ex qua boni sapientesque expelluntur! Hephaestiōnem Alexander plurĭmi fecit.

14. Virtue makes pleasure of very little account. My conscience is of more account to me than the talk[1] of all men. Homer was very highly valued by Alexander the Great. Gold and gems on account of[2] (their) scarceness and beauty have always been esteemed of more value than other metals which are more useful to men. Knowledge is certainly[3] to be highly valued, but we justly[4] esteem virtue of more value. To act with consideration[5] is worth more than to think wisely. My warning does not seem to have been of great account to you, nor do I wonder at it[6], for you thought nothing even[7] of what your father had told you. One eye-witness[8] is of more account than ten ear-witnesses[9]. No possession, no mass[10] of gold and silver is to be valued[11] more highly than virtue. Certain[12] philosophers have thought nothing of pain and pleasure.

[1]sermō, -ōnis [2]ŏb [3]sānē [4]jure [5]consīdĕrātē [6]*at it*, hoc [7]ĕtĭăm [8]testis oculātus [9](testis) aurītus [10]vīs [11]aestĭmandus [12]quīdam

Genitive with Verbs of *Accusing*.

SYNTAX *43*.

Miltiădes capĭtis absolūtus tanta pecunĭa multātus est, quantam solvĕre non potĕrat. Themistŏcles absens proditiōnis damnātus est. Caesar Cornelĭum Dolabellam repetundārum postulāvit. Piso incusāvit Germanĭcum luxus atque superbĭae.

15. The jury[1] condemned Socrates to death. So live that you can convict all calumniators[2] of falsehood. Even[3] a daring person we do not[3] wholly[4] acquit of fear. Cicero so eloquently defended Sextus Roscius (who was)[5] accused of parricide, that he was acquitted of that crime by the unanimous decision of the judges[6]. The judges were so inflamed[7] by the answer of Socrates that they condemned a most innocent man to death: many of the judges wished to acquit him of the capital charge[8] and mulct him in a (sum of) money[9]. During[10] civil wars the best citizens have often been accused of treachery, the innocent[11] have been condemned to death, the guilty[12] have been acquitted of many crimes. Claudius invited many of those whom he had condemned to death, to[13] a banquet on the following day[14].

[1]jūdĭcēs [2]mălĕdĭcŭs, -ī [3]nĕ. .quĭdĕm; the emphatic word, here *daring person*, comes between them [4]prorsŭs [5]not to be translated [6]omnĭum judĭcum sententĭis, *by the unanimous decision of the judges* [7]exardescō, -ĕrĕ [8]căpŭt, -ĭtis [9]pĕcūnĭă, -ae, *sum of money* [10]intĕr [11]insons, -tis [12]sons, -tis [13]ăd [14]Abl. without Prep.

Genitive with essĕ and fĭĕrī.

SYNTAX *44*.

Adulescentis est majōres natu verēri. Virōrum fortĭum est dolōrem aequo anĭmo pati. Insŭla Megarensĭum Atheniensĭum facta est. Nostrum est parentes amāre. Asĭa Romanōrum facta est.

16. It is the duty of children to reverence their parents, and of parents to love (their own)[1] children and to correct their[2] faults. It is the duty of a judge to assist[3] innocence. In the time[4] of Augustus almost the whole world[5] was in possession of the Romans. It is your duty to reverence your parents. It is the part of a sincere friend not to forsake a friend in adversity. The whole kingdom of the Persians came under

Alexander's dominion[6]. It is the duty of every[7] man to speak the truth. It is our duty to love our parents. Nothing is so characteristic[8] of a narrow and little mind as[8] to love riches. In the Gallic war[9], all things except the Capitol and the citadel were (in the possession)[10] of the enemy. Condemning is (the function)[10] of the judges, punishment that[10] of the law. Lycurgus wished that[11] the highest honors should belong not to the rich but to the old.

[1]Not to be translated [2]eōrum [3]subvĕnīō, -īrĕ, with the Dat. [4]Abl. Plur. without Prep. [5]orbis terrārum [6]Translate: *became Alexander's* [7]quīvis [8]Translate: *of so narrow and so little a mind as*, tăm..quăm [9]Abl. without Prep. [10]not to be translated [11]Translate: *the highest honors to be not of* &c.

Genitive with Impersonals.

Syntax 45.

Me piget stultitĭae. Pudĕat te neglegentĭae. Athenienses crudelitātis paenitŭit. Me malōrum civitātis morum taedet. Misĕros saepe taedet vitae. Me misĕret paupĕrum.

7. Diligent scholars will not be disgusted with even the greatest labor. He is a fool who is ashamed of his parents; but[1] virtuous[2] parents are justly ashamed of their wicked[3] sons. I am not only grieved but also ashamed of my folly. The wretched are often weary of life. This boy is neither ashamed nor tired of his indolence[4]. No one will repent of industry. These men are neither ashamed nor weary of their dishonor. A good citizen will never be sorry to undergo the greatest dangers for his country. After[5] Alexander had slain[6] (his) friend Clitus, he began to be sorry for the deed. An inconstant man very often repents of his first design[7]. You will never be sorry for having learned much[8], but if you let slip[9] the opportunity to learn[10], you will certainly hereafter[11] be sorry for this indolence. He who[12] is sorry for having sinned is almost innocent.

[1]ăt [2]prŏbŭs, -ă, -ŭm [3]imprŏbŭs, -ă, -ŭm [4]ignāvĭă, -ae [5]postquăm [6]trŭcīdō, -ārĕ, Perfect [7]consĭlĭŭm, -ī [8]multă, -ōrŭm [9]praetermittō, -ĕrĕ (*to let slip*) [10]ad discendum (*to learn*) [11]mox [12]qui (*he who*)

Genitive with intĕrest.

SYNTAX *46—48.*

Magni intĕrest mea cum amīco una esse. Atheniensīum plus interfuit, firma tecta in domiciliīs habēre quam Minervae signum ex ebŏre pulcherrīmum. Boni viri multum intĕrest, quid post mortem suam futūrum sit.

18. It very much[1] interests not only parents but also the country itself that[2] children should be well educated. It is the interest of all to do right. It makes no matter[3] how many books you have[4] but how good they are[5]. It concerns me nothing what ignorant[6] people may speak of[7] me. What matter is it how long[8] you have lived[4], unless you have lived[4] well? I am much concerned what other people think[4] of[7] me. The Spartan[9] state was much interested in the maintenance[10] of the laws of Lycurgus. It concerns the common safety very much that[11] there be two consuls in the state. It is the interest of all citizens to obey the laws. When we are thirsty, it makes no difference[12] whether[13] it be[4] wine or[14] water (we drink)[15], nor does it matter whether[13] it be[4] a golden cup or[14] a glass (one we use)[15], or[14] the hollow of the hand[16].

[1]permultum [2]Translate: *children to be well educated;* Acc. w. Inf. [3]non refert [4]Subjunct. [5]Translate: *how good (ones)* [6]impĕrītus, -a, -um [7]dē [8]quamdīu [9]Say: *of the Spartans* [10]Translate: *the laws to be maintained*, Acc. w. Inf. [11]Translate: *two consuls to be*, Acc. w. Inf. [12]nihil intĕrest [13]utrŭm [14]ăn [15]not to be translated [16]Say: *the hollow hand*

Accusative with Transitives, Intransitives and Compounds.

SYNTAX *49—53.*

Deus est, qui omnem hunc mundum regit. Panem et aquam natūra desidĕrat. Adeunda sunt pericŭla decŏris honestātisque causa. Convenīo cotidīe plurīmos amīcos. Piscis ipsum mare sapit. Vulgatīor fama est, Remum ludibrīo fratris novos transiluisse muros.

19. Themistocles did not escape[1] the envy of his fellow-citizens. We are wont to imitate those with whom we keep company[2]. The wives and the children of the Germans were accustomed to follow the army. Sulla who had formerly taken[3] the side of Marius, afterwards became his[4] most bitter enemy. Soldiers emulate the example of (their) leader. All men laugh at folly; all men grieve[5] at misery. Appius Claudius, the censor, brought[6] the Appian water into the city, and laid[7] the Appian way. Happy is he who has never thirsted for pleasures. He who loves his children, also[8] chastises them. In Africa many animals are found which thirst for blood. An upright and just man will not shudder[9] at death. Alexander the Great emulated Achilles chiefly[10] among[11] the Greek heroes. Death will pass by nobody. Hannibal led 90,000 foot-soldiers and 12,000 horse across the Ebro. A coward lives the life of a hare.

[1]effŭgiō, -ĕrĕ [2]versŏr, -āri, *to keep company* [3]sĕquŏr, -ī [4]ejus [5]dŏlĕō, -ērĕ [6]indūcō, -ĕrĕ [7]aedĭfĭcō, -āre [8]ĕtiăm [9]horrĕō, -ērĕ [10]maxĭmē [11]ĭn, w. Abl.

Accusative with Impersonals; in Exclamations.

SYNTAX *54—57.*

Irasci judĭcem non decet. Modestum esse decet juvĕnem. Aliēna me non decent. Quod patrem decet, idem filĭum saepe dedĕcet. O vim maxĭmam errōris! Id nobis onĕris, hominĭbus id aetātis (= ejus aetātis) imponĭtur.

20. It becomes an upright man to assist his country in every way[1]. It becomes a youth to be modest[2]. It becomes the wise[3] to live according[4] to nature. What becomes boys is often unbecoming to men. O fool (that thou art)[5] if thou fearest death at the time when[6] it thunders. O glorious day, when[7] I shall go[8] to[9] the assembly and company of those who lived before me! The Suevi live for the greatest part on milk and meat[10]. O the folly of men, and (his) uncertain fortune, and our idle[11] hopes! I do not fail to observe[12] that[13] practice is the best teacher of speaking. O excellent protector of the sheep, a wolf! Many things[14] are becoming for men which are unbecoming for women. It becomes good citizens to obey[15] the laws and to undergo all hardships and dangers for the safety of their country.

[1]omni ratiōne [2]vĕrēcundŭs, -ă, -ŭm [3]săpĭens, -tis [4]sĕcundŭm [5]not to be translated [6]tŭm. . cŭm, *at the time when* [7]cŭm [8]profĭciscŏr, -ī [9]ăd [10]Abl. without Prep. [11]ĭnānis, -ĕ [12]me praetĕrit, *I fail to observe* [13]Say: *practice to be the best teacher of speaking*, Acc. w. Inf. [14]Neut. Plur. [15]pārĕō, -ērĕ, w. Dative,

Accusative with Verbs of *Naming*.

SYNTAX 58.

Romŭlus urbem ex nomĭne suo Romam vocâvit. Nerōnem senātus hostem judicâvit. Cicerōnem universus popŭlus consŭlem declarâvit. Dionysĭus superbum se praebŭit in fortūna.

21. Apollo judged Socrates (to be)[1] the wisest of men[2]. Golden bits do not make a horse better. Crœsus, king of Lydia, on account of[3] his riches considered himself the happiest of men[2]. David appointed[4] his son, Solomon, as his successor. Alexander founded in Egypt a city which from[5] his own name he called Alexandria. Our father gave us the most distinguished men as teachers. Boys in (their)[1] play name him king who appears to be the most distinguished. Demosthenes showed himself an ardent defender of common liberty. I show myself grateful to those who have deserved well of[6] me. Necessity makes even the timid brave. Anthony called his flight victory, because he had come off[7] alive. Wisdom offers herself to us as the surest guide to[8] pleasure. Socrates considered himself an inhabitant and citizen of the whole world. Poverty makes a man in a measure[9] more fitted[10] for[11] many virtues.

[1]Not to be translated [2]omnēs [3]proptĕr [4]dēsignō, -ārĕ [5]ex [6]dē [7]exēō, -īrĕ [8]ăd [9]quodammŏdo [10]aptŭs, -ă, -ŭm [11]ăd

Accusative with Verbs of *Teaching*.

SYNTAX 59.

Dionysĭus musĭcam docŭit Epaminondam. Cicerōnem Minerva omnes artes edocŭit. Catilīna juventūtem mala facinŏra edocēbat. Eumĕnes iter, quod in anĭmo agitābat, omnes celāvit.

22. They are silly[1] who teach others what they have not tried[2] themselves. Pythagoras taught boys modesty and a love[3] of letters. Isocrates, an Athenian orator, who taught many youths eloquence, never delivered[4] a speech himself. Who taught men agriculture? Good boys conceal nothing from their parents. Saturn first taught the Italians the cultivation of the land. In the schools of the Romans the teachers taught the boys the Latin and Greek languages[5], history and music. Many wish to teach others what[6] they have not sufficiently learned themselves. He is a sincere friend who conceals nothing from a friend. You teach the eagle to fly, the dolphin to swim. Hunger teaches many a lesson[7]. Dionysius, that[8] he might not[8] trust[9] his neck to a barber, taught his daughters to shave. Divine providence has wisely concealed from us future events[10]. The deserters[11] acquainted Caesar with all the plans[12] of the enemy[13].

[1]rīdĭcŭlŭs, -ă, -ŭm [2]expĕrĭŏr, -īrī [3]stŭdĭŭm, -ī [4]hăbĕō, -ērĕ [5]Sing. [6]ea quae [7]multă, -ōrŭm [8]nē, with Subj. [9]committō, -ĕrĕ [10]rēs, rĕī [11]transfŭgă, -ae [12]consĭlĭŭm, -ī [13]Plur.

Accusative with Verbs of *Asking*.

SYNTAX *60—62.*

Idem te rogāvi, quod pater tuus me rogavĕrat; non quemquam idem interrogārem. Visne ut de vita Aristīdis te Latīne interrŏgem? Racilĭus consul in senātu me primum sententĭam rogāvit. Caesar eădem, quae antĕa ex Lisco quaesivĕrat, secrēto quaerēbat ab alĭis.

23. The boys and girls of the Gauls from[1] the wall of the town besought[2] peace of the Romans. He who was first asked his opinion in the senate was called "princeps senātus." The Athenians entreated[2] aid from the Lacedaemonians. Verres demanded[3] from parents a price[4] for[5] the burial of (their) children. The Campanians were compelled to entreat help from the Romans. Why do you ask me about that[6] which I have so often explained to you? Cæsar quickly dismissed the council; he detained Liscus; he inquired from him alone what he had spoken in the meeting; he inquired privately from the others the same things[8]; he found them to be true. A friend will ask of another[9] nothing except[10] what is honorable. An upright man, when asked[11] for his opinion, will either be silent or speak the truth. God demands from us nothing else than what is useful to us. Ask[12] nothing of God except[10] what you can ask openly.

[1]ex [2]pĕtō, -ĕrĕ [3]poscō, -ĕrĕ [4]prĕtĭŭm, -ī [5]prō [6]ĕă [7]quaerō, -ĕrĕ [8]eădem [9]Say: *from a friend* [10]nĭsĭ [11]*when asked*, rogātus [12]Pres. Subjunct.

Dative. Indirect Object. With Intransitives.

SYNTAX *63. 64.*

Medĭci medentur morbis. Frater tuus mihi maledixit. Paucis Trojānis ferrum Graecōrum pepercĕrat. Obtrectāre altĕri nihil habet utilitātis. Numquam mihi persuadebĭtur, anĭmos esse mortāles.

24. Old age is a disease which no physician can cure. I could never be convinced that[1] our souls are mortal. Riches are more frequently envied than virtue. A perfect man never curses fortune. The condition of those whom fortune excessively[2] favors is extremely[3] dangerous. Pleasure w.ns upon[4] our senses. The soldiers spared neither women nor children. Lycurgus recommended[5] frugality to all. The upright man envjes nobody. Let us imitate the example of Christ who blessed his very[6] enemies. Those who devote themselves[7] to virtue are alone rich. Demosthenes could not say the first letter of that art to which he devoted himself. We seldom envy the honors of those whose power[8] is not feared. Once the same physician treated[9] both[10] wounds and[10] diseases. No one has ever come up[11] to Dionysius in cruelty[12]. Some people seem to envy not only the living, but even the dead. He who spares the rod hates his son.

[1]Acc. w. Inf.; say: *our souls to be mortal* [2]immodĭce [3]Superlat. [4]blandĭŏr, -īrī [5]suādĕō, -ērĕ [6]ipse [7]stŭdĕō, -ērĕ [8]vīs [9]mĕdĕŏr, -ērī [10]ĕt, .ĕt [11]aequō, -ārĕ [12]Abl. without Prep.

Dative with Adjectives.

SYNTAX *65.*

Amo veritātem, etsi mihi jucunda non est. Respublĭca Romāna adĕo erat valĭda, ut cuilĭbet civitātum finitimārum bello par esset. Ineptum id dicĭtur, quod nec tempŏri, nec homĭni, nec loco aptum est.

25. The soil of their country is dear to all. Next to[1] God men can be most[2] useful to men. Nothing is more pleasing, nothing more acceptable to God than a pious mind[3] and (one) mindful of benefits. Nothing is more adapted[4] to man's nature than beneficence and liberality. Old age is burdensome to most men. Death is common to every age. Every animal seeks[5] that which is adapted to its nature. No place ought to be more agreeable[6] to us, than our country. True friends are never troublesome to us. Truth is to many people troublesome and hateful. The cultivation of the fields is beneficial to the whole[7] human race. Every one[8] loves himself[8], for every one is for his own sake[9] dear to himself. It is easy for an innocent man to find words, difficult for the unfortunate to observe[10] a limit[11] in his words[12]. Pain appears to be the bitterest enemy to virtue. Bravery is especially[13] peculiar to men. I am of the same age[14] as thy brother.

[1]sĕcundŭm [2]maxĭmē [3]ănĭmŭs, -ī [4]accommŏdātŭs, -ă, -ŭm [5]appĕtō, -ĕrĕ [6]dulcĭs, -ĕ [7]ŭnĭversŭs, -ă, -ŭm [8]ipsĕ sē quisquĕ [9]per sē, *for his own sake* [10]tĕnĕō, -ērĕ [11]mŏdŭs, -ī [12]Genit. Object. [13]maxĭmē [14]aequālĭs; Say: *I am a contemporary of thy brother*

Dative of Advantage. Ethical Dative.

SYNTAX *66. 67.*

Non scholae sed vitae discĭmus. Pisistrătus sibi, non patrĭae Megarenses vicit. Filĭus meus, si quid peccat, mihi peccat. Plures in Asĭa mulĭĕres singŭlis viris nubĕre solent. Quid sibi vult haec oratĭo?

26. To the unhappy man time is very long, to the happy man very short. We wish to be rich not only for ourselves, but for our children, relatives, friends and especially[1] for our country. Solon established[2] laws for the Athenians, Lycurgus for the Spartans. Vulcan made weapons for Achilles. Orgetorix gave his daughter in marriage[3] to Dumnorix, the brother of Divitiacus. Dumnorix was a friend to the Helvetians, because[4] he had taken[5] from[6] that state the daughter of Orgetorix in marriage; and, led by a strong desire[7] for power[8], he was anxious[9] for a revolution[10], and wished[11] to have as many[12] states as possible[12] under obligation[13] for his kindness[14]. Octavia, the sister of Augustus, was married to Anthony. From[15] some roots[16] and herbs we cull[17] remedies for diseases and wounds. He is a thief in my opinion[18].

[1]maxĭmē [2]instĭtŭō, -ĕrĕ [3]in matrimonĭum dare [4]quŏd [5]ducĕre in matrimonĭum [6]ex [7]cŭpĭdĭtās, -ātĭs [8]regnŭm, -ī [9]stŭdĕō, -ērĕ [10]rēs novae [11]vŏlō, vellĕ [12]quam plurĭmi, *as many..as possible* [13]sibi restrictus, *under obligation* [14]bĕnĕfĭcĭŭm, -ī, Abl. without Prep. [15]ex [16]stirps, -ĭs [17]ēlĭgō, -ĕrĕ [18]*in my opinion*, say: *to me*

Dative or Accusative. With Compounds.

SYNTAX *68. 69.*

Natūra sensĭbus ratiōnem adjunxit. Ratiōne antecellĭmus bestĭis. Antonĭus leges civitāti per vim imposŭit. Interpōne tuis interdum gaudĭa curis. Manlĭus posthabŭit filĭi caritātem publĭcae utilitāti. Leonĭdas, rex Spartanōrum, occūris Persis supervĕnit.

27. Not to be on one's own guard[1], and to give advice to others is foolish. Beware of the dog! Hannibal struck a great terror into the Roman army. To every virtue is opposed a vice. We often put[2] ducks' eggs under[2] hens. What greater or better service can we render[3] the state than that[4] of teaching and instructing youth? The nose appears to be, as it were[5], a wall thrown in[6] between the eyes. Certain signs precede[7] certain events[8]. Those who consult the interests of a part of the citizens and neglect a part, introduce[9] into the state sedition, a most pernicious evil[10]. In India a woman is placed[11] on the funeral pile along with[12] her dead husband. The Roman censors were accustomed to take the horse away[13] from a too fat knight. Compare[14] our longest life with eternity, and it will be found short. It is mean to prefer money to friendship.

[1]căvĕō, -ēre [2]suppōnō, -ĕre [3]adfĕrō, -rĕ [4]Say: *when we teach and instruct* [5]quăsĭ [6]interjĭcĭō, -ĕre [7]praecurrō, -ĕre [8]rēs [9]indūcō, -ĕre [10]rēs [11]impōnō, -ĕre [12]ūnā cŭm [13]ădĭmō, -ĕre [14]confĕrō, -rĕ

Dative of Possession. With Verbs of *Giving* and *Putting*.

SYNTAX *70. 71.*

Dionysĭus fossam latam cubiculāri lecto circumdĕdit. Semper in civitāte ii, quibus opes nullae sunt, bonis invĭdent, malos extollunt, vetĕra odēre, nova exoptant. Romāni Q. Metello cognōmen Numidĭcum (Numidĭco) indidērunt.

28. The lion has (its) greatest strength[1] in (its) breast. The Lydians had many kings before Crœsus. Semiramis founded Babylon and surrounded the city with a wall. Tall[2] trees have deep roots. Crocodiles have the upper[3] part of the body hard and impenetrable, the lower[4] part soft and tender.

As[5] among trees each[6] has its own fruit, so[5] among men each has its own gifts. Flowers have not always the same color. My father has many sons and (only) one daughter. Publius Cornelius Scipio who overcame Hannibal and destroyed Carthage was surnamed[7] Africanus. In a state those who have no means[8] always envy the better classes[9]. To Tarquinius was given the surname "Overbearing". A sick man has always hope. The name of this disease is avarice. Nature had surrounded the town with a broad and deep river. Maecenas presented Horace with a country-house. Cicero had a great resemblance to[10] Demosthenes.

[1]vīs [2]prŏcērŭs, -ă, -ŭm [3]sŭpĕrĭŏr, -ŭs [4]infĕrĭŏr, -ŭs [5]ŭt..ĭta [6]quisquĕ [7]Say: *had the surname* (cognōmen) [8]opēs, -ŭm [9]bŏnī, *the better classes* [10]cŭm

Dative with Gerund. Two Datives.

SYNTAX 72. 73.

Hortensĭo, quod bello civīli numquam interfuisset, ignavĭae tribūtum est. Timolĕon Syracusānis auxilĭo erat missus. Caesar quinque cohortes castris praesidĭo relīquit. Vitis arborĭbus decŏri est. Iter mihi faciendum est.

29. Attalus, a king of Asia, gave his kingdom to the Romans as a present. Avarice is a[1] great evil to men. Virtues bring[2] glory and honor to men. A thousand Plataeans came to the help of the Athenians[3] against the Persians. Poverty is a[4] disgrace to no one. God is not wont to come to the help of[5] those who bring[6] themselves inconsiderately into danger. Many men count it[7] as a praise to themselves what[7] they owe to fortune. Pericles made a present of his lands to the state. A roomy house often becomes a[8] disgrace to its owner, if solitude reign[9] in it. The hope of a future life is a[10] great consolation to the wretched. Virtue alone is neither given nor received as a present. The disciples of Plato were to be silent[11] for[12] five years. To many distinguished men the fortune of war has proved[13] a reproach, the envy of the people a disaster. Every one must bear[14] his own trouble.

[1]Say: *for a great evil* [2]*are for* [3]*to the Athenians* [4]*for a disgrace* [5]Dat. [6]mittō, -ĕrĕ [7]ĕă..quae [8]*for a disgrace* [9]Say: *is* [10]*for a great consolation* [11]tăcendŭm ĕrăt [12]pĕr [13]Say: *has been for a reproach. for a disaster* [14]fĕrendŭm est.

Ablative of Cause.

SYNTAX *74—78.*

Trahĭmur omnes laudis studĭo et optĭmus quisque maxĭme glorĭa ducĭtur. Socrătis responso judĭces sic exarsērunt, ut capĭtis homĭnem innocentissĭmum condemnārent. Parentes salūte liberōrum laetantur.

30. Many comets we do not see, because they are obscured by the rays of the sun. Xerxes was conquered more[1] by the prudence[2] of Themistocles than by the arms of Greece. Friendships are known[3] by affection and love. By the prudence and valor of Scipio Hannibal was compelled to depart[4] from Italy. Alexandria was founded by Alexander the Great. The world is governed by God's providence. The liberty of the Romans was crushed by Tarquin the Overbearing, but was restored by means of Brutus. We have[5] to obey the laws[6] from love of virtue, not from fear of punishment. Hannibal was inflamed with hatred against the Romans. Servius Tullius began to reign, not by the order, but by the wish and permission of the citizens. Catiline was born of a noble house[7]. We rejoice in the recollection of past pleasures. Many rejoiced at the death of Cæsar. Parents bear many hardships, not for their own, but for their children's sake, because they rejoice most in their children's welfare.

[1]măgĭs [2]consĭlĭŭm, -ī [3]cognoscō, -ĕrĕ [4]dēcēdō, -ĕrĕ [5]dēbĕō, -ērĕ [6]Dat. [7]lŏcŭs, -ī

Cimon Thasĭos opulentĭa fretos adventu suo fregit. Virtūte qui praedĭti sunt, soli sunt felīces. In vobis, boni cives, salus civitātis nitĭtur. Quidam vitĭis suis gloriantur.

31. Who can confide in strength of body? All good men mourn over the loss[1] of their beloved ones[2]. As[3] wise old people are delighted with youths endowed[4] with a good disposition[5], so[3] youths delight in the precepts of the old by which they are led to[6] the pursuit of virtue. They are to blame[7] who desert their duties from effeminacy of temper[8]. Nero on account of the remembrance of his crimes was never free from fear[9]. The safety of the state rests on the loyalty, piety and virtue of the citizens. Blessed is he who is content with honorable mediocrity. No one can trust either to the strength of body or to the stability of fortune. Verres had committed a great many[10] crimes incited by avarice and relying on his riches. Who can boast of stability of fortune? Orgetorix, the richest and most noble of the Helvetians, led on[11] by the desire of reigning, formed a conspiracy of the nobility.

[1]intĕrĭtŭs, **-ūs** [2]sŭī, **-ōrŭm** [3]ŭt..ĭtă [4]praedĭtŭs, **-ă, -ŭm** [5]**Abl. without Prep.** [6]ăd [7]ĭn culpā, *to blame* [8]mollĭtĭă, **-ae**, *effeminacy of temper* [9]**Abl. without Prep.** [10]permultŭs, **-ă, -ŭm** [11]inductŭs, **-ă, -ŭm**

Ablative of Means or Instrument.

Syntax 79.

Cornĭbus tauri, apri dentĭbus, morsu leōnes se defendunt. Ocŭlis vidēmus, aurĭbus audīmus. Per patrem tuum pericŭlo liberātus sum.

32. The earth has been clothed with flowers, plants, trees (and) fruits. Every one measures dangers by his own fear. The sun illuminates all things with a most bright light. Happy is he who cultivates (his) paternal fields with his own oxen. Birds are covered with feathers, quadrupeds with hairs, fish with scales. Not by (their) fortune, but by (their) character[1] I will value men. Men are caught by pleasure as[2] fishes with a hook. Italy was fortified against barbarian nations by the Alps, as it were[3] by a natural rampart. Truth is corrupted either by a lie or by silence. Great things are done not by strength or speed of body, but by counsel and valor. No one received the fugitives[4] into the city or[5] into (his) house. Among the Parthians[6] the signal in battle was given not with the trumpet but with the drum. Pompey crossed the sea with all the soldiers which he had with him. The enemy has devastated[7] the whole region with fire and sword[8]. The Roman boys, like[9] our own, played with ball and hoop.

[1]mōrēs [2]ŭt [3]quăsī, *as it were* [4]fŭgĭens, **-tĭs** [5]- vĕ, appended to its word, here, *house* [6]Say: *to the Parthians* [7]pŏpŭlŏr, **-ārī** [8]ferrŭm ignisquĕ (**Abl.** of ignĭs in **ī**) [9]ŭt

Ablative of Limitation.

SYNTAX *80.*

Boni vix totĭdem numĕro sunt quot Thebārum portae. Isocrătis glorĭam nemo, meo quidem judicĭo, est postĕa consecūtus. Nemĭnem Thrasybūlo praefĕro fide, constantĭa, magnitudĭne anĭmi, in patrĭam amōre. Crine ruber, niger ore, brevis pede.

33. My brother is lame in (his) right foot. It is the duty of a youth to reverence (his) elders. Ariovistus was by nation a German. Of all companionships none is more excellent[1], none firmer than when[2] good men, similar in character, are united in intimacy[3]. The horse on which I rode through the city was lame in (his) right foot. By our civil law no one can be a citizen of two states. In appearance[4] Crœsus was very happy indeed[5], in reality[6] very[7] unhappy. Aristotle was, according to the opinion of all, the most learned man of all[8] antiquity. Amulius left the kingdom to his brother Numitor who was the elder. Socrates, according to the testimony of all learned men, and the judgment of all Greece, was the prince[9] of philosophers. The Lacedaemonian Agesilaus was king in name, not in power like[10] the rest[11] of the Spartans. Love of truth is, according to my opinion, the foundation of all virtues. The Roman people was marked off[12] according to income[13], rank[14] (and) age[14].

[1]praestans, -tis [2]cŭm [3]Abl. without Prep. [4]spĕcĭēs, -ēī [5]quĭdĕm [6]rēs vērā [7]admŏdŭm [8]tō ŭs, -ă, -ŭm [9]princeps, -cĭpĭs [10]sĭcŭt [11]cētĕrī, -ae, -ă [12]descrībō, -ĕrĕ [13]censŭs, -ūs [14]Plur.

Ablative of Manner.

SYNTAX *81. 82.*

Malo cum dignităte potĭus cadĕre, quam cum ignominĭa servīre. Legiōnes profecti sunt alăcri anĭmo et erecto. Sulla maxĭmo cum labōre Athēnas cepit.

34. The earth revolves around its axis with the greatest swiftness. Cicero always began to speak with great fear. The wise man bears an injury with an even mind. Those who live honestly and virtuously (with virtue) can never be quite unhappy. Orators are heard with severe judgment[1], poets with pleasure. Those who are thirsty drink in[2] silence. Marcus

Crassus perished on the other side of the Euphrates in[1] shame and disgrace. Swans die amid[2] song and pleasure. Plato lived to extreme old age in[2] the best health. Hares sleep with (their) eyes open. You have written this letter with great care and diligence. The leader of the Gauls determined[3] to fortify (their) camps after the manner of the Romans. The Massilians kept[4] (their) treaty with the Romans with the greatest fidelity. In[2] anger nothing can be done well. The Gauls suffered the army of Hannibal to pass through[5] their territory[6] in[2] peace and quiet[7]. The tribune of the commons excited[8] the feelings[9] of the commons in every way.

[1]sĕvērĭtās, -ātĭs, *severe judgment* [2]Say: *with* [3]stătŭō, -ĕrĕ [4]servō, -ārĕ [5]transmittō, -ĕrĕ, *to pass through* [6]fīnēs, -ĭŭm [7]bŏnă pax, *peace and quiet* [8]accendō, -ĕrĕ [9]ănĭmŭs, -ī

Ablative of Measure and Comparison.

SYNTAX *83. 84.*

Omnis sensus homĭnum multo antecellit sensĭbus bestiārum. Nihil in homĭnum genĕre rarĭus perfecto oratōre invenīri potest. Nihil est laudabilĭus, nihil magno et praeclāro viro dignĭus virtūte. Homĭnes quo plura habent, eo plura cupĭunt.

35. What is more desirable than wisdom, what better for man? No one is dearer to me than my parents. The simpler food[1] is, the more useful it is for man. The air is denser, the nearer (it is) to the earth. Ireland is less by half than Great Britain. The wiser any one[2] is, the more modest (he is). The peacock is handsomer than other[3] birds, not more useful. Every portion of time[4] seems the shorter the happier it is. It is much more difficult to conquer one's self than an enemy. No place ought to be dearer to thee than thy country. The smoke of our own country is brighter[5] than fire abroad[6]. The weaker an enemy is, the greater is the disgrace[7] if one[8] is conquered by him. Cicero was some[9] years younger than Hortensius. Lacedaemon bore no man[10] either[11] better or[11] more useful than Lycurgus. My country is much dearer to me than life. There is nothing more perfect than the world, nothing better than virtue.

[1]cĭbŭs, -ī [2]quisquĕ [3]cētĕrī, -ae, -ă [4]tempŭs, *portion of time* [5]lūcŭlentŭs, -ă, -ŭm [6]ălĭēnŭs, -ă, -ŭm [7]ignōmĭnĭă, -ae [8]quĭs [9]ălĭquŏt [10]nēmō, *no man* [11]aut. aut

Ablative of Price.

SYNTAX *85.*

Viginti talentis unam orationem Isocrătes vendĭdit. Emit hortos tanti quanti volŭit. Venditōri expĕdit rem venīre quam plurĭmo. Multo sanguĭne victorĭa Poenis stetit. Agrum emi talento, vendĭdi duplo pluris.

36. We cannot buy virtue and wisdom with gold. In large and crowded[1] cities houses are let at a very high price. Jugurtha, king of Numidia, had purchased peace from[2] the Roman generals with a large sum of money[3]. Our house was bought for a very high price. We sell our corn not dearer than every body else[4], perhaps even cheaper, since[5] we have[6] a larger stock. Nothing[7] costs dearer than what is bought with prayers. The victory cost the enemy[8] much blood and wounds. So great was the terror of the Gallic name that[9] kings of their own accord[10] bought peace with an immense sum of money[11]. Those who are besieged by an enemy are sometimes compelled to buy a pint of water with a large amount of money. The best books are often sold at a very low price. No plague has cost the human race[8] as much as anger. My father sold his horse for less than he purchased (him). No one will sell at a low price what he has bought himself at a high price. My father sold his horse at the same price at which he bought (him).

[1]frĕquens, **-tĭs** [2]ā [3]magna pecunĭa [4]cētĕrī [5]cŭm, w. **Subjunct.** [6]essĕ [7]nulla res [8]**Dat.** [9]ŭt, w. **Subjunct.** [10]ultrō, *of their own accord* [11]ingens pecunĭa

Ablative of Separation.

SYNTAX *86.*

Nihil est praestabilĭus viro quam pericŭlis patrĭam liberāre. Alexander vix a se manus abstinŭit. Apud Germānos quemcunque mortalĭum arcēre tecto nefas habētur. Lacedaemonĭi de diutĭna contentiōne destitērunt.

37. The fear of punishment deters many from wrong. Death releases men from all cares. Timoleon with incredible good fortune drove Dionysius from the whole of[1] Sicily. We are taught to restrain all our desires, to protect our property[2], to keep our minds, eyes and hands from other people's property[3]. The Athenians drove[4] their best deserved citizens from the state. The Red Sea does not differ[5] in color[6] from other seas. The Aedui could not defend themselves and their property[7] against[8] the Helvetii. Ariovistus excluded[9] the Romans from all Gaul. The Roman people forced Lentulus to lay down[10] the office of praetor[11]. The soldiers of the ninth and tenth legions[12] quickly drove the enemy from the higher position into the river, and they themselves crossed the river and put[13] the enemy to flight[13]. Deliver me from a bad man, from myself. Death delivers the diseased[14] from all evils. Scarcely did the soldiers keep off the onslaught[15] of the enemy from the gates and walls.

[1]Not to be translated [2]nostră, -ōrŭm [3]ălĭēnă, -ōrŭm, *other people's property* [4]ējĭcĭō, -ĕrĕ [5]ăbhorrĕō, -ērĕ [6]Abl. of Limitation [7]sŭă, -ōrŭm [8]ā [9]interdīcō, -ĕrĕ [10]sē abdĭcārĕ [11]praetūră, -ae, *the office of praetor* [12]Singular [13]in fugam vertĕre [14]aegrōtans, -tĭs [15]impĕtŭs, -ūs

Ablative of Plenty and Want.

Syntax 87.

Regno carēbat Tarquinĭus, cum regno esset expulsus. Virtus plurĭmae exercitatiōnis indĭget. Abundārunt semper auro regna Asĭae. Sapĭens eget nulla re. Omnĭbus fortūnis privāri malo quam carēre tranquillitāte anĭmi.

38. If we shall be free[1] from passions, we shall be able to depart from life with a tranquil mind. We all need[2] God's help. Verres had an abundance of gold and silver vessels of which he had plundered the temples of the gods. Neither men nor animals can do without[3] air. America abounds in gold and silver. Old age is not without[3] (its) pleasures and joys. The sun fills the whole world with its light. The cold north-wind strips[4] the trees of (their) leaves. Children need[2] the advice of (their) parents. In Sulla's time[5] the Roman commonwealth was deprived[6] of many illustrious men. No one's life is always filled with joys. Old age is free[1] from those services which cannot be assumed without strength[3]. Fear of death most disturbs those who abound in all good things. The most necessary things do not require[9] skill so much as labor. Prusias was robbed[10] of (his) kingdom and forsaken even[11] by his friends. Nothing can be honorable what is void[7] of justice. Arion had filled all lands with the glory of his name. A bad man is never free[12] from fear. The city was surrendered to Cæsar empty[13] of (its) garrison, but filled[14] with stores.

[1]lībĕr, -ă, -ŭm. [2]ĕgĕō, -ērĕ [3]cărĕō, -ērĕ, *to do* or *be without* [4]nūdō, -ārĕ [5]Sullae temporĭbus [6]orbō, -ārĕ [7]văcō, -ārĕ [8]Plur. [9]indĭgĕō, -ērĕ [10]spŏlĭō, -ārĕ [11]ipsĕ [12]văcŭŭs, -ă, -ŭm [13]nūdŭs, -ă, -ŭm [14]rĕfertŭs, -ă, -ŭm

Ablative with ŏpŭs est.

SYNTAX *88*.

Auctoritāte tua nobis opus est et consilĭo. Magistratĭbus opus est, sine quorum prudentĭa et diligentĭa esse civĭtas non potest. Corpŏri et cibo et potiōne opus est. Attĭcus, quae amĭcis suis opus erant, omnĭa ex sua re familiāri dabat.

39. How much[1] money do you need? There is need not of many books, but of good (ones). To body and mind there is sometimes need of recreation. There is need of good laws for[2] the common safety of citizens. For carrying on war[3] there is need of forces, arms and money. We are in need of our senses in order[4] to perceive things; of our mind, to be[4] able to judge right. When a violent storm has arisen, ships are in need of a skilful pilot. What do you need in order[4] to be good? To be willing. He who has a daughter needs money; he who has two, needs more[5], he who has several[6], still more. The unhappy have need not only of pity but also of assistance. Not only men and beasts but also plants have need of air. The body needs much food and much drink. As soldiers are in need of arms, so scholars are in need of books.

[1]quantŭm [2]ăd [3]ad bellum gerendum, *for carrying on war* [4]Translate: *that we may perceive*, etc.; *that*, ŭt with the Subjunct. [5]mājŏr, -ŭs [6]plūrēs, -ă

Ablative with Adjectives and Deponents.

SYNTAX *89. 90.*

Quem non pudet, hunc ego non reprehensiōne solum, sed etĭam poena dignum puto. Dolĕo, te a studĭo litterārum alĭēnum esse. Multi beneficĭis Dei perverse utuntur. Civĭtas Atheniensĭum rerum potīta est.

40. The ship which employs the most skilful pilot, best accomplishes (its) course. The virtue of excellent citizens is worthy of imitation, not of envy. Flies are no less worthy of admiration than elephants. How many are unworthy of light and nevertheless[1] the sun rises! The laws which the Athenians obeyed[2] were given by Solon. All the works of God are worthy of the highest admiration. That is every one's[3] own, which every one enjoys and uses. Alexander made himself master of the empire of the whole (of) Asia. Many men make bad use of riches. Fraud is foreign to a good man. The old painters used but[4] few[5] colors. Most[6] people will enjoy greater happiness in heaven, than they have enjoyed upon[7] this earth. The elder[8] Cato ate the same food and drank the same wine with his servants. The light which we enjoy is given to us by God. Those who free men from superstition are not less worthy of respect[9] than those who banish[10] slavery from among them. The Scythians carried[11] their wives and children with them in wagons which they used for[12] houses. He who enjoys good health, does not require[13] (any) medicine. Valor is praiseworthy even[14] in an enemy.

[1]tămĕn [2]ūtŏr, -ī [3]quisquĕ [4]tantŭm [5]paucī, -ae, -ă [6]plērīquĕ [7]ĭn [8]mājŏr [9]vĕnĕrātĭō, -ōnĭs [10]dēpellō, -ĕrĕ [11]vĕhō, -ĕrĕ [12]prō [13]indĭgĕō, -ērĕ [14]vĕl

Use of Prepositions.

Prepositions construed with the **Accusative.**— SYNTAX *92.*

antĕ, ăpŭd, ăd, adversŭs,
circŭm, circā, cĭtrā, cĭs;
ergā, contrā, intĕr, extrā,
infrā, intrā, juxtā, ŏb,
pĕnĕs, (pōnĕ), pōst & praetĕr,
prŏpĕ, proptĕr, pĕr, sĕcundŭm,
suprā, versŭs, ultrā, trans.

41. Against death we have no weapons. Let children be thankful unto[1] (their) parents and teachers. Sailing hard by[2] the shore is dangerous. Physicians have remedies against diseases; against death they have no remedy. Your good-will toward me, and mine toward you are equal. There is a great variety of[3] languages among men. During night we see the stars. There were many holidays with[4] the Romans. Fish swim through the water. Among the blind the one-eyed is king. To live according to nature is the best life, but many men live against nature. The teacher praises these scholars on account of their diligence; he blames those an account of their laziness. The women commonly attend to the houses and household things, the men to the occupations without the house. Those who remove across the sea change the sky, not their mind. The most pleasant sailing is hard by the land, the most pleasant walk is hard by the sea. All things are frail beneath[5] the moon. Few men live above[6] ninety years. Before noon we attend to our occupations, after noon we walk through the meadows and woods. Rich people have magnificent country houses near the city.

[1]ergā [2]juxtā [3]vŏluntās, -ātis [4]ăpŭd [5]infrā [6]suprā

42. The earth turns[1] around its axis. The empire over[2] the whole world is in the hands of God. Above us we see a multitude of stars. Sleep after dinner is not salutary. A fool digs a well hard by a river. Many men obey the laws[3] from fear. If boys are well, they should not[4] sleep[5] over seven hours. Men are more prone to pleasure than to virtue. Sicily is situated over against Italy. In summer[6] we shall live out of town. That loss is most shameful which happens through carelessness. The Romans were accustomed[7] immediately after dinner to play at dice. The Argonauts sailed over the Black Sea for[8] the golden fleece. To-day your brother will come to us to dinner. After Romulus Numa was made king of the Romans. A good judge will judge according to the laws. All animals defend themselves against violence with their own weapons[9]. Most graves of the Romans were close by the Appian Way. According to the opinion of the ancients the Islands of the

Blessed were situated beyond mount Atlas toward the West. By heavy cares and continuous labor men grow old before (their) time. Nature produced[10] all things for the use of men.

[1]se convertĕre [2]Object. Genit. [3]Dat. [4]nē [5]Imperat. *should not sleep = let them not sleep* [6]Abl. without Prep. [7]sŏlĕō, -ēre [8]ăd [9]Instrum. Abl. [10]gignō, -ĕre

43. Nature has provided[1] the greatest abundance of things for the use of men. The sons of Brutus were slain by the lictor before the eyes of (their) father. Pompey finished the war of the pirates within 90 days. A good man obeys the laws from[2] duty, a bad man from fear. Next to God men can be most useful to men. Sophocles lived to extreme[3] old age. Comets are wonderful on account of their infrequency and appearance. All animals live according to nature, man alone often lives against reason and nature. Julius Cæsar was capable of enduring labor beyond belief. The Athenians brought the Ionians help against the Persians. You will find this verse twice in Virgil. The city (of) Marseilles was founded near the mouth of the Rhone. Britain is opposite the coast of Gaul. Let us be grateful towards our parents from whom we have received most benefits. The right of an embassy used[4] to be sacred among all nations. Lycurgus divided the lands of all equally among all. The Rhine is between Gaul and Germany. The Romans called the land this side the Alps Cisalpine Gaul, the land beyond the Alps Transalpine Gaul. The Romans by means of their ambassadors declared war on[5] the Carthaginians.

[1]compărō, -āre [2]proptĕr [3]summŭs, -ă, -ŭm [4]adsuescō, -ĕre [5]Say: *to the Carthaginians.*

Prepositions construed with the **Ablative.** — Syntax *93.*

ā, ăb, abs, cŭm, dē,
cōrăm, prō, ex, ē,
tĕnŭs, sĭnĕ, prae.

44. No man's life is without pain. The Atlantic ocean separates[1] America from Europe. It is sweet and glorious to die for one's country. The citizens fight for their country, for freedom and the laws. Out of all the animals which live with us dogs are the most faithful. The deeds of men do not always agree[2] with their words. A dog is small in comparison with an elephant and large in comparison with a mouse. We hear the song of birds with pleasure. You are safe if God is with you. It is pleasant to me to walk with my friends through fields and woods. Nothing of[3] all that we see remains. The passage from virtue to vices is easier than from vices to virtue. With a friend we deliberate respecting the least and the greatest affairs. There is sometimes more danger from the doctor than from the disease. I have a friend with whom I am accustomed[4] to share[5] all joys and sorrows. Tacitus wrote a little book[6] on the situation, customs, and peoples of Germany. The Britons sent ambassadors to Cæsar concerning peace. A blind man cannot judge of[7] colors. On account[8] of tears I cannot speak.

[1]dīvĭdō, -ĕrĕ [2]congrŭō, -ĕrĕ [3]ex [4]sŏlĕō, -ērĕ [5]partĭŏr, -īrī [6]lĭbellŭs, -ī [7]dē [8]prae

45. Who has ever lived without danger, without sorrow, without joys? A Persian said to a Spartan: You will not see the sun on account of[1] the multitude of the javelins. The latter answered: All right[2], then[3] we shall fight in the shade. Cicero wrote a beautiful book on friendship. The first recommendation of a youth arises[4] from modesty. From the larger ox the smaller (one) learns to plow. Out of nothing nothing comes[5]. We write from the left hand to the right, the Hebrews from the right to the left. For so many and so great benefits which we have received we owe the greatest thanks to our parents. Souls do not die with (their) bodies. The Romans before a battle implored victory from the immortal gods and goddesses. The Scythians used wagons for houses. The innocent man can live even within the door and threshold of the prison without pain and torture. Man consists of[6] soul and body. The Athenians were distinguished[7] by eloquence above[8] the other[9] Greeks. Let youths be modest in presence of old people. The Gauls despised the low stature[10] of the Romans in comparison with the size of their own bodies. Anthony in presence of the people shed tears for[11] Caesar.

[1]prae [2]bĕnĕ hăbĕt [3]ergō [4]prŏfĭciscŏr, -ī [5]fīō, -ĕrī [6]ex [7]flōrĕō, -ērĕ, *to be distinguished* [8]prae [9]cētĕrī [10]brĕvĭtās, -ātis, *low stature* [11]dē

Prepositions construed with the **Accusative & Ablative.**

SYNTAX *94.*

sŭb, sŭpĕr, subtĕr, ĭn.

46. Beneath[1] the earth there are many useful things. Over[2] our heads there are numberless stars. War is often concealed[3] under the name of peace. It is not pleasant to all to live in the city. The nightingale does not always remain in the same land. Toward winter many birds migrate into other lands. Nobody should[4] be a witness in his own cause. There is often wisdom under a shabby coat. An upright life is the road into Heaven. Birds fly under the clouds, fish swim in the water, and worms creep upon the earth. Many birds hide (their) heads under[1] (their) wings when[5] they sleep. There is nothing new under the moon. Even under a golden roof there lodges care. Many birds migrate before winter to warmer countries. We do not see all things which come under our eyes. Not all the rivers which are upon this earth flow into the ocean. It is not troublesome to soldiers to live under the open sky[6]. Some animals dwell under ground[7], fish in the water. The air is purest and most salubrious on a mountain. We have other peoples'[8] vices before our eyes, our own behind[9] (our) back. Eagles have (their) nests on high rocks, swallows under the roofs of houses.

[1]subtĕr [2]sŭpĕr [3]lătĕō, -ērĕ, *to be concealed* [4]dēbĕō, -ērĕ [5]quandō [6]caelŭm, *the open sky* [7]terră, -ae [8]ălĭēnŭs, -ă, -ŭm [9]ā

47. Eclipses of the sun and likewise[1] of the moon are predicted for[2] many years. Beasts of prey mostly abide in deserts. Merchants make journeys to[3] various countries. When the sun sets, birds hide themselves under the leaves of trees. Vice increases from day to day. Frogs live in marshes. The sources of rivers are usually[4] in mountains. The boys of the Lacedaemonians remained up to (their) seventh year under the care of (their) mothers. The souls of the pious after this life will pass into heaven, as it were[5] their home. In a good citizen love of country is especially praised. Mad dogs bend their tail under the belly. A thatched roof[6] covers the free; servitude dwells under marble and gold. Pliny wrote a letter to the emperor Trajan on[1] the manners of the Christians. The battle was cruel; they were slain one[8] upon another[8]. Virtue holds all things beneath itself. Toward evening most birds go to sleep and they waken up shortly before[9] daybreak[10]. In the assembly you speak of valor, in battle you cannot bear the sound of the trumpet on account of[11] (your) cowardice.

[1]Itemquĕ [2]in [3]*to = into* [4]*use to be* [5]quăsī, *as it were* [6]culmŭs, -ī, *a thatched roof* [7]sŭpĕr [8]aliī..aliī [9]sŭb, *shortly before* [10]prīmă lux [11]prae

Place. Names of Towns.

SYNTAX *95. 96.*

Hannĭbal in Hispanĭam profectus est. Hannĭbal in Hispanĭa impĕrător electus est. Plato Tarentum venit et Locros. Talis Romae Fabricĭus, qualis Aristīdes Athēnis fuit. Pompējus Lucerĭa proficiscĭtur Canusĭum atque inde Brundisĭum.

48. The Apostle Paul was born at Tarsus, but lived for a long time at Jerusalem. Curius first brought four elephants to Rome. The largest libraries were in former times at Alexandria and Pergamum. Tarquin the Proud, the last king of the Romans, died at Cumae. Plato came from Athens to Syracuse. The emperor Severus died at York in Britain. After the battle of Cannae[1] Hannibal sent to Carthage three pecks of gold rings which he had drawn from[2] the fingers of the Roman knights. Pompey had been seriously ill at Naples. He who travels from Venice to Naples passes over[3] the Apeninnes. The trade-winds are very unfavorable to those who sail from Alexandria. At Athens and Sparta the children of those who had fallen for their country, were brought up at the expense of the state[4]. The poet Archias came from Antioch to Rome. Alexander the Great died at Babylon. A slave ran away[5] from Rome to Athens; thence[6] he came to Asia, afterwards he was arrested[7] at Ephesus and sent back to Rome. Cadmus came from Phoenicia to Thebes, Cecrops from Egypt to Athens.

[1]Cannensĭs, -ĕ [2]dē [3]transcendō, -ĕrĕ [4]publĭcē, *at the expense of the state* [5]aufŭgiō, -ĕrĕ [6]indĕ [7]dēprĕhendō, -ĕrĕ

Apposition with Names of Towns. domus and rus.

SYNTAX *96.* 1—5. *97.*

Cimon in oppĭdo Cittĭo est mortŭus. Tres sunt viae ad Mutĭnam. Antiŏcho licŭit remigrāre in domum vetĕrem e nova. Ego rus abĭbo, atque ibi manēbo. Archĭas poēta Antiochĭae natus est celĕbri quondam urbe et copiōsa.

49. Crœsus, king of Lydia, sent ambassadors to Delphi; in Delphi there was a very celebrated oracle of Apollo. Alcibiades was born at Athens and educated in the house of Pericles. Hannibal being driven from Carthage came to Ephesus to king Antiochus. Cato killed himself with his own hand at Utica, a town of Africa. My uncle has determined to pass his life in the country. All those whom their shameful deeds[1] had driven from home flocked into Rome. Cimon of his own accord set out from Athens to Lacedaemon and brought about[2] peace between the two greatest states of Greece. Aristides conducted[3] public affairs[4] excellently in peace and in war. My friend who lived with me, died lately at my house. When my son returns[5] from the country, I will send him to thee. He who comes from home, knows not whether[6] he is going to return[7] home. Cæsar departed from Tarraco and came by land[8] to Narbo and thence to Massilia. The weary sleep well even on the ground.

[1]flāgĭtĭŭm, -ī, *shameful deed* [2]concĭlĭō, -ārĕ [3]gĕrō, -ĕrĕ [4]rēs [5]Say: *shall have returned* [6]ăn [7]rĕdĭtūrŭs sit, *is going to return* [8]pedĭbŭs.

Ablative and Accusative of Place.

SYNTAX *98—100.*

Caesar nuntĭos tota Aeduōrum civitāte dimittit. Erant omnīno itinĕra duo, quibus itinerĭbus domo exīre possent. Impĭi cives unum se in locum, ad curĭam congregābant.

50. Light is diffused[1] over the whole world. My uncle has departed by sea for California. The sun does not always rise or set in the same place. Order is the arrangement of things in fitting and convenient places. The Athenians led out (their) forces from the city and pitched (their) camp in a suitable place. A stone falling is borne downwards in a straight line. The Romans conquered the Carthaginians by land and by sea. As long as[2] my father lived, our affairs were in a very good condition[3]. Nature herself has stamped the idea of God in the minds of all men. Xerxes being warned[4] of danger by Themistocles returned into Asia in 30 days[5] by the same route by which he had made his journey into Greece in six months[5]. The Egyptians and Babylonians bestowed[6] all (their) attention on astronomy[7]. Cæsar embarked[8] his legions and (his) cavalry at Brundisium.

[1]diffundō, -ĕrĕ, with Abl. [2]dōnĕc [3]lŏcŭs, -ī [4]Perf. Part. [5]Abl. of Time [6]pōnō, -ĕrĕ [7]sidĕrum cognĭtĭo [8]in naves imponĕre

Extent of Space.

SYNTAX *101. 102.*

Milĭtes duxĕrunt fossam viginti pedes longam. A recta conscientĭa transversum, ut ajunt, digĭtum non oportet discedĕre. Ariovisti copĭae a Romānis milĭbus passŭum quattŭor et viginti abĕrant.

51. The soldiers built[1] a mound 300 feet broad and 80 feet high. The trunk of the elephant is seven or eight feet long. The city (of) Naples is distant[2] five English miles from Vesuvius. Zama is[3] five days' journey from Carthage. The Saguntines (when) besieged by Hannibal made a rampart three hundred feet long (and) twenty feet high. The highest pyramid is 450 feet high; the single sides are 800 feet broad at[4] the lowest part. Susa was distant from the sea a journey of three months. The soldiers made trenches 100 feet long and 5 feet deep. The town (of) Saguntum was by far the most opulent of the Spanish towns, situated nearly a mile from the sea. The temple of the Ephesian Diana is said to have been 400 feet long and two hundred broad. The Arabians have slender swords each four cubits long. The elephant is eight or nine feet high.

[1]exstrŭō, -ĕrĕ [2]distō, -ārĕ [3]absŭm, ăbessĕ [4]in, w. Abl.

Time *When? How long?*

SYNTAX *103. 104.*

Quo anno Carthāgo delēta est, eōdem interĭit Graecĭa. Pyrrhi temporĭbus jam Apollo versus facĕre desiĕrat. Decem annos Troja oppugnāta est ob unam muliĕrem ab universa Graecĭa.

52. Rome was founded in the 754th year before Christ. Corinth was destroyed by Mummius, and Carthage by Scipio on the same day. Forsake those by whom you will be forsaken in a short time. In autumn storks migrate to other lands and return in spring. The city (of) Veii was besieged during ten summers and winters. The Arabs wander over[1] the plains and mountains winter and summer. Augustus died in the 76th year of his age. Mithridates reigned 60 years, lived 72 years and maintained[2] war against the Romans for forty years. During the morning hours the rainbow appears towards the west, in the afternoon hours it appears towards the east. Some birds sing through the whole year, others only[3] at certain[4] seasons. Barbers came from Sicily to Italy in the 454th year after the founding of Rome[5]; before that[6] the Romans were unshaved. Rome was built in the 431st year after the destruction[7] of Troy. At the time[8] of the Gallic war all things except the citadel had fallen into the hands of the enemies.

[1]perăgrō, -ārĕ, *to wander over* [2]hăbĕō, -ērĕ [3]nonnĭsĭ [4]quĭdăm [5]post Romam condĭtam [6]antĕā, *before that* [7]excĭdĭŭm, -ī [8]Plur.

Distance of Time.

SYNTAX *105—109.*

Corpus Alexandri paucis annis post Alexandrĭam translātum est. Germāni intra annos quattuordĕcim tecta non subiĕrant. Aristīdes sexto fere anno postquam expulsus erat, in patrĭam restitūtus est. Quaestor fui abhinc quattuordĕcim annos. Ad cenam invitātus sum in postĕrum diem.

53. King Numa lived very many years before Pythagoras. The planet Saturn completes its course in nearly thirty years. Cyrus reigned thirty years; (he was) forty years old (when) he began to reign. Carthage by order of the senate was restored[1]

22 years after it had been overthrown[2] by Scipio. Hannibal having been made general, subdued all the tribes of Spain in the next[3] three years. Romulus in the eighteenth year of his age founded a small city on the Palatine hill. How many years ago was the art of printing invented? Charles lived with us for more than a year. Arganthonius came to the throne at the age of 40 years, reigned 80, and lived 120 years. Alexander died thirty three years and one month old. Cæsar returned to Rome nine years after he had gone to Gaul. My friend's father died almost twenty years ago. Cicero was some years younger than Hortensius. Among the Suebi it was not allowed to stay longer[4] than one year in the same place.

[1]rĕpărō, -ārĕ [2]ēvertō, -ĕrĕ [3]proxĭmŭs, -ă, -ŭm [4]longĭŭs

Special Uses of Adjectives.

Syntax *118—127.*

Conscientĭa saepe bonum a malo rectĭus discernit quam doctrīna. In summis Alpĭbus nix sempiterna est. Vide ne oratĭo tua iniquĭor sit quam verĭor. Carthāgo urbs opulentissĭma a Romānis incendĭo delēta est.

54. Hear much, speak little. The past cannot be changed. What we wish, we readily believe. Either be silent or tell the truth; he who despises truth is worthy of the greatest contempt. The splendid city of Athens did not recover its former[1] magnificence after the Peloponnesian war. Hannibal of Carthage has not gained so[2] great fame by (his) victory at Cannae as[2] Epaminondas of Thebes by (his) battle of Leuctra. Hannibal left Spain with a great army in the beginning of spring and arrived in[3] Italy at the end of summer. No general of the Romans was able to penetrate into the heart[4] of Germany. At the break[5] of day[6] the tops of the mountains are illuminated by the rays of the sun. The clamor of a great crowd is more troublesome than dangerous. The rebuke of a kind friend is more useful than bitter.

[1]pristĭnŭs, -ă, -ŭm [2]tantŭs..quantŭs [3]in w. Acc. [4]intĭmŭs, -ă, -ŭm [5]prīmŭs, -ă, -ŭm [6]lux, lūcĭs

Personal and Demonstrative Pronouns.

Syntax ***128—131.***

Flebat filĭus de patris morte. Demosthĕnes non tam dicax fuit quam facētus; illud acriōris ingenĭi, hoc majōris artis est. Cave Catōni antepōnas Socrătem; hujus (Catōnis) facta, illĭus dicta laudantur.

55. Carthage and Corinth were destroyed in the same year, the former by Scipio, the latter by Mummius. You possess my estates, I live on the charity[1] of others. Cæsar and Hannibal were very famous leaders in war, upon the former[2] the conspiracy of Brutus, Cassius (and) others brought[3] destruction, the latter killed himself by poison. I say this, my opponent that. He whom we now call foreigner, in our fathers' time[4] was called enemy. How many narrators of his exploits had that famous Alexander the Great with him! Who will ever be dearer to you than your parents! Cato bore the death of his son, a perfect and tried man with the greatest wisdom. Cæsar and Pompey contended long together[5], the former because he could not[6] endure any[6] superior, the latter, because he could not bear any equal. The Capitol was built of hewn stone[7], a work to be admired[8] even in the present[9] magnificence of the city. I will present to you this book, keep[10] it; (it is) the same (that) we are reading in school.

[1]Abl. [2]Dat. [3]părō, -ārĕ [4]apud majōres nostros [5]inter se [6]nēmo, *not any* [7]Abl. saxum quadrātum [8]adspĭcĭendŭs, -ă, -ŭm, *to be admired* [9]hic [10]rĕtĭnĕō, -ērĕ

Determinative Pronouns.

Syntax ***132—136.***

Polemarchus est vir bonus atque honestus; is ad Verrem in jus eductus est. Erant in Torquāto plurĭmae littĕrae nec eae vulgāres. Bona externa cum corpŏris comparantur. Virtus per se ipsa placet. Quidquid honestum est, idem est utĭle.

56. All naturally[1] love themselves. By our own faults[2] times are bad. Cato died just 86 years before Cicero's consulship[3]. Men must be most annoyed[4] by those evils which have been contracted by their own fault. Angry men are not masters of themselves. Nobody easily knows himself, because every one willingly forgives his own faults. The brilliancy of the same stars delights the country-people and the city-people. This sea is called the Atlantic, that the Pacific, between them lies[5] America. Many through tedium[6] of life have brought[7] death upon themselves. Cato stabbed himself in the breast[8] with his sword. Instances of virtue are found everywhere, and, indeed, the most in the hardest times. Socrates instructed many young men in the most important things, and that without (any) recompense. Virtue wants no other reward except[9] that of praise. Nothing helps[10] that may not likewise[11] hurt. (He) takes away the greatest ornament of friendship who takes away from[12] it mutual respect[13].

[1]natūrā (Abl.) [2]culpă (Sing.) [3]consŭl [4]molestissĭme ferre alĭquid, *to be most annoyed by something* [5]Say: *is* [6]Abl. of **Means** [7]sibi mortem consciscĕre [8]Say: *stabbed the breast to himself* [9]praetĕr [10]prōdessĕ [11]īdĕm [12]ex [13]vĕrēcundĭă, -**ae**, *mutual respect*

Relative Pronouns.

SYNTAX *137—140.*

Est profecto Deus, qui quae nos gerĭmus, audit et videt. Malum est consilĭum, quod mutāri non potest. Quem di dilĭgunt adulescens morĭtur. Quod vides accidĕre puĕris id nobis quoque majuscŭlis puĕris evĕnit. Spero te quae tua prudentĭa et temperantĭa est, jam valēre.

57. The pleasure which is derived[1] from[2] base actions[3] passes away quickly. That indeed is welcome[4] praise which comes[5] from those who themselves have earned true and just praise. What fortune has not given she does not take away. All ancient nations formerly obeyed kings, a kind of government which was at first conferred on[6] the justest and wisest men. He who loves his children also chastises them. The evils we suffer in common with[7] many, seem to us lighter. The earth never returns without interest what it has received. Those are good citizens who adorn the state by (their) warlike glory and their own homes by (their) virtues. Cæsar, such[8] was his ambition, preferred to be the first in the smallest town than the second in Rome. Neoptolemus in[6] his cruelty spared neither old men nor boys. America was discovered by the aid[9] of the magnetic needle, the use of which the ancients did not know.

[1]capĕre [2]ex [3]turpĭa, *base actions* [4]jūcundŭs, -ă, -ŭm [5]proficisci [6]de-ferrĕ ăd [7]*in common with*, cŭm [8]Relative [9]ŏpĕ

Interrogative and Indefinite Pronouns.

SYNTAX *141—146.*

Nuda fere cacumĭna Alpĭum sunt et, si quid est pabŭli, obrŭunt nives. Noli quidquam sequi, quod assĕqui non queas. Alcidămas quidam scripsit laudatiōnem mortis. Suae quisque fortūnae faber est. Optĭmus quisque maxĭme glorĭa ducĭtur.

58. What was the cause of war? Which do you consider the greatest general, Cæsar, Scipio or[1] Hannibal? Which the better orator, Cicero or[1] Demosthenes? Who is better than God? No one. What man is most like God? The best[2]. Credulity is an error rather[3] than a fault and creeps most readily into the minds of the best[2]. Some nations live on[4] fish and birds' eggs. To every body his own manners are the most pleasing. It is the custom of fools to say anything. Laziness is shameful to every one, but especially to young men. Every man's life has some troubles. Whatever is honest is useful. There are some animals which live only one day. Youth is a certain part of life. (He) who teaches learns. I write this letter to some one of my friends. The manners of some young men are not pleasing to us. Every body looks out for[5] his own profit. Certain animals have a very long life. Every one loves his parents and to every one his parents are dear. All the arts which belong[6] to[7] cultivation have a certain common bond. The better one is, the more modest he is.

[1]ăn [2]Say: *each best* [3]măgĭs [4]Abl. [5]quaerō, -ĕrĕ, *to look out for* [6]per-tĭnĕō, -ērĕ [7]ăd

PART III. — Syntax of the Verb.

Tenses. Present and Perfect.

Syntax 147—151.

Scribo epistŭlam. Malum vas non frangĭtur. Invēni portum, spes et fortūna valēte, sat me lusistis, ludĭte nunc alĭos. Milo domum venit, calcĕos et vestimenta mutāvit, paulĭsper commorātus est. Tantum bellum Pompējus extrēma hiĕme apparāvit, ineunte vere suscēpit, medĭa aestāte confēcit.

59. Cæsar in the Pontic triumph amid the decorations of the procession carried before (him) an inscription of these three words: I came, I saw, I overcame. The Romans conquered the Corinthians and carried their[1] works of art to their own city. Italy first saw elephants in the war of king Pyrrhus and called them Lucanian oxen, because they first appeared in Lucania. The flashes of lightning reach[2] our eyes before we hear the crash of the thunders. Hannibal (as) general subdued in war all the tribes in Spain, stormed Saguntum, an allied city, and raised three armies. Of these he sent one into Africa; the second he left with his brother Hasdrubal in Spain, the third he brought with himself into Italy. I hold a wolf by the ears. The camel asking[3] for horns lost also (his) ears. Nature gave the fields, human art built the cities. The love of money grows as[4] money itself grows. When we are in good health[5] we all give easily good advice to the sick. Meanwhile Rome increases by the demolition of Alba; the number of citizens is doubled; the Caelian mount is added to the city.

[1]Say: *of them* [2]pervenīre ad, *to reach* [3]desiderāre, *to ask for* [4]quantŭm. [5]valēre, *to be in good health*

Imperfect, Pluperfect, Future. Periphrastic Conjugation.

Syntax 152—157.

Donec eris felix, multos numerābis amīcos; tempŏra si fuĕrint nubĭla, solus eris. Ansĕres Romae publĭce alebantur in Capitolĭo. Scripsĕram epistŭlam, cum amīcus adfŭit. Scribam epistŭlam cum otĭum nactus ero. Morĕre, Diagŏra, non enim in caelum ascensūrus es.

60. I used to read[1] the books of the ancient writers with great zeal and diligence in school. From[2] the tongue of Nestor, as Homer says[3], speech flowed more sweet than honey. The Lacedæmonians had two kings. Men will be more easily taught by examples than by precepts. Will you not[4] be moved by the prayers and tears of your parents? Augustus after the civil wars never called his soldiers "fellow-soldiers" but "soldiers". Why[5], if I shall ask you anything, will you not[4] answer? Agesilaus, king of the Lacedæmonians, sometimes played with his children whom he greatly loved. The Romans engraved the laws, which the senate and people had sanctioned, on[6] brass tables. Ariovistus, chief of the Germans, was about to occupy all Gaul. When I come[7] to New York, I will write to you about what[8] I shall see[7]. Verres used to live in the winter months at Syracuse. In spring he gave himself up[9] to work and travelling[10]; he was carried in a litter, in which there was a pillow[11] stuffed with roses[12].

[1]Imperf. [2]ex [3]ait [4]nonnĕ [5]quĭd [6]Abl. [7]Fut. Perf. [8]*about what*, Acc. [9]sē dărĕ [10]ĭtĭnĕră, -ŭm [11]pulvīnŭs, -ī [12]rosă, -ae (Sing.)

Tenses of the Indicative.

Syntax *158—163*.

Chabrĭas dum primus studet portam intrāre, ipse sibi perniciēi fuit. Ignāvus miles simŭlac hostem vidit, fugit. Cum ad villam veni, hoc ipsum nihil agĕre me delectat. Gratissĭmum mihi fecĕris, cum ad me venĕris.

61. Whilst Hannibal threatened (to) the city of Rome, the Romans sent (their) forces out of the city into Spain. While Pompey was deliberating, Cæsar with the utmost speed approached Rome. The false friend who promised aid to you against being fettered[1], as soon as the chain shall have clanked, will fly away. After the war was finished[2], the consul returned to Rome and triumphed. Cimon was recalled to his country five years after he was banished. Gnaeus Scipio was killed eight years after he came to Spain, and twenty nine days after the death of his brother. As often as each[3] cohort charged[4], a great number of the enemy fell. Young ducks[5] leave the hens, by which they have been hatched[6], as soon as they see the water. After Hannibal had taken Saguntum and subdued all the nations of Spain in war, he raised three armies, and sent one of them to Africa, the second he left with his brother Hasdrubal in Spain, the third and best he took with him to Italy. As soon as Pelopidas recognizes[7] the tyrant in the battle, he spurs on his horse against him, and falls pierced[8] with darts far away from his followers[9].

[1]Say: *against fellers* [2]confĭcĭō, -ĕrĕ [3]quisquĕ [4]prōcurrō,-ĕrĕ, Pluperf. [5]pulli anătum [6]exclūdō, -ĕrĕ [7]ănĭmadvertō, -ĕrō [8]confossŭs, -ă, -ŭm [9]sŭī, -ōrŭm

Sequence of Tenses.

Syntax *164—176.*

Nullum est anĭmal praeter homĭnem, quod habĕat alĭquam notitĭam Dei. Audīvi, quid agas. Nihil ex sapiente viro discet adulescens, quod nescisse rectĭus fuĕrit. Morāti melĭus erĭmus, cum didicerĭmus, quae natūra desidĕret. Natūra praescripsit homĭni, ut nihil pulchrĭus quam homĭnem putāret. Libertas ut laetĭor esset, ultĭmi regis superbĭa fecĕrat.

Words to be expressed by the Subjunctive are in *Italics.*

62. Have you[1] learned so little[2] in school that you *do not understand* this? So great is the multitude of stars that they *cannot* be numbered. Life is short, even if it *lasts* over[3] 100 years. Sometimes there is need that we *be reminded* of human frailty. Our ancestors often fought that they *might free* their country. Sometimes men praise others only[4] for the reason[5] that they *may be praised* by them. We carry on war that we *may enjoy* peace. We see every day how great *is* the goodness of God. Alexander had never said whom he *was about to make* his heir. Who does not know in how great honor music *was held*[6] among the Greeks? The boy fell down from the roof so that he *broke* his leg. For this reason[7] we have two ears and one mouth that we *may hear* much[2] and *speak* little[2]. There is no state that *has* not wicked citizens. Dogs are kept in houses that they *may give notice* if thieves *come*[8]. Tell me, I beseech you, what page the teacher *gave* us to be copied[9]. Caligula wished that the Roman people *had* one neck that he[10] *might fill* his cruelty by one stroke and at one day. Alexander, (when) about to die[11], to those asking whom he *wished* to make his heir answered: The worthiest. Plato calls pleasure a bait, because men *are caught* by it as fishes with a hook. Cæsar (when) dictator adjusted the year according to[12] the course of the sun, so that it *might be reckoned* (as consisting[13]) of 365 days, and one day *should be interpolated* every fourth year. So great a terror of the Germans prevailed[14] in Cæsar's camp that even wills *were written* by the Roman soldiers. The Pythagoreans rehearsed in the evening what[15] they *had said, heard* and *done* every day. Augustus was so great that he *despised* triumphs.

[1]tūnĕ [2]Neut. Plur. [3]suprā [4]tantŭm [5]ĭdĕō [6]Say: *was* [7]idcircō [8]Perf. [9]describendŭs, -ă, -ŭm [10]ipsĕ [11]mŏrĭbundŭs, -ă, -ŭm [12]ăd [13]not to be translated [14]Say: *was* [15]quĭd

Indicative Mood.

Syntax *177—180.*

Optandum est, ut aliquando alĭam viam ingrediāre. Erat amentis, cum acĭem vidēres, pacem cogitāre. Haec qualiacunque erant, reticenda non fuērunt. Brutum non minus amo quam tu: paene dixi quam te.

63. The time of death will come, and indeed quickly, whether you shall delay or hasten (it). It would be tedious to enumerate the battles of Hannibal. It would have been the best thing either to drive[1] those wicked men from[2] the state or to condemn (them) to death. The war ought either not have been undertaken, or been carried on consistently with[3] the dignity of the Roman people. Whether we live or die, we are in the hands[4] of God. I could enumerate many examples of rich men who have not been happy. It would lead too far to name all the Romans who willingly died for their country. It would be best to shun the company of bad people of whatever rank they may be. A flatterer likes sumptuous[5] dinners more than a rich man does[6], I had almost said, as the rich man himself. Tiberius Gracchus ended by a premature[7] death a life which he could have led most gloriously. It would have been just not to condemn Socrates to death, but to bestow upon[8] him the highest praise.

[1]ējĭcĭō, -ĕrĕ [2]Abl. [3]prō, *consistently with* [4]*in the hands of God*, Dei, Gen. *of property* [5]lautŭs, -ă, -ŭm [6]not to be translated [7]immātūrŭs, -ă, -ŭm [8]conferre in alĭquem, *to bestow upon*

Subjunctive Mood.

SYNTAX *181—186.*

Quis tibi hoc concessĕrit? Hoc di bene vertant. Quidquid ages, prudenter agas et respĭce finem. Ne difficilĭa optēmus. Ego tibi irascĕrer? Quo me confĕram, milĭtes, cui caput meum credam?

64. Cæsar could conclude the affair without a battle; why should he try[1] his luck? If we are Christians, let us have[2] Christian morals and speech[3]. In prosperity let us avoid[4] pride and haughtiness. Let every one know his own disposition[5] and show himself a sharp judge both of his good qualities[6] and his faults I should praise no virtue of Socrates more than his patience. Let us imitate our ancestors; let us remember that[7] justice is to be observed even towards the lowest. You may expel nature with a pitchfork, nevertheless it will ever[8] be returning[9]. Let not[10] your right hand know[10] what[11] your left hand doeth[12]. Valerius used to sing every day, because he was a stage-player; what else[13] should he do? Let him who has granted a favor, speak not of it[14]; let him who has received (one), proclaim[15] (it). Solon very well said[16]: Let others keep[17] riches for themselves, we virtue. Let us show ourselves worthy of our ancestors, let us love our country, let us obey our parents, let us worship God. Who would not admire the splendor and beauty of virtue? May I not be safe if I write otherwise than[18] I think!

[1]pĕrīclĭtŏr, -ārī [2]ūtŏr, -ī [3]vōcēs, Plur. [4]fŭgĭō, -ĕrĕ [5]ingĕnĭŭm, -ī [6]bŏnă, -ōrŭm, *good qualities* [7]justitĭam esse servandam, Acc. w. Inf. [8]usquĕ [9]rĕcurrō, -ĕrĕ [10]nescĭō, -īrĕ [11]quĭd [12]Subjunct. [13]alĭud [14]Say: *be silent* [15]narrō, -ārĕ [16]not to be translated [17]hăbĕō, -ērĕ [18]ăc

Consecutive Conjunctions.

SYNTAX *188—191.*

In eo statu res nostrae sunt, ut non possint esse miseriōres. Sequĭtur, ut de magnitudĭne belli dicam. Quis est tam demens, ut sua voluntâte maerĕat?

65. Atticus so lived that he was deservedly most dear to all the Athenians. Italy is so planted with trees that the whole (of it) appears an orchard. It happens, I know not how, that we see the faults of others more sharply than our own. So great was Cato's diligence that he, (when) an old man, learned the Greek language. Mithridates had so learned the languages of 22 nations which were under his rule, that he could speak without an interpreter with all whom he governed[1]. There is this common vice in great and free states that envy is the companion of glory. The kings of the Persians, for the sake of (their) pleasure, so divided the year that they spent the winter in Babylon, the summer in Media. Bears during winter are overcome with so heavy a sleep that they cannot be aroused even by wounds. He is rich who has so much that he desires nothing more[2]. Geese are too heavy of body[3] to be[4] able to fly conveniently. Socrates on[5] his trial for life so spoke for himself that he seemed not to be the defendant, but the master of his judges. Xanthippe, the wife of Socrates, was very cross and quarrelsome so that she was troublesome to her husband day and night.

[1]imperāre, w. Dat. [2]amplīus [3]Abl. [4]ŭt w. Subjunct. [5]in

Final Conjunctions.

Syntax *192—193.*

Pylădes Orestem se esse dixit, ut pro eo necarētur. Cura ut valēas. Omne anĭmal id agit, ut se conservet. Concēdo ut ea praetermittas, quae dum taces, nulla esse concēdis. Monēo te desīnas furĕre.

66. The Romans took[1] Cincinnatus from the plow that he might be dictator. Parents send their children to school in order to learn something. He who runs a race ought to strive[2] to conquer. Always think of death[3] that you may never fear it. Boys are exercised in labors[4] that they may become[5] strong in mind[4] and stout in body[4]. If we are not moved by honesty[6] itself to be good men, but by utility, we are smart, not good. Mirrors were invented, to make man acquainted with himself[7]. That you may be loved, be lovable. Reason has been given to us to be able to judge and to act rightly. You have often been admonished by your masters not to desire the company of bad people. Before old age let us see to it[8] that we live well, in old age that we die well. Alexander made an edict[9] that no one[10] should paint him except Apelles. Metellus persuaded the ambassadors of Jugurtha to deliver to him[11] the king alive or dead[12]. We ought to eat that we may live, not live that we may eat. Aeneas that he might win[13] the hearts[14] of the Aborigines, called both the nations Latins.

[1]abdūcĕre [2]contendĕre [3]Acc. [4]Abl. [5]evadĕre [6]hŏnestŭm, -ī [7]Say: *that man might know himself* [8]cūrārĕ, *to see to it* [9]ēdīcĕrĕ, *to make an edict* [10]nĕ quĭs [11]sĭbĭ [12]Say: *either alive or dead* (aut..aut) [13]sibi conciliāre [14]anĭmus

Verbs of *Hindering* and *Fearing*.

Syntax *194—200.*

Cura, ne in morbum incĭdas. Metŭo ne frustra labōrem suscepĕris. Opĕram dat Clodĭus, ut judicĭa ne fiant. Timĕo, ut hunc labōrem sustinĕas.

67. We fear that we cannot discharge[1] our duty. The fear at Rome was great that the Gauls would again come to Rome. Hannibal left Carthage through fear[2] that he might be betrayed[3] to the Romans. The physician feared that you would not recover from[4] this disease. The organ of hearing has a crooked passage, that nothing may be able to enter. We often patiently suffer[5] griefs that we may not fall into greater (ones). I fear that you are not diligent enough. The Athenians were in great fear that Xerxes would destroy the town. The citizens of the town besought the commander with tears[10] that he would not burn their town. I fear that my brothers will not come to the city. Herod gives orders[6] for the children to be slain. Take care lest you fall anew into sickness. There is no danger that he who can paint[7] a lion or a bull skilfully could not do the same thing[8] with[9] many other quadrupeds. The army begged Alexander with tears[10] to put an end to the war. The miser fears lest his goods may be snatched away[11] from him. Romulus, lest the greatness of the city should be void, opened a certain place (as) an asylum.

[1]satisfacĕre w. Dat. [2]Abl. [3]tradĕre [4]ex [5]perpĕti, *to suffer patiently* [6]imperāre, *to give orders* [7]*can paint*, Pres. Subjunct. [8]Idem [9]in [10]lacrĭmans [11]eripĕre, w. Dat. sibi

Subjunctive after quō, quīn.

Syntax *201—204.*

Leges breves sunto, quo facilĭus teneantur. Nemo est, quin hoc intellĕgat. Numquam accēdo, quin abs te abĕam doctĭor. Epaminondas non recusāvit, quomĭnus legis poenam subīret. Dubitandum non est, quin numquam possit utilĭtas cum honestāte contendĕre.

68. Nothing is found in the whole world that has not been most wisely ordained[1] by God. Xerxes did not doubt that with his forces he would easily overcome the Greeks. There is no doubt that God rules the world. We never sin without our conscience reminding[2] us. There is no doubt that all the bad are wretched. What hinders us from everywhere practising[3] virtue? The rain hinders us from walking. Nothing will prevent a good man from freely stating[4] his opinion. There is no man but knows that all things are ruled[5] by God. What prevented you from coming? Nothing is so difficult but that it can be found out by inquiring[6]. Nature has covered the trunks of trees with bark that they might be more secure from cold[7] and heat[7]. Old age does not hinder us from keeping up[8] literary[9] studies even to the last moment of our life. A defect of speech did not hinder[10] Demosthenes from becoming the greatest orator. Aristippus did not hesitate to call pain the greatest evil.

[1]instituĕre [2]monēre [3]colĕre [4]dicĕre [5]Say: *all things to be ruled*, omnĭa regi [6]quaerendo (Abl. of Gerund.) [7]Plur. [8]tenēre [9]literārum [10]officĕre w. Dat.

Temporal Conjunctions.

Syntax *205—210.*

Cæsar, cum Pompējum apud Pharsālum vicisset, in Asĭam trajēcit. Is qui non defendit injurĭam cum potest, injuste facit. Aegrōto dum anĭma est, spes esse dicĭtur. Alexander paullisper exercĭtum consistĕre jussit, donec considĕret pulvis.

69. When we are in good health[1], we easily give good advice[2] to the sick. After bees have alighted on[3] flowers, they suck honey from[4] them. When Diogenes saw the splendid gates of the little city (of) Myndus, he said to the townspeople: Shut your gates lest your city move out[5]. We see the lightning before we hear the thunder. The day before I came to London, my brother had departed for America. When the Roman ambassadors said to Ariovistus, chief of the Germans, "Come to Cæsar", he replied "Who is that Cæsar? If (he) likes[6], let him[7] come to me." Let boys be silent when wiser people speak. When Cicero was quaestor in Sicily, he discovered the tomb of Archimedes. Cæsar after his violent death[8] lay lifeless some time, until three slaves carried[9] him home. Labor while you can that you may rest when you become[10] feeble. Fortune is like glass[11]; at the very time[12] when it is bright, it is broken. When the Nile restrains[13] its overflow of waters, the Egyptians vainly expect[14] fertility of lands. Aristides lived in exile until he was recalled by his fellow-citizens. The Spartans were wont to consult the oracles before they went[15] to war.

[1]valēre [2]Plur. [3]In [4]ex [5]ēgrĕdĭŏr, -ī [6]lĭbĕt [7]ipse [8]nex, nĕcĭs, *violent death* [9]referre [10]esse, Fut. [11]vitrĕŭs, -ă, -ŭm, *like glass* [12]tŭm [13]Perfect [14]sperāre [15]proficisci

Causal Conjunctions.

Syntax *211—217.*

Mater irāta est, quia non rediĕrim. Bene facis quod littĕras voluptatĭbus antepōnis. Quod mihi de nuptĭis filĭae gratulāris, agnosco humanitātem tuam. Quonĭam de genĕre belli dixi, nunc de magnitudĭne pauca dicam. Non reprehendo: quippe cum ipse istam reprehensiōnem non fugĕrim.

70. He who forsakes you has never been your friend, because true friendship never ceases. Since the soul of man is immortal, it can in no manner[1] perish. Those things which[2] are to be done to-day, do to-day, since the morrow[3] is uncertain. (There are) many crimes (which) bad men do not commit, because they fear that they may be punished. Why shall I hear words since I see deeds? Zopyrus was laughed at[4] by the others, because he blamed vices in Socrates, which the latter had not. Many comets we do not see, because they are obscured by the rays of the sun. Men wonder at[5] eclipses of the sun, because they happen rarely, and they wonder at eclipses of the sun more than of the moon, since the latter are more frequent[6]. There was an immense number of captives whom

Hannibal sold since they were not redeemed by their folks. No one loves his country because it is great, but because it is his own. Cicero was called the father of his country, because by his[7] prudence and vigilance the conspiracy of Catiline had been detected. The Aeduans complained that Ariovistus had led a great army of Germans across the Rhine into Gaul.

[1]nullō mŏdō [2]quae, *those things which* [3]dies crastīnus [4]dērīdĕrĕ [5]mīrŏr -āri [6]crēbĕr, -ră, -rŭm [7]Say: *of him*

Conditional Sentences.

Syntax *218—224.*

Manent ingenĭa senĭbus, modo permanĕat studĭum et industrĭa. Si dies est, lucet. Si quis id fecĕrit, imprudentem eum dixĕris. Facĕrem si possem. Si verum respondĕre velles, haec erant dicenda. Parvi sunt foris arma, nisi est consilĭum domi. Aequĭtas tollĭtur omnis, si suum cuĭque habĕre non licĕat.

71. You will be sad if you are[1] alone. If the masters of the houses are not at home, danger more easily threatens the houses[2]. Physicians if they could cure all diseases, would be very happy. Many neglect every thing[3] honorable and virtuous[4], provided they attain power. Provided we are sheltered and clothed against the storm, we care little for[5] ornament. If you dwell[6] near[7] a lame person, you will learn to limp. The Gauls suffer with an even mind all the outrages of war, provided only they ward off the outrage of slavery. A countryman once hired a piece of land from Jupiter on this condition[8] that he should yield up to Jupiter half[9] of the fruits if the god would do every thing, would send rain, make a clear sky, send breezes, at his pleasure[10]. Laws were invented for no other reason[11] than that[12] citizens might be kept safe. If all people[13] had collected their misfortunes into one place, each one would prefer to carry[14] his own back[14] home rather than accept his hears from[15] the common heap of miseries. An innocent person, if he is accused, can be acquitted; a guilty person, unless he shall have been accused, cannot be condemned.

[1]Fut. [2]Dat. [3]omnĭa [4]rectŭs, -ă, -ŭm [5]Acc. [6]Subjunct. [7]juxtā [8]Abl. [9]dimidĭa pars [10]ad ipsĭus nutum, *at his pleasure* [11]nulla alĭa de causa [12]nisi ut [13]cuncti, *all people* [14]reportāre [15]ē, ex

Concessive Conjunctions.

Syntax *225—229.*

Licet fremant omnes, ego non tacēbo. Quamquam festīnas, non est mora longa. Nihĭlo minus eloquentĭae studendum est, etsi ea quidam perverse abutuntur. Attĭcus honōres non petĭit, cum ei patērent.

72. No one, however rich he may be, can dispense with[1] the help of others. A good man will not do what is base although it may bring[2] him money. Although the Romans were the conquerors of almost the whole world, nevertheless their[3] greed was not yet satisfied. Beware[4] of telling a falsehood; for God hears every thing, although[5] men may not hear. Socrates although he was the most innocent of all men, nevertheless was accused and condemned. Although[6] truth obtains no patron or defender, yet it is defended by[7] itself. A dwarf is not great, although[6] he stand[8] on a mountain; a colossus will retain[9] its magnitude, even if[10] it stand[11] in a well. Though[6] ambition itself be a fault, yet it is often a cause of virtues. Although the ground[12] was unfavorable[13], nevertheless Cæsar determined to attack the enemy. Granted that Rome was founded before the time of Romulus, nevertheless the Roman historians begin with[14] him. However full thy coffer may be, I do not consider thee rich while I see thee unsatisfied[15]. Though[16] glory may not[17] possess[18] anything[17] in itself, yet it follows virtue like[19] (its) shadow.

[1]carēre w. Abl. [2]afferre, Fut. [3]Say: *of them* [4]cavēre nē [5]etsī [6]lĭcĕt [7]pĕr [8]consistō, -ĕrĕ, Perf. [9]servō, -ārĕ [10]ĕtĭamsī [11]stārĕ, Perf. [12]lŏcŭs, -ī [13]ĭnīquŭs, -ă, -ŭm [14]ā [15]ĭnānĭs, -ĕ [16]etsī [17]nĭhĭl [18]habēre [19]tamquăm

Comparative Conjunctions.

Syntax *230. 231.*

Ita tibi rem commendo, tamquam si tua res agātur. Ut aurum igni, sic benevolentĭa fidēlis pericŭlo alĭquo perspĭci potest. Metelli sperat sibi quisque fortūnam, proinde quasi plures fortunāti sint, quam infelĭces.

73. Apelles, a very illustrious painter, had painted Alexander the Great on horseback[1]. The king praised the likeness less than it deserved. But when Alexander's horse neighed to the painted horse as if it were a real steed, "Your horse, O king," said Apelles, "appears to be a better judge[2] of the art of painting than you (are[3])". So live with men as if God saw you; so speak with God as if men heard you. We ought to live[4] as if we lived in the sight of all men. We should so think[5] as if some one could look into our inmost breast. It is foolish in grief[6] to pluck out one's hair, as if sorrow[7] could be lessened[8] by baldness. Like swallows in summer time, so false friends are at hand in the serene time of life. Xerxes sent 4000 armed men to Delphi to plunder[9] the temple of Apollo, as if he were carrying on war not only with the Greeks but with the immortal Gods. Many noble Romans, for instance Camillus, Curius Dentatus, Cincinnatus and others, cultivated their fields. My brother treats me as if I were a king. Virtuous men always act in such a manner[10] as if all (men) were looking at them. Those who injure[11] some[12] in order to be liberal towards others[12], are guilty of[13] the same injustice as if they appropriated[14] other people's property.

[1]ĕquĭtans, -tĭs [2]pĕrītĭŏr, *a better judge* [3]not to be translated [4]vivendum est [5]cogitandum est [6]luctŭs, -ūs [7]maerŏr, -ōrĭs [8]lĕvō, -ārĕ [9]Say: *who might plunder* [10]sīc [11]nŏcĕō, -ērĕ [12]alĭus [13]*guilty of = in the same injustice* [14]in suam rem aliēna convertĕre, *to appropriate other people's property*

Relative Clauses with Subjunctive.

Syntax *232—238.*

Pyrrhus ad Românos legâtum misit, qui pacem aequis condicionĭbus petĕret. Artaxerxes comparāvit exercĭtum quem in Graecĭam mittĕret. Nulla vis tanta est, quae non debilitāri possit. Ea est Romāna gens, quae victa quiescĕre nescĭat.

74. You may read a good book again and again; but many books do not deserve[1] to be read a second time. Words were devised not to conceal but to reveal truth. There is no speed which can be compared with the speed of the mind. Nothing is so useful that it cannot become hurtful by abuse. There is no grief which length of time may not diminish and assuage. There is nothing which God cannot accomplish and indeed without any[2] labor. What lurking place is there into which the fear of death may not enter! There have been many found who were ready to give up[3] not only their money but even life for their country. There are some who seek[4] money more ardently than learning. There is no one who hates himself. There is hardly a[5] night during which[6] we may not dream. The old man plants trees to benefit[7] the next generation. Aristides was expelled by the Athenians, because he was called the Just in preference[8] to others[9]. Cæsar gave rewards to brave soldiers, that they might defend more bravely what they had acquired.

[1]non satis digni sunt [2]ullus [3]profundĕre [4]appetĕre [5]nulla fere [6]quā [7]Say: *which may benefit* [8]praeter [9]cētĕrī, -ae, -ā

75. If there is anything which feels neither pleasure nor pain, that cannot be an animal. The government of the world has nothing in it[1] that can be found fault with[2]. If you wish[3] to compare riches with virtue, riches will appear hardly fit[4] to be the waiting-maid of virtue. Caninius was (a man) of wonderful wakefulness[5], since during his whole consulship he did not see sleep. Nero was given to[6] uncommon luxury since he fished with golden nets. King Philip called in Aristotle (to be) the teacher of his son Alexander that he[7] might receive from him both rules for[8] acting and speaking. The losses of reputation and credit are greater than can be estimated. There is none of all whom I now wish to see more than you. Laws have been invented that they[7] might speak with all in one and the same language[9]. In all times fewer have been found who conquered their desires than the forces of the enemy. Although Aristides distinguished himself so much[10] in moderation[11], that he alone, as far as we have heard, was surnamed[12] the Just, yet he was punished with an exile of ten years. I fear I shall increase the labor while I wish to diminish it. There is nothing that cannot be bought if you will give as much as the seller wants. There is nothing more disgraceful than to carry on war with those with whom you have lived on intimate terms[13].

[1]sē [2]reprehendĕre [3]vellĕ, Fut. [4]vix satis idonĕus, *hardly fit* [5]Abl. of quality [6]*given to* = *of*, Gen. of quality [7]that he = quī [8]Gen. Gerund. [9]vox, Abl. [10]ădĕō [11]Abl. without Prep. [12]cognomĭne appellāre [13]fămĭlĭārĭtĕr

Imperative.

SYNTAX *240—245.*

Dic cur hic. Cura, ut valĕas. Apud judĭces vera loquĭtor. Nihil gratĭae causa fecĕris. Puer ne telum habĕat. Nocturna sacrificĭa ne sunto. Noli me tangĕre. Cave credas. Fac ne quid alĭud cures.

76. Pray and work. Get up, boys, right early in the morning[1]. Learn or depart[2]. Philip, king of the Macedonians, used to say: Fight with silver weapons, and you will conquer every thing. Attalus, king of the Pergameans, left this will: The Roman people shall be the heir of my goods. Let the other[3] side also[4] be heard. A good book you should read a second time. Reverence God, reverence (your) parents and those whom nature has given you in place[5] of (your) parents. Do not admire all things which have a show of glory. Let us imitate the example of Christ who blessed his very enemies. Look to[6] the mind of a man, not his forehead. Let no one despair, God will give to every one what will benefit him most. Of[7] two evils choose[8] the less, of two vices neither. Do not put off a pressing affair till[9] to-morrow[10]. Let the right hand carry the sword, the other display[11] peace. Add not fire to fire. Be ye not[12] disheartened[13] even[12] in the greatest danger! The conqueror should spare the enemy. Let there be a sound mind in a sound body. Before old age take care[14] that you live well, in old age, that you die well.

[1]bene mane, *right early in the morning* [2]discedĕre [3]altĕr [4]ĕt [5]lŏcō [6]spectāre [7]e, ex [8]elĭgĕre [9]In w. Acc. [10]dies crastĭnus [11]monstrāre [12]ne. . quĭdĕm, *not even* [13]anĭmos dimittĕre, *to be disheartened* [14]curāre

Infinitive.

SYNTAX *246—250.*

Imperāre sibi maxĭmum est imperĭum. Necesse est mori. Non esse cupĭdum pecunĭa est. Omnes homĭnes student beāti fiĕri.

77. It is easy to do harm, difficult to do good. It is the first virtue to fly vice. To dwell in the city is irksome to him who has been accustomed to live in the country. It is beautiful to speak the truth[1], it is more beautiful to hear (it) willingly. To die is not to perish. All who wish to live according to nature, will obey[2] divine and human law. If you wish to subject all things to yourself, subject yourself to reason. It is mean to prefer money to friendship. He who has accustomed himself to lie, will easily steal. I have never wished to please the people[3], for what I know the people do not approve, what they approve I am ignorant of. To lose a friend is the greatest of losses. Very many cannot govern their passions, and yet they wish to rule others. Life itself teaches very many to be wise. Nothing is more miserable than on account of money[4] to despise God. I have often been sorry for having spoken, for having been silent, never. All who wish to transact[5] great affairs[6] are accustomed to think long. All men strive for[7] liberty, but not all have learned to be free. It is better a thousand times to perish than not to be able to live in one's own state without a guard of armed men. To be content with one's own possessions[8] is the greatest riches. It is always advantageous[9] to be a good man, because it is always honorable.

[1]vērŭm, -ī [2]părēre, w. Dat. [3]pŏpŭlŭs [4]nummī, -ōrŭm [5]ăgĕrĕ [6]nĕgōtĭŭm, -ī [7]pĕtĕrĕ, *to strive for* [8]rēs [9]ūtĭlĭs, -ĕ

Accusative with the Infinitive. (Subject)

Syntax *254*.

Verum est amicitĭam nisi inter bonos esse non posse. Omnĭbus bonis expĕdit salvam esse rempublĭcam. Legem brevem esse oportet. Constat ad salūtem civĭum inventas esse leges. Illis timĭdis et ignāvis licet esse.

78. It is certain that children are loved by (their) parents. It is agreed that laws were invented for the safety of citizens. It is true that upon this earth no one is always happy. It can easily be understood that the mind both hears and sees, and not those parts which are, as it were[1], the windows of the mind. A liar should[2] have a good memory[3]. It can be truly[4] said that a magistrate is a speaking law, but a law a mute magistrate. It is agreed among all writers that Romulus was the first king of the Romans. It is handed down[5] to us by the poets that a woman was the cause of the Trojan war. It is known that the Romans were often conquered by Hannibal.

It is probable that most[6] stars are suns. It is certain that the world is the work of God. It is a crime for[7] children to be ungrateful towards (their) parents. It is evident that nobody is without faults. To have been rich is a small consolation. It was not lawful[8] for a patrician to be made tribune of the people. It was known that Cæsar would make war[9] upon theBritons. It is right that a victor spare the vanquished.

[1]quăsĭ, *as it were* [2]ŏportĕt [3]memŏrem esse, *to have a good memory* [4]vērē [5]tradĕre [6]plerīque [7]Acc. [8]lĭcĕt [9]bellum inferre alicui

79. How foolish it is to trust too much to prosperity! It is credible that the world was made for the sake of men. It becomes all men who consult about[1] doubtful affairs to be free[2] from anger and partiality. It is necessary that the world be governed by God. It is well known that the inhabitants of the Balearic Islands implored the aid of the Roman army against an excessive multitude of rabbits. It is more difficult to bear wisely good fortune than bad[3]. It has never been heard that a crocodile was injured by an Egyptian. Certain it is that many people die daily. There is a story that Remus, in mockery[4] of his brother, leaped across the new walls of Rome. It is fitting[5] that a narrative should have three things[6]: that[7] it be short, clear and probable. It is well known that all Sicily had been anciently dedicated to Ceres and Prǫserpina. Nothing is more difficult for friendship[8] than to continue down to[9] the last day of life. It is necessary that every mortal body should perish some time[10]. Would it not[11] be better[12] for you[8] to be dumb than to be eloquent to[13] the ruin of others? It concerns me much that you all should be good boys. It is becoming that our country should be dearer to us than our very selves[14]. It is an excellent precept of wisdom, that each one of us ought[15] to have a greater regard[16] for that time[17] which will follow[18] after our death than for that short and scanty (time) which[19] we have in this life.

[1]dē [2]vacŭus, w. Abl. [3]Say: *good than bad fortune* [4]Dat. [5]convĕnit [6]trĭa [7]ŭt [8]Acc. [9]usquĕ ăd [10]alĭquo tempŏre [11]nonnĕ [12]praestat [13]ĭn, w. Acc. [14]nosmet ipsi [15]debēre [16]cūra [17]Gen. [18]consĕqui [19]quō

Accusative with the Infinitive. (Object)

SYNTAX *255.*

Spero me mox reditūrum esse. Alexander dicēbat se filĭum Jovis esse. Sentĭmus calēre ignem, nivem esse albam, dulce mel. Orphĕum poētam docet Aristotĕles numquam fuisse.

80. I know that I am mortal. We know that we are mortal. We know that the sun is larger than the moon. You see that there is nothing so like death than sleep. Who has not heard that the Romans were conquered by Hannibal near[1] Cannae? We know that the sun is very far[2] distant from the earth. Anaxagoras denied that snow is white. We see that fire is the cause of heat. We see that the moon is sometimes eclipsed by the shadow of the earth. All believe that the knowledge of future things is not very[3] useful to us. History relates that Rome was founded by Romulus. Every body considers his own misfortune[4] the most grievous[5]. We see that death is common to every age; still[6] a youth hopes that he will live long which he[7] cannot hope for (when[8]) old. Know you not that kings have long hands? Experience teaches that our life is subject to many dangers. We know that the alternation[9] of day and night is caused by the revolution[10] of the earth around its axis. Demaratus informed[11] the Lacedæmonians by letter that Xerxes was getting ready for war[12]. There is no hope of his returning soon. You have never heard that fools are pleasing to sensible people. Who will deny that virtue is the greatest riches?

[1]ăpŭd [2]longissĭme [3]parum, *not very* [4]călămĭtās, -ātis [5]mĭsĕr, -ă, -ŭm [6]ăt [7]ĭdĕm [8]not to be translated [9]vĭcissĭtūdŏ, -ĭnis [10]mōtŭs, -ūs [11]certiōrem facĕre [12]bellum parāre

Use of the Infinitive after Verbs of *Declaring* and *Perceiving*.

SYNTAX *256—258.*

Credo eum scribĕre; credēbam eum scribĕre. Credo eum scripsisse; credēbam eum scripsisse. Credo eum scriptūrum esse; credēbam eum scriptūrum esse. Romāni putābant fore ut Galli vincerentur.

81. The ancient Greeks and Romans thought there were many gods. We perceive by the touch that stones are hard.

Alexander hearing that Dareus was raising[1] immense[2] bodies[3] of soldiers, said: One wolf is not afraid of many sheep. Aristotle asserts[4] that there never was a poet Orpheus. Most people[5] say that their own dangers are nearer to them than those of others[6]. Solon said that before death no one ought to be called[7] happy. Many Romans believed that Germany could not be inhabited[8] on account of the cold. Who does not know that griefs[9] are assuaged by tears? They say that Romulus was brought up among shepherds. Lucilius says that Crassus once laughed in (his) life. The Epicureans said that nothing was better[10] than a life of ease[11]. Socrates used to say that the appetizer of food was hunger, of drink thirst. The oracle of Delphi said that Socrates was the wisest of all men. Cæsar and Tacitus write that the Germans were of immense bodily[12] stature. Cæsar found that most[13] (of) the Belgians were sprung[14] from[15] the Germans and anciently brought across[16] the Rhine. Herodotus says that by the Persians nothing was judged baser[17] than lying.

[1]parāre [2]innŭmĕrābĭlĭs, -ĕ [3]copĭae [4]docēre [5]plurĭmi [6]aliēnus [7]Gerundive [8]incolĕre [9]dolor [10]praestabĭlĭs, -ĕ [11]ōtĭōsŭs, -ă, -ŭm [12]Say: *of the body* [13]plerīque [14]ŏrĭŏr, -īri [15]ā [16]transdūcō, -ĕrĕ [17]turpĭs, -ĕ

Accusative with the Infinitive after Verbs of *Will* and *Desire*.

Syntax *259—261.*

Cupĭo me non dissolūtum vidēri. Milĭtes quod jussi sunt facĭunt. Lex recte facĕre jubet, vetat delinquĕre. Meum factum abs te probāri gaudĕo.

82. A youth commonly[1] hopes that he will live long. In war times we hope that the good cause shall at length[2] triumph. Crœsus, king of Lydia, ordered all his treasures to be shown to Solon. Xerxes ordered the sea to be scourged[3]. Your parents wish you to be diligent and pious, they do not wish you to have bad friends. We hope that from this life we shall go[4] to another and happier life. Nature herself bids us to be thankful. All wish to live happily. You promised to come, but you did not come. Remember that you will die. One[5] of the consuls was ordered to go with an army to Africa. The Romans ordered the Carthaginians to leave the town and to live somewhere else[6]. The thirty tyrants caused the best citizens of Athens to be thrown[7] into prison. We rejoice that our country is saved from those perils. I have often wondered that the countless army of the Persians was vanquished by the small handful[8] of Greeks. The Pythian Apollo bids us know ourselves. The father forbids his son to come into his sight[9]. Your teachers praise you for[10] learning so diligently. The Egyptians believed that the souls migrated from[11] the bodies of men into the bodies of animals.

[1]plerumque [2]tandem [3]flagellis caedĕre [4]venīre [5]alter [6]ălĭcŭbī [7]conjicĕre [8]mănŭs, -ūs [9]conspectŭs, -ūs [10]quŏd [11]ex

Nominative with the Infinitive.

Syntax 262—267.

Adesse equĭtes nuntiabantur. Omnĭbus vidēmur recte fecisse, quod amīci causam defenderĭmus. Ne fando quidem audītum est crocodīlum aut ibim aut felem violātam esse ab Aegyptĭo. Te suspĭcor iisdem rebus, quibus me ipsum, commovēri.

83. Xanthippe, the wife of Socrates, is said to have been cross and quarrelsome in a high degree. Lycurgus persuaded the Lacedæmonians that he had received his laws from Apollo. It seems as if Sicily was once joined[1] to Italy. They say that Plato came to Italy to[2] make the acquaintance[3] of the Pythagoreans. The Phœnicians it is said were very experienced sailors. Philip, king of the Macedonians, used to say[4] that all forts could be captured into which only[5] a donkey laden with gold could climb up. Most people love those friends most from[6] whom they hope they will gain[7] the greatest advantage[8]. Ceres is said to have first taught men the use of corn. Tacitus who has most accurately described the manners of the Germans and the situation of their country, is believed to narrate not only what he heard[9] but also what he himself saw[10]. Thales of Miletus is said to have first predicted an eclipse of the sun. A miser is grieved[11] that his neighbor is richer than himself.

Homer is said to have lived in the time[12] of Lycurgus. The discipline of the Druids is supposed to have been devised in Britain and hence brought across[13] into Gaul.

[1]adhaerēre, *to be joined* [2]ŭt [3]cognoscĕre [4]Imperf. [5]mŏdŏ [6]ex [7]capĕre [8]fructŭs, -ūs [9]audīta, -ōrŭm, *what he heard* [10]Perf. Subjunct. [11]aegre patī [12]Plur. [13]transferre

Simple Questions.

Syntax *268—275.*

Quis non paupertātem extimescit? Unde dejectus est Cinna? ex urbe. Quare vitĭa sua nemo confitētur? Potestne hic tacēre? Num vespertilĭo avis est? Nonne poētae post mortem nobilitāri volunt? Numquid duas habētis patrĭas?

84. What is the sun? Is not iron far more useful than gold? Is the body mortal? Is the soul immortal? Is gold more excellent than wisdom? Are crocodiles fishes? Do we not owe the greatest thanks to our parents? Why were you not in school yesterday? Were you sick? Is man alone on this earth endowed with reason? Where are those who have been in the world before us? Shall a wise man be wretched when he is poor? Were you in school when I was at your house yesterday? Who was more eloquent than Demosthenes? What is sweeter than honey? To whom have you lent your book? How many years did Alexander the Great reign? Of what parts[1] does man consist[2]? In what year did the first Punic war break out[3]? Are they worthy of life who do nothing praiseworthy? Is each one the[4] happier the[4] richer he is? Are they all cowards who are taken in battle? Did the Athenians do right[5] in driving[6] Aristides from the state? Does anybody be angry with boys[7] whose age does not yet know[8] the distinctions[9] of things? If a father should try[10] to betray his country, will the son be silent? Where or of what sort[10] is your mind? Can you tell?

[1]Abl. [2]constāre [3]exardescō, -ĕrĕ [4]ĕō..quō [5]rectē facĕrĕ [6]Say: *that they drove* [7]Dat. [8]nōvī, -issĕ [9]discrīmĕn, -īnis [10]cōnŏr, -āri, Fut. [11]quālĭs, -ĕ

Disjunctive Questions.

SYNTAX *276—280.*

Vosne Domitĭum, an Domitĭus vos desernit? Utrum hoc tu parum meministi, an ego non satis intellexi? Quid istic tibi negotĭi est? Mihīne? Ita. — Estne frater intus? Non est. — Dic, quaeso, tune es Myconĭus? Non sum.

85. Is the sun or the moon the greater? Whether is gold or silver the heavier? Have you been at home or at school? Have you been at home or not? Is the bat a bird? By no means. — Does not the perusal of this book delight you? It delights me, indeed. — Is there anything more excellent[1] than virtue? Nothing, indeed. — Is the sun larger or smaller than the earth? Is the mind immortal, or will it perish together with the body? Are you laughing or crying? Is this your house? Yes. — Is the world governed by the providence of God or by chance? Does wisdom alone make us happy or not? Do not men often despise the better[2]? Did you read the book which I sent you the other day[3]? No, I did not. Did you write this letter or your brother? All wicked men are slaves[4]; or is he free who is a slave[5] to his lust? Don't you see the large flock of sheep in our meadow? Yes, I see the sheep, and the dog, but no shepherd. Are we not children of one parent? Certainly. How long have you been in the city, my friends? Six days. Are these your words or not? Is Fabricius unhappy because he himself digs his own ground[6]? Was your friend in need[7]? Nay[8], he was wealthy.

[1]praeclārŭs, -ă, -ŭm [2]mĕlĭōră, -ŭm [3]nūpĕr, *the other day* [4]servŭs, -ī [5]servīre, *to be a slave* [6]rūs, rūrĭs [7]ĕgĕō, -ērĕ [8]immō

Indirect Questions.

SYNTAX *239. 275. 276.*

Nescĭo num pater domi sit. Dubĭto, num idem tibi suadēre quod mihi debĕam. Quaerĭtur, utrum Carthāgo diruātur, an Carthaginiensĭbus reddātur, an colonĭa eo deducātur. Disce quid sit vivĕre. Dii utrum sint, necne sint quaerĭtur.

86. Charles, bring me word[1] whether your brother is at home. The mind itself does not know what the mind is. Where have you been? Tell me whether you were in school yesterday? Your father does not know where you have been. It is doubtful whether he is a good[2] man or a bad one. In former times it was a question whether the earth was round. It is uncertain how long the life of every one of us will be. People do not understand how great an income[3] frugality is. All ask if he be rich, no one if he be good. It is uncertain what shall be to-morrow. How long man shall be on earth is unknown to him. Whether the[1] number of stars be even or odd is uncertain. Which[4] of you is the older? I do not know which of you is the older. Why did you not come to me? Tell me why did you not come to me. Will the physician ask a sick person whether he will[5] be healed? Tell me does it hail in summer or in winter? Whether or not wisdom makes men happy is a question[6]. It makes great difference[7] whether an injury was done by chance or on purpose[8]. It is uncertain in what place death is looking for[9] you; therefore[10] do you look for it in every place. Is there one world or several[11]? The question is whether there is one world or several.

[1]rĕnuntiāre [2]probus [3]vectīgal [4]uter [5]velle [6]quaerĭtur, *it is a question* [7]multum intĕrest, *it makes great difference* [8]de industrĭa [9]exspectāre [10]ităque [11]plures

87. Xenocrates when he was asked why he was almost always silent replied: Because I have been sorry[1] sometimes[2] for having spoken, for having been silent never. Thales being asked what was most[3] common to men replied: Hope, for even they have that who (have[4]) nothing else. Who has read this book? Tell (me[4]) who has read this book. Is it not plain[5] that this whole world is governed by God? It can hardly be told with how many and how great dangers human life is surrounded[6]. Judges are accustomed to ask the defendants by what causes they were driven[7] to[8] those crimes of which they are accused. Can the fish love the angler? Are you so foolish that you should believe all these things to have been made by chance? It is uncertain what each night or day may bring forth. The magnet is a stone which lures[9] and attracts[10] iron; the reason why it happens I cannot tell[11]; that it actually[12] happens you will not deny. Many tribes do not know why the moon is eclipsed[13]. Alexander's friends asked him[14] whom he made heir of the throne. I am inclined to think[15] that Hannibal was more wonderful in adversity than in prosperity. It is asked whether virtue can be secured[16] by nature or by education[17]. Faustulus compelled by necessity, informed Romulus who was (his) grandfather, who (his) mother. We will consider what he has done, what he is doing, what he is going to do.

[1]paenĭtet [2]aliquando [3]maxĭme [4]*not to be translated* [5]perspicŭus [6]circumdăre (Perf.) [7]impellĕre [8]ăd [9]allicĕre [10]ad se attrahĕre [11]afferre [12]omnīno [13]dĕficĕre, *to be eclipsed* [14]Say: *the friends asked Alexander* [15]haud scio an [16]efficĕre [17]doctrīna.

Oratĭo recta. — Syntax *281.*

88. A certain man flogged his servant principally on account of his laziness. The latter began to cry out: "Why do you flog me? I have done nothing." — "Exactly for this very reason[1] I flog you", replies the master, "because[2] you have done nothing."

[1]proptĕr ĭd ipsŭm, *for this very reason* [2]quŏd

An ant in winter time dragged from her hole the grains which she had prudently[1] collected in summer and was drying them. A hungry cricket asked her to[2] share[3] something with him[4], to whom the ant said: "What were you doing in the summer?" Then the other answered: "I had no time[5] to[6] think of[7] the future, I roved about chirruping among[8] the hedges and pastures." The ant laughing and carrying the grains back spoke thus: "If you chirruped in summer, go[9] dance now in winter."

[1]Adject. [2]ŭt [3]impertīre [4]Dat. [5]ŏtĭŭm est [6]ŭt [7]dĕ [8]pĕr [9]ăgĕ

A lion stricken in years[1] feigned sickness. Then several beasts came to[2] visit the sick king who immediately devoured them. But the wily fox stood before the cave at a distance saluting the king. The lion asked: "Why do you not enter?" The fox replied: "Because I see many footsteps of those[3] entering, but none of those[3] departing."

[1]Abl. [2]ăd w. Acc. Gerundive [3]not to be translated

89. A gnat perched[1] on the horn of a bull said: "If I oppress you by my weight[2], I will fly off immediately[3]." But the bull replied: "It is no matter[4] to me whether you stay or fly off, for I have not felt you at all[5].

[1]sĕdens [2]mōlēs, -īs [3]prōtĭnŭs [4]nihil intĕrest [5]prorsŭs.

A cuckoo questioned a starling which had flown from the city: "What do people say of my song? What of the nightingale?" — "They praise the song of the nightingale most particularly", says the starling. "What about the lark?" — "A great many[1] praise its[2] song also," answers the starling. "And what do they say about the quail?" — "Some also are delighted with its voice." — "What, pray[3]," asks the cuckoo, "do they think of me?" — "That," replied the starling, "I cannot say, for nobody makes mention of you." The cuckoo angry says: "Therefore, I will always speak of myself[4].

[1]permultī [2]hīc [3]tandĕm [4]de me ipsĕ.

Aristides, among the Athenians, and Epaminondas among the Thebans, are said to have been such lovers[1] of truth that they never told a lie even in jest. Atticus, likewise, with whom Cicero lived in the greatest intimacy, never told nor could bear[2] a lie. "I hate the man", Achilles used to say, "as much as I do[3] the gates of Pluto, who says one thing[4] and thinks another[4]." — "Liars", Aristotle was wont to observe, "gain[5] this, that when they have spoken the truth, they are not believed[6]."

[1]adĕo amans [2]pătī [3]aequē ăc, *as much as I do* [4]ălĭŭd..ălĭŭd [5]consĕqui [6]Say: *it is not believed to them.*

Oratĭo Oblīqua.

Syntax *282—283.*

Apud Hypănim fluvĭum, inquit Aristotĕles, bestiŏlae quaedam nascuntur, quae unum diem vivunt.

Apud Hypănim fluvĭum Aristotĕles ait bestiŏlas quasdam nasci, quae unum diem vivant.

90. Bitter enemies deserve better of[1] some people than those friends who seem obliging; the former[2] often tell the truth, the latter[2] never.

Cato used to say that bitter enemies deserved better of some people than those friends who seemed obliging, that the former often told the truth, the latter never.

Scipio when he was styled king by the Spaniards said: "The name of general which[3] my soldiers have called me, is to me the greatest; the kingly name, elsewhere great, is intolerable at Rome; I beseech you to[4] abstain from the appellation of king.

Scipio when he was styled king by the Spaniards said that the name of general which the soldiers called him, was to him the greatest, the kingly name, elsewhere great, was intolerable at Rome; he besought them to abstain from the appellation of king.

Diogenes used to boast how much[5] he excelled even[6] the king of Persia in happiness. "To me", says he, "nothing is wanting, to him nothing will be ever enough; I do not desire his pleasures, he can in no manner attain[7] to mine."

Diogenes used to boast how much he excelled even the king of Persia in happiness (by saying) that to himself nothing was wanting, to the king nothing would be enough; that he did not desire the king's pleasures, and the king could in no manner attain to his.

Tiberius wrote to the governors of the provinces the following[8]: It is the duty of a good shepherd to shear, not to skin, his sheep.

Tiberius wrote to the governors of the provinces that it was the duty of a good shepherd to shear, not to skin, his sheep.

[1]dē [2]illĕ..hīc [3]quō [4]ŭt [5]quantō [6]ipsĕ [7]consĕqui, *to attain to* [8]haec

Oratĭo oblīqua into oratĭo recta.

91. Inter alĭa clara somnĭa tradĭtur hoc: cum duo quidam Arcădes familiāres iter facĕrent, et Megăram venissent, altĕrum ad caupōnem devertisse, ad hospĭtem altĕrum. Qui ut cenāti quiescĕrent visum esse in somnĭis ei, qui erat in hospitĭo, illum altĕrum orāre ut subvenīret, quod sibi a caupōne interĭtus pararētur; eum primo perterrĭtum somnĭo surrexisse; dein cum se collegisset, idque visum pro nihĭlo habendum esse duxisset, recubuisse; tum ei dormienti eundem illum visum esse rogāre, ut quonĭam sibi vivo non subvenisset, mortem suam ne inultam esse paterētur; se interfectum in plaustrum a caupōne esse conjectum, et supra stercus injectum; petĕro ut mane ad portam adesset priusquam plaustrum ex oppĭdo exīret. Hoc vero eum somnĭo commōtum, manē bubulco praesto ad portam fuisse; quaesisse ex eo, quid esset in plaustro; illum perterrĭtum fugisse, mortŭum erŭtum esse; caupōnem re patefacta poenas dedisse.

Matrem Phalarĭdis scribit Pontĭus Heraclīdes, doctus vir, audĭtor et discipŭlus Platōnis, visam esse vidēre in somnis simulacra deōrum, quae ipsa domi consecravisset: ex his Mercurĭum e patĕra, quam dextra manu tenēret, sanguĭnem visum esse fundĕre: qui cum terram attigisset refervescĕre viderētur sic ut tota domus sanguĭne redundāret.

Quod matris somnĭum immānis filĭi crudelĭtas comprobāvit.

Hannibălem Caelĭus scribit, cum columnam aurĕam, quae esset in fano Junōnis Lacinĭae auferre vellet, dubitaretque utrum ea solĭda esset, an extrinsĕcus inaurāta, perterebravisse, cumque solĭdam invenisset, statuissetque tollĕre, ei secundum quiētem visam esse Junōnem praedicĕre, ne id facĕret, minārīque si fecisset, se curatūram ut eum quoque ocŭlum, quo bene vidēret, amittĕret; idque ab homĭne acūto non esse neglectum. Ităque ex eo auro, quod exterebrātum esset, bucŭlam curasse faciendam, et eam in summa columna collocavisse.

Apud Agathŏclem scriptum in historĭa est, Hamilcărem Carthaginiensem, cum oppugnāret Syracūsas, visum esse audīre vocem, se postridĭe cenatūrum Syracūsis: cum autem is dies illuxisset, magnam seditiōnem in castris ejus inter Poenos et Sicŭlos milĭtes esse factam; quod cum sensissent Syracusāni, improvīso eos in castra irrupisse, Hamilcăremque ab iis vivum esse sublātum.

Ita res somnĭum comprobāvit.

Oratĭo recta into oratĭo oblīqua.

92. Ubi ad fines Scythārum pervēnit Alexander, unus ex eōrum legātis haec inter alĭa multa dixit:

Quid nobis tecum est? Numquam terram tuam attigĭmus. Annon licet nobis, qui in vastis silvis vivĭmus, ignorāre quis sis, et unde venĭas. Nec servīre ulli possŭmus, nec imperāre desiderāmus. Major fortĭorque es fortasse quam quisquam, tamen alienigĕnam domĭnum pati nemo vult. Tu, qui te gloriāris ad latrōnes persequendos venisse, ipse omnĭum gentĭum latro es. Lydĭam cepisti, Syrĭam occupasti; Persĭdem tenes, Indos petisti, jam etĭam ad pecŏra nostra avāras manus porrĭgis. Quid tibi divitĭis opus est, quae te esurīre cogunt, ita ut, quo plura habes, eo acrĭus cupĭas, quae non habes? Denĭque si deus es, tribuĕre mortalĭbus beneficĭa debes, non sua eripĕre; sin homo es, id quod es, semper esse te homĭnem cogĭta.

Cum Astyăgi mirum viderētur, quod Cyrus puer, pincernam Sacam egregĭe imitātus in porrigendo sibi pocŭlo ad bibendum, non praegustasset vinum, ut ille solēbat, causam ab eo quaesīvit. Cui Cyrus:

Metuēbam, inquit, ne vino admistum venēnum esset. Nam cum tu nuper die natāli amīcos convivĭo excipĕres, Sacam istum venēnum vobis infudisse animadverti. Vidēbam vos nec anĭmis nec corporĭbus constāre. Quae nos puĕros facĕre vetātis, ea faciebātis ipsi; omnes simul vociferabamĭni, neque quisquam, quid ab altĕro dicerētur, attendēbat. Cantabātis ridicŭle admŏdum, jurabātis tamen cantum illum esse optĭmum. Quin etĭam, cum surrexissētis ad saltandum, non modo non saltāre ad numĕros, sed ne recte quidem stare poterātis, prorsusque oblīti erātis, et tu et illi, regem esse te.

Tum Astyăges: An vero, inquit, fili mi, pater tuus cum bibit, non fit ebrĭus? — Numquam profecto, respondit ille, sitīre enim tantum desĭnit.

Amāsim, Aegyptiōrum regem, cum admonērent amīci, eum parum e regĭa dignitāte facĕre, quod inter epŭlas jocarētur:

Qui, inquit, arcum habent, eum, cum est opus, intendunt, mox remittunt: si enim perpetŭo intentus sit, frangātur necesse est, ita ut eo amplĭus uti non possint. Eădem est homĭnis ratĭo. Si assidŭe serĭa tractāre et nihil sibi ad lusum indulgēre velit, sensim membris aut anĭmo captus fiet.

Reflexive and Reciprocal Pronouns.

SYNTAX *284—288.*

Deum testantur opĕra sua. Ubĭi orābant, ut Caesar sibi auxilĭum ferret. Caesar se ad suos recĕpit. Ariovistus ait nemĭnem secum sine sua pernicĭe contendisse.

93. Alcibiades carried on war not against his country, but against his enemies. His good fortune accompanied Caesar into Spain. I expect the father with his sons. Many through tedium[1] of life have brought death upon themselves[2]. Cato stabbed himself in the breast[3] with (his) sword. Physicians cannot heal themselves. Hannibal's own countrymen drove him from the state. A fight has its end when the foe is down[4]. By[5] his works we recognize God who confers benefits on every one[6]. Tiberius Gracchus and his brother were killed by the senators. Cicero himself relates[7] that the tomb of Archimedes was found by him. When Solon was asked why he had appointed[8] no punishment for[9] him who should have killed a parent, he replied that he thought no one would do that. Who is there that although he be young, knows[10] he will live till evening? Antoninus Pius had this celebrated sentence of Scipio often in (his) mouth that he had rather save one citizen than slay a thousand enemies. To Fabia Dolabella saying that she was[11] thirty years old, "it is true" replied Cicero, "for I am hearing that now these 20 years[12]". Caesar declared that he had conquered not for himself, but for (his) country. Caesar's friends declared that he had conquered not for himself, but for (his) country. After the battle of Allia[13] a great number of Romans fled to Veii, where they thought that they were safer[14] than at Rome.

[1]Abl. [2]Dat. [3]Say: *to himself the breast* [4]jacērĕ, *to be down* [5]ex [6]Dat. [7]narrāre [8]constituĕre [9]in w. Acc. [10]Subjunct. [11]habēre [12]jam viginti annos, *now these* 20 *years* [13]Allĭensĭs, -ĕ [14]tūtŭs,-ă, -ŭm

Participial Sentences.

SYNTAX *297.*

Caesar laudāvit milĭtes fortĭter pugnantes. Caesar auxilĭum tulit urbi ab hostĭbus obsessae. Quocunque te flexĕris, ibi Deum vidēbis occurrentem tibi.

94. The master punishes the scholars who learn carelessly. Get yourself[1] riches which will last forever. The happiness of a man who is still[2] living is not less uncertain and doubtful than the victory of a soldier who is still fighting. The examples of varying fortune are innumerable. The lion, being hungry, roars. A bow too much[3] bent[4] is broken. No one who looks at[5] the whole earth, can doubt of[6] the divine providence. A wise man gives with the greatest consideration choosing[7] the worthiest. Clouds are formed[8] from[9] vapors which ascend into the air. An opportunity once lost[10] will never return. The mind of him[11] who does evil[12] is never free [13] from fear. The body of one[11] who sleeps lies like[14] that[11] of one dead, but the mind lives. Flatterers do not praise less what should be blamed[15] than what is praiseworthy. Alexander called the city which he had founded[16], Alexandria. It is the way of timid people to fear those things which ought not to be feared[15]. Four hundred cavalry of the Helvetians fighting bravely put to flight four thousand of the Romans. He who has been struck by lightning does not see the flash of lightning. All the remedies you have applied[17] sometimes do the sick more harm than good. Misers hide in chests their money which they have scraped together[18] from every quarter.

[1]sibi parāre [2]adhuc [3]nimĭum [4]tendĕre [5]intuēri [6]dē [7]eligĕre [8]nasci [9]ex [10]praetermittĕre [11]not to be translated [12]male agĕre [13]sine [14]ut [15]**Gerundive** [16]Say: *founded by him* (sē) [17]**Perf. Part.**, *which have been applied* [18]*which has been scraped together.*

SYNTAX *298.*

Alexander morĭens anŭlum suum dedĕrat Perdiccae. Quis potest, mortem metŭens, beātus esse? Socrătis morti illacrimāre solĕo, Platōnem legens. Romāni, complurĭbus proelĭis ab Hasdrubăle fugāti, tamen spem salūtis non amisērunt.

95. Plato died while writing in the 81st year of (his) life. While sitting I plucked these grapes. Lions when satiated and not provoked are perfectly harmless. The nightingale sings while sitting, the lark during flight[1]. Word was brought[2] to Cincinnatus while plowing that he had been made dictator. Hannibal having been made commander subdued in war[3] all the tribes of Spain. Boys, while playing, are sometimes accustomed to imitate those things which[4] are most serious.

Death overtakes[5] many men without their thinking[6] of it[7]. A rich man can often help a poor one, without robbing himself. The stars appear small to us, because they are separated[8] from us by an immense space. Ducks cannot live without water, because they seek a great deal of food in the water. In the morning (time)[9] and when declining[10] towards the west, the sun has less (of) strength[11]. Tigers attack all animals because they are always thirsting for[12] blood. Bees when provoked sting[13] furiously[14]. Though ordered by the senate, yet Caesar did not disband his army. The unicorn is rightly regarded as fabulous, because it has never been seen. Caesar having got possession of Alexandria, gave the government[15] to Cleopatra.

[1]Say: *flying* [2]nuntiāre [3]bello superāre [4]ea quae [5]opprimĕre [6]opīnārī [7]not to be translated [8]sējungĕre [9]tempus matutīnum [10]vergĕre ad [11]minus virīum [12]sitīre [13]aculĕis pungĕre [14]vehementer [15]regnŭm, -ī

Syntax *299—301.*

Homĕrus et Hesiŏdus ante Romam condĭtam fuĕrunt. Darēus pervenĕrat ad Arbēla vicum, nobīlem sua clade factūrus. Miltiădes capĭtis absolūtus, pecunĭa multātus est.

96. We are accustomed to pass over[1] very many things[2] even though they are put before our eyes. Storks, when about to go away, assemble[3] in a particular place[4]. A friend had come to take[5] breakfast with me. The murder of Caesar, the dictator, appeared to some the worst, to others the most glorious[6] deed. He who is about to purchase land must before[7] all things look upon[8] the water, the roads and the neighbors. The rhinoceros, when about to fight with an elephant is said to sharpen (its) horn on rocks[9]. He is a fool who when he is going to buy a horse does not examine the (animal[10]) itself but its cloth and bridle. Numa was made king in the forty first year after the founding of the city. The Greeks burnt Troy when taken. The soldiers of Anthony overtook Cicero in his flight[11]. King Pyrrhus sent an ambassador to Rome to sue for peace. Tullus Hostilius in the 31st year of his reign (was) struck by lightning (and) burnt[12] with his house. When the Roman soldiers first saw elephants rushing[14] against[14] them, they were astonished and did not offer resistance[15]. The

Helvetii when they were about to seek new settlements, had burned[16] all their towns and villages. Many people leave their country to seek other settlements. The return[17] of the storks announces spring.

[1]transīre [2]multa [3]congregāri [4]Abl. without Prep. [5]sumĕre [6]pulchĕr [7]prae [8]intuēri [9]Abl. [10]not to be translated [11]fugĕre [12]ardēre [13]irruĕre [14]in [15]alicŭi resistĕre [16]incendĕre [17]redīre

Ablative Absolute.

SYNTAX *302—304.*

Pythagŏras, Tarquinĭo Superbo regnante, in Italĭam venit. Bello Helvetiōrum confecto, legāti omnĭum civitātum ad Caesărem convenĕrunt.

97. When danger increases, strength increases. When the cause of disease has been found out, the physicians think that the cure has been found. When the sun rises, the stars flee. In summer the days are longer than the nights, because the sun shines[1] longer. When spring returns, the swallows return. After Troy was taken by the Greeks, Aeneas came (in)to Italy. Our labor is fruitless[2] when Nature opposes[3]. The Romans when (their[4]) city was taken by the Gauls retreated (in)to the Capitol. Day breaks[5] when the sun rises; when it sets, night comes on. A wise man having lost all his goods, remains rich and that saying of Bias is known: "I carry my all with me." Excepting virtue nothing is more excellent than friendship. In many countries[6] grapes do not ripen, the heat of the sun not being sufficient[7]. When one yawns, another yawns, too. Arts and precepts avail nothing without the help[8] of nature. Tears fall inspite[9] of us. With the melting[10] of the snows rivers usually[11] swell. Among the Spartans nothing brought greater disgrace than to return from battle without[12] one's shield. What would restrain[13] wicked men from crime if the fear of punishment were taken away? Hannibal having crossed the Alps came into Italy. Even[14] after the wound is healed, a scar remains.

[1]lucēre [2]irrĭtus [3]reluctāri [4]not to be translated [5]lucescit [6]rĕgĭŏ, -ōnĭs [7]deficĕre, *not to be sufficient* [8]adjŭvāre [9]nōlens [10]solūtus [11]Say: *are wont* [12]Say: *having lost one's shield* [13]cohibēre [14]etĭam

98. What enjoyment of life can there be when friendship is taken away? Jerusalem was demolished during the reign of Vespasian. Nothing can happen[1] unless[2] a cause precedes. At the approach of winter the swallows migrate (in) to warmer countries. If one dog barks, another also will at once bark. The Greeks, on the approach[3] of the Persians, occupied Thermopylae. After the expulsion of the kings, the first consuls at Rome were Brutus and Collatinus. We cannot doubt that there is a God as nature herself teaches (it[4]). Schools are a great hope of one's country; when they flourish, the state also thrives[5]. For 44 years Mithridates carried on war with often varying fortune. We ought[6] to be free[7] from all fear, since God regulates human affairs. A wise man though he have lost all things, is to be considered rich. A rumor[8] having been spread abroad that Numa Pompilius, a Sabine, was prominent for virtue and wisdom[9], the Roman people passing over[10] their own citizens made him, though[11] a foreigner, king. The judge who decrees[12] anything[13] without hearing the other side, is charged with injustice. Eclipses are not seen everywhere, sometimes on account of the clouds, more frequently the globe of the earth intervening[14]. After the Carthaginians had been driven out, Sicily became a Roman province. The Gauls routed[15] the army of the Romans on[16] the Allia and approached the walls of the city. Cæsar after spending[17] a few days in Syria, gave Sextus Cæsar, his friend and kinsman, the command[18] of the legions and the province.

[1]evenīre [2]nisi [3]advenīre [4]not to be translated [5]vigēre [6]debēre [7]expers, **-tis** [8]fama [9]**Abl.** [10]praeterīre (**Abl. Absol.**) [11]quamquăm [12]statuĕre [13]alĭquid [14]obstāre [15]fundĕre (**Abl. Absol.**) [16]ăd [17]consumĕre [18]praeficĕre w. **Dat.**, *to give the command of*

Ablative Absolute with Nouns.

SYNTAX *305.*

Deo adjutōre omnĭa efficĕre poterĭmus. Pausanĭa duce Graeci ingentes Mardonĭi copĭas apud Plataeas fugavērunt. Tranquillo mari quilĭbet gubernātor esse potest.

99. The ancient Germans wore skins, a great part of the body being naked. I do not send your son to New York against your will. It thunders sometimes when the sky is serene. The Greeks under the leadership of Themistocles conquered the Persians at[1] Salamis. Pythagoras who first called himself a philosopher, flourished when Servius Tullius was king of the Romans. Under the guidance of nature the ancients comprehended that there was a God, but it was not agreed[2] among them what God was. Chilo, one of[3] the seven wise men, because his son was victorious at Olympia, expired of excessive joy[4]. While Hannibal lived, the Romans did not consider that they were safe from[5] treachery. Under the leadership of P. Cornelius Scipio the Romans crossed into Africa where, after a battle fought[6] at[1] Zama, peace was granted[7] to the Carthaginians seeking[8] (it). From[9] how many dangers has God delivered[10] your life without your being aware[11] (of it)! The son died in (his) father's lifetime. The Gallic war was carried on under the command[12] of Cæsar. In the consulship of Manlius Torquatus and Gaius Atilius there was a triumph[13] over the Sardinians, and peace being made in all places, the Romans had not a war on their hands[14], a thing which[15] happened but once from the[16] foundation of the city to that time[16], namely[17] in the reign of Numa Pompilius.

[1]ad [2]convĕnit [3]ex [4]**Abl.** [5]ā [6]committĕre [7]dare [8]petĕre [9]e [10]eripĕre [11]sentīre [12]imperātor [13]triumphātum est [14]habēre [15]*a thing which*, quod [16]inde ab, *from..to that time* [17]not to be translated

Genitive of Gerunds and Gerundives.

SYNTAX *310. 311.*

Studĭum venandi apud Persas magnum fuit. Discipŭli discendi cupĭdi sunto. Multi propter glorĭae cupiditātem cupĭdi sunt bellōrum gerendōrum.

100. The art of writing was invented by the Phenicians. In a magnet there is[1] a wonderful power of attracting iron. Clothing[2] was at first invented for the purpose of keeping out cold. There are various ways[3] of teaching and learning. The art of being silent and speaking at the right[4] time is very difficult. Few men possess[5] the ability to answer well and readily. God made the animals for the sake of men, as for instance the horse for carrying, the ox for plowing, the dog for hunting and watching. Frugality is the knowledge of avoiding[6] needless expenses. What cause for carrying on war is more just than the repulse of slavery! A desire seized[7] Romulus and Remus of founding a city in those places where they had been exposed and brought up. Many men are more desirous of buyin books than of reading (them[8]). The custom o against religion is bad and impious. The only art o the memory is practice. We came into the garden for the sake of taking a walk. Remember that youth is the time for learning. Monuments are erected for the purpose of testifying our admiration, respect and love. Cimon for the purpose of establishing[9] peace between the Athenians and Lacedaemonians proceeded[10] to Sparta. Nature has given us the means[11] of seeing ourselves: a clear fountain reflects[12] to every one his image. Wisdom is to be considered the art of living.

[1]inest, *there is* [2]vestēs, -ĭŭm [3]mŏdŭs [4]suus [5]esse, w. Dat. [6]vitāre [7]capĕre [8]not to be translated [9]confirmāre [10]contendĕre [11]facultas [12]reddĕre

Dative and Accusative of Gerunds and Gerundives.

SYNTAX *312. 313.*

Aqua nitrōsa utĭlis est bibendo. Tribūto plebs liberāta est, ut divĭtes conferrent, qui onĕri ferendo essent. E terrae cavernis ferrum elicĭmus, rem ad colendos agros necessarĭam.

101. Not all water is good for[1] drinking. No age is too late[2] for learning. Blotting paper is not fit[3] to write (upon). A husbandman ought to attend to tilling his fields. Nighttime is more suited to sleeping than to studying. Brave soldiers are ready to undergo all dangers. We are not only inclined to learn but also to teach. Twilight is more suitable for conversing than for reading or writing. Goose quills are more adapted to writing than reed-pens which the Greeks and Romans used. Amusements will benefit boys, because boys after amusements bring more energy to (their) studies[4]. Oxen are not proper for carrying burden. Pythagoras went to Babylon to learn[5] the motions of the stars and inquire into[6] the origin of the world; thence he proceeded to Crete and Lacedaemon to become acquainted with[7] the laws of Minos and

Lycurgus. The short period of life is long enough for living virtuously[8] and honestly. Stormy weather[9] is not suitable for catching fish. Iron is necessary for the cultivation of the land[10]. The character[11] of boys reveals itself[12] in[13] (their) games[14]. By nature we are inclined to love men. There are some games ... very useful[15] for sharpening the wits[16] of boys.

...s, *too late* [3]inutĭlis [4]discĕre; say: *to learning* [5]perdiscĕre [6]spec- ...ĕre [8]probe [9]tempestātes [10]Plur. [11]mores [12]detegĕre [13]inter [14]Translate *while playing*, inter.. [15]non inutĭlis, *very useful* [16]ingenĭum

Ablative of Gerunds and Gerundives.

SYNTAX *314.*

Homĭnis mens discendo alĭtur et cogitando. Virtūtes cernuntur in agendo. Superstitiōne tollenda religĭo non tollĭtur. Hannĭbal visenda urbe (Capŭa) magnam diēi partem consumpsit.

102. The mind is nourished not only by reading books but also by thinking and by writing. Elegance in[1] speaking and writing is increased by reading the works of orators and poets. I am occupied writing[2] letters. Virtue is especially discerned in despising pleasure. Many persons use care in getting[3] horses but are careless in choosing friends. Socrates was accustomed to draw out by questioning the opinions of those with whom he discoursed. Sailors by taking in sails lessen the dangers of a storm. He who exceeds measure in eating and drinking easily contracts[4] disease. In reading we must imitate the bees. He who is not skilled in governing a house will be far less fit for ruling a state. Justice has to do with[5] protecting human society and giving to every one his own. The deliberation in[6] choosing a line of life is the most difficult of all. There is often more misfortune[7] in the fear[8] than in the misfortune itself. Old age draws (us) off[9] from active life[10]. By doing nothing men learn to do ill[11]. The fortified walls[12] he had seen[13] deterred Hannibal from besieging Naples. There is often too little pains taken[14] in teaching the first elements of letters. By persuading and dissuading many have already drawn[15] enmities upon themselves[15]. By giving and receiving benefits friendships are made[16]. The Athenians without waiting for assistance went[17] to[18] battle against the immense army of the Persians. The third part of our life is lost in sleeping[19]. Many men find fault with[20] books without understanding[21] (them). I never drink without being thirsty; many men drink without being thirsty. The precepts of art are of little avail[22] to[23] form an orator without the assistance of nature. A drop hollows a stone, not by force, but by falling often; so a man becomes learned not by force but by constant study[24]. Philosophers in those very books which they write on contempt[25] of glory, write[26] their own names.

[1]Say: *of* [2]Say: *in writing letters* [3]parāre [4]sibi contrahĕre [5]versāri in, *to have to do with* [6]dē [7]malŭm, -ī [8]Say: *in fearing* [9]abducĕre [10]res agendae [11]male [12]moenĭa, *fortified walls* [13]**Perf. Part.** [14]parum laborātur, *too little pains is taken* [15]sibi conciliāre [16]parāre [17]ēgrĕdi [18]in [19]**Abl.** [20]vituperāre, *to find fault with* [21]**Perf. Part.** [22]parum valēre, *to be of little avail* [23]ăd [24]Say: *by studying often* [25]contemnĕre [26]inscribĕre

103. We eradicate the noxious weeds of fields by plowing. The opportunity to learn is not always at hand. The ancients used a stilus for[1] writing. No one can have a just cause for[2] bearing arms against his country. This pupil is more inclined to play than to learn. By hoping misfortune is made lighter. There is always opportunity of reading, not always of hearing. My brother being unaccustomed to[3] sailing fears the sea. Man is born for understanding and thinking. A man should do nothing without reflection[4]. Trees afford wood not only for burning, but also for building and other necessary things. From whom did the spider learn the art of weaving (its) nets? Three things[5] are especially to be respected by youths: God, one's parents, the laws. In the most ancient times many peoples did not yet know[6] the art of writing. Misers are tortured not only by a desire of increasing (their) riches but also by the fear of losing (them). If rain freezes while[7] falling[8] it becomes hail. There is no lot so hard[9] that[10] a brave man may not overcome it by prudently enduring. In the contest at[11] Thermopylae the Persian soldiers were finally forced to[12] fight by the strokes of scourges. The greatest pleasure is received from[13] learning. As a horse is of no use to one who does not understand[14] riding, so books are of no use to those who do not know[15] how to read.

[1]ăd [2]Say: *of* [3]Say: *of* [4]ratĭo [5]tria, *three things* [6]cognōvi, *I know* [7]inter [8]decidĕre [9]aspĕr, -ă, -ŭm [10]qui w. Subj. [11]ăd [12]ăd [13]ex [14]imperītus, *he who does not understand* [15]ignārus, *he who does not know*

Passive Periphrastic Conjugation. Gerundive as Predicate Accusative.

Syntax *315. 316.*

Suō cuīque judicīo ūtendum est. Puĕros magistro erudiendos trado. Perfŭgam Fabricīus reducendum curāvit ad Pyrrhum.

104. Secret enmities are more[1] to be feared than open (ones). New friends ought not to be preferred to old (ones). I return the greatest thanks to my parents because[2] they took care[3] that I was instructed[4]. Virtues as such[5] ought to be practised[6], and herein we must follow duty, not advantage[7]. We ought to pray that we may have a sound mind in a sound body. Men should never depart[8] from the straight way. Young men ought to acquire[9], old men ought to enjoy. One should not fight with two. In times of peace we should think of[10] war. Riches are to be lightly esteemed. The Egyptians give (their) dead to the priests to embalm. At the request of Artaxerxes Diomedon undertook to bribe[11] Epaminondas. When Catiline was planning[12] a revolution two knights undertook to kill Cicero in his house and to bribe his slaves. My brother was sent to Germany for his education[13]. The conquered must be spared. God is to be honored not with sacrifices, but with a pure heart[14]. Caesar had all the old ships repaired[15] and new ones built in Gaul. No one is good by chance, virtue is to be learned. Even after a bad crop we must sow. Certainly we must die, but on what day we must die, is uncertain.

[1]magis [2]quod [3]curāre [4]Say: *me to be instructed* [5]per sē [6]colĕre [7]fructus [8]discedĕre [9]parāre [10]dē [11]pecunīa corrumpĕre [12]mōlīŏr, -īrī [13]*to be educated* [14]mens [15]reficĕre

Supine.

Syntax *317. 318.*

Totīus fere Gallīae legāti ad Caesārem convenĕrunt congratulātum. Tu pro tua prudentīa, quid optĭmum factu sit vidēbis.

105. Do you wish to go with me to hunt? I know that many have come to me, not to congratulate (me) but for the sake of eating and drinking. This book is most difficult to understand. The shorter a narrative (is[1]), the clearer it is and the easier to understand. What is pleasanter to hear than a fine speech? The people of Veii sent envoys to Rome to sue for peace. Few women had come to look, most came[1] that they might be looked at[2]. The Aedui sent ambassadors to Caesar to ask assistance. You yourselves will see what is best to be done, my[1] friends. A vast multitude of men crowded[3] into the city to view the public games. Pears are sweet to the taste[4]. Merchants go to market either to buy or to sell various wares. Cicero was about to set out for Rome to view the games when friends came to his Tusculan farm to pay their respects[5]. Virtue is difficult to find out, it requires a master[6] and leader, but vices are learned even without a master. Do you not[7] see yourselves what is necessary[8] to be said and to be done in this affair?[9] Things which[10] are pleasant to you to tell are often not at all pleasant to another[11] to hear. Pompey was (a man[1]) of so great humanity that it is difficult to say whether enemies more feared[12] his bravery or loved his mildness.

[1]Not to be translated [2]spectāre [3]convenīre [4]gustāre [5]salutāre alīquem, *to pay one's respects* [6]rector [7]nonne [8]opus est [9]negotīum [10]quae [11]alter [12]Perf. Subjunct.

Copulative Conjunctions.

Syntax *320. 321.*

Quadrupĕdum celerĭtas atque vis nobis ipsis affert vim atque celeritātem. Recte judĭces, et, ut vetĕres loquuntur, rem acu tetigisti. Ibi mortŭus sepultusque Alexander. Opiniōne vulgi rapĭmur in errōrem, nec vera cernĭmus.

106. God sees and rules all things. Our mind is immortal and will not perish along with the body. Avoid[1] avarice, loquacity, gaming, hatred, and the rest of vices. Ancus Marcius subdued the Latins in war, enlarged the city of Rome and surrounded it with new walls. We had rather be poor and honest than rich and wicked. Naked I came into this world and naked I will return. Virtue is highly to be valued even in an enemy. Hannibal was forced to leave Carthage and never returned. "I hate that man who says one thing and thinks another," Achilles used to say, "as much[2] as I do the gates of Pluto." The Romans carried on severe wars against the Gauls and Spaniards. Friends are also suspected by[3] tyrants. Reason teaches what ought to be done and what avoided[1]. Dionysius, the tyrant, very greatly favored[4] Dio and did not love him otherwise[5] than as his own brother. Verres utterly racked and ruined Sicily for three years. God alone can be the maker and ruler of heaven and earth. Hadrian could hear, write, dictate and speak at one and the same time. The Romans engraved the laws which the senate and the people had passed[6] on[7] tables of brass.

[1]fugĕre [2]aequē [3]Say: *to tyrants* [4]indulgēre [5]secus [6]sancīre [7]Dat.

Disjunctive Conjunctions.

SYNTAX *322. 323.*

Pugnantĭbus puncto tempŏris mors aut victorĭa obtingit. Stupōrem homĭnis vel dicam pecŭdis attendĭte. Esse ea dico, quae cerni tangĭve possunt. Consŭles alter ambōve ratiōnem agri habĕant.

107. All things have been well ordained by nature or rather by God. The hours and months and days glide away, nor does time past ever return, nor can it be known what may follow. Aeneas left Troy and made for Italy; even in Italy great dangers threatened Aeneas; but these also he overcame and established a kingdom in Italy. Nothing hinders recovery so much[1] as the frequent change of remedies. In the upper part of the body or the breast, are the heart and lungs; in the lower part, or abdomen, is the stomach with the intestines. They are foolish who pride themselves on (their) figure or wealth. The Parthians were ignorant how[2] to fight in line hand to hand, or how to storm besieged cities. The 30 tyrants stood around Socrates and could not break his spirit. Friendships are formed[3] by mutual favors or by virtue. The immortality of the soul is very reasonable[4] or rather very certain. Much can be changed in three or four days. Metals are either precious or base. The precious metals are silver and gold; the base ones brass or copper, lead, quicksilver. Here, soldiers, we must conquer or die! In battle swift death comes or joyful victory.

[1]aequē [2]not to be translated [3]jungĕre [4]veri simĭlis

Adversative Conjunctions.

SYNTAX *324.*

Saepe ab amīco tuo dissensi, sed sine ulla ira. Pater, prout ipse amābat littĕras, fīlĭum erudīvit. Erat autem in puĕro summa suavĭtas oris et vocis. Brevis a natūra nobis vita data est, at memorĭa bene reddĭtae vitae sempiterna. Pausanĭas accusātus capĭtis absolvĭtur, tamen multātur pecunĭa.

108. Although the Romans were the conquerors of almost the whole world, yet their craving for more[1] was not satisfied. Not he who has little, but he who desires more than he has, is poor. Virtue cannot be obtained by wealth, but wealth (can)[2] by virtue. Ariovistus had crossed the Rhine, not of his own accord, but having been requested and summoned by the Gauls. Tears mostly indicate sorrow, but[3] sometimes also[3] joy. The hives of bees are most artificial; nothing, however, is sweeter or more wholesome than honey. Nature has given serpents dull eyes and has put them not in the forehead, but in the temples. Wisdom is acquired not by age, but[4] by natural disposition[5]. All things pass away, not into nothing[6], but into their elements. All the stars which appear to be fixed in the sky[7] move[8] nevertheless. Fear not[9] bitter, but flattering words! Caesar himself indeed had been butchered by the conspirators, but[10] his will had not been abolished. Cicero saved his country, but he received no thanks for this service. Men do not know many things; God, however, knows all. All our riches consist in[11] virtue; but virtue makes men happy. Many men neglect virtue itself, but seek the appearance of virtue. Every thing perishes, yet virtue will remain. Although fortune is blind. still she commonly favors virtue.

[1]cupīdo, *craving for more* [2]not to be translated [3]vero etĭam [4]verum [5]ingenĭum, *natural disposition* [6]nĭhĭlŭm [7]Dat. [8]Pass. [9]nōn [10]neque tamen [11]continēri, w. Abl.

Causal and Illative Conjunctions.

SYNTAX *325. 326.*

Nos omnes nati sumus, ergo etĭam moriēmur. Virtus sola numquam perībit, hanc igĭtur expetĕre debēmus. Noli confidĕre fortūnae;

namque fortŭna nihil mutabilĭus est. Recte Romāni Martis filĭi nominantur; nullus enim popŭlus Martem magis colŭit.

109. Because nature cannot be changed, therefore true friendships are eternal. If you want to be liked[1], be grateful, for all hate an ungrateful person. God has not a body, and on that account, although he is everywhere, he can nowhere be seen. Mind conscience more than public opinion[2]; for public opinion can[3] often be mistaken, conscience never. Cyrus (when) a child was delivered by Astyages to Harpagus that he might be exposed in the woods[4]; but his lot was exchanged with the lot of a little one of the king's shepherd; for the former[5] was educated for the son of the shepherd, the latter[6] was exposed as the king's grandson. A friend is not known at a feast; he errs therefore, who judges of[7] a friend at a feast. A disregard of public utility is contrary to nature; for it is unjust. There is[8] a kind[9] of natural warfare between the kite and the raven; therefore the one breaks the other's eggs wherever it gets (them). The senses are admirably situated[10], for the eyes, like[11] watchmen, occupy the highest post. Themistocles restored the walls of Athens with risk to himself[12]; for the Lacedaemonians endeavored to prevent (it). We are all brethren, for we are all children of God. This sentence is not true; therefore it is false. Hannibal was recalled by the Carthaginians; for this reason he left Italy.

[1]gratiōsus [2]fama [3]Fut. [4]saltŭs, -ūs [5]ipse [6]ille [7]probāre [8]Say: *to the kite is. . warfare with the raven* [9]quīdam [10]collocātus [11]tamquam [12]suo pericŭlo

Copulative Correspondents.

SYNTAX *327.* I.

Romanōrum et in bellĭcis et in civilĭbus officĭis vigēbat industrĭa. Mentīri nec possum nec, si possem, cupĕrem. Dicendi vis cum in omnĭbus rebus humānis tum in civitatĭbus regendis plurĭmum valet.

110. There is in fact a God who both hears and sees what we do[1]. Tullus Hostilius was not only unlike the last[2] king, but even more warlike than Romulus. The tiger fears neither the lion nor the elephant. Many men can neither read nor write. Pure water has neither taste, nor smell, nor color. What birds can both swim and fly? Olives and vines thrive[3] neither in very cold nor in very hot climate[4]. You violate[5] not only human but also divine law by perjury. They are justly despised who do good neither to themselves nor to others. Fortune can neither give nor take away probity from any one. An effeminate education breaks the nerves both of body and mind. Envy carps at[6] not only the living but also the dead. Accustom yourself both to speak the truth[7] and to hear (it). Not only fortune helps the brave as it is in an old proverb, but much more reason. We change[8] every day; neither have we been what we are, nor shall we be to-morrow. Formerly agriculture was practised[9] both by kings and by the sons of kings. Orpheus by his song not only tamed[10] wild beasts, but also drew after him[11] the rocks and woods. The Roman populace were sorely pressed[12] both by want and by military service. Many flowers delight us both by their beauty and by (their) odor.

[1]gerĕre [2]proxĭmus [3]provenīre [4]Say: *lands* [5]laedĕre [6]rodĕre [7]verum [8]Pass. [9]exercēre [10]mulcēre [11]ductāre, *to draw after* [12]urgēre, *to press sorely*

Disjunctive Correspondents.

SYNTAX *327.* II.

Omne enuntiātum aut verum est aut falsum. Nihil est tam conveniens ad res vel secundas vel adversas quam amicitĭa. Ad has littĕras addiscendas tibi sive comes sive dux fui.

111. An injury is done in two ways[1], either by violence or by fraud. The nobles can either corrupt or correct the morals of the state. Whether we work or play, or sleep or wake, our life doth pass. Almost all wars among mortals have arisen[2] on account of either power or riches. It is the mark of true friendship both to advise and to be advised. A woman either loves or hates. The moon either increases or decreases. Brave soldiers are willing either to conquer or to die. The motion of the animals is different: either they walk and run, or they fly, or they swim. Man is to man either a god, or a wolf. Many indeed know what is just, but they do it not. You do not work, therefore you have nothing. Who does not know of[3] that most wicked emperor Nero, whose impious hands were stained[4] with the blood as well of many other persons as of his own mother? Let this law be sacred among friends that they neither ask base things[5] nor do (them) when asked[6]. The wise man not only sees the present and holds in memory the past, but also looks into[7] the future. Xerxes before the naval battle in which he was defeated by Themistocles had sent four thousand armed men to[8] plunder the temple of Apollo as if he were carrying on war, not only with the Greeks but also with the immortal gods.

[1]Abl. [2]orĭŏr, -īrī [3]ignorāre [4]imbuĕre [5]turpĭa [6]Participle [7]prospicĕre [8]ăd w. Gerundive.

VOCABULARY

of all English words occurring in the Exercises, with their special meanings as used in this book.

NOTE. Changeable parts of words are printed in **bold-faced** type, so as to indicate the manner of forming the Genitive and the Gender-endings, and to show the principal parts of Verbs.

The - simply added to a noun indicates that the Genitive is like the Nominative.

(m.), (f.), (n.), (pl.) mean: masculine, feminine, neuter, Plural, respectively.

The signs of quantity are given, unless the syllable is long by position or contains a diphthong.

A.

the abdomen, abdōm**ĕn**, -**ĭnĭs** (n.)
to abide, commŏr**ŏr**, -**ārī**
ability, făcult**ās**, -**ātĭs** (f.)
to abolish, toll**ō**, -**ĕrĕ**, sustŭlī, sublātŭm
the Aborigines, ăbŏrīgĭn**ēs**, -**ŭm** (f. pl.)
to abound, ăbund**ō**, -**ārĕ**
about, dē (w. abl.)
above, sŭpĕr (w. acc. & abl.); sŭprā (w. acc.)
abroad, fŏrīs; *a fire abroad*, ignĭs ălĭēnŭs
to abstain, abstĭn**ĕō**, -**ērĕ**
abundance, ăbundantĭ**ă**, -**ae** (f.); *to have abundance*, ăbund**ō**, -**ārĕ**
abuse, ăbūs**ŭs**, -**ūs** (m.)
to accept, accĭp**ĭō**, -**ĕrĕ**, accēp**ī**, accept**ŭm**
acceptable, accept**ŭs**, -**ă**, -**ŭm**
easy access, făcĭlĭt**ās**, -**ātĭs** (f.)
accidental, fortŭĭt**ŭs**, -**ă**, -**ŭm**
to accompany, cŏmĭt**ŏr**, -**ārī**
to accomplish, confĭc**ĭō**, -**ĕrĕ**, confēc**ī**, confect**ŭm**
of one's own accord, spontĕ, ultrā
according to, ăd (w. acc.), sĕcundŭm (w. acc.)
on account of, ŏb (w. acc.); proptĕr (w. acc.); prae (w. abl.); *on that account*, ĭdĕō; *to be of great account*, magnī essĕ; *to be of more account*, plūrĭs essĕ; *of very little account*, mĭnĭmī

accurate, accūrāt**ŭs**, -**ă**, -**ŭm**
to accuse, accūs**ō**, -**ārĕ**
to be accustomed, sŏl**ĕō**, -**ērĕ**, sŏlĭt**ŭs** sŭm
Achilles, Achill**ēs**, -**ĭs** (m.)
to acquaint, ēdŏc**ĕō**, -**ērĕ**, ēdŏc**ŭī**, ēdoct**ŭm**
to become acquainted, *to make the acquaintance*, cognosc**ō**, -**ĕrĕ**, cognōvī, cognĭtŭm
to acquire, ădĭpisc**ŏr**, -**ī**, ădept**ŭs** sŭm; acquīr**ō**, -**ĕrĕ**, acquīs**īvī**, acquīs**ītŭm**
to acquit, absolv**ō**, -**ĕrĕ**, absolv**ī**, absŏlūt**ŭm**
across, trans (w. acc.)
to act, ăg**ō**, -**ĕrĕ**, ēg**ī**, act**ŭm**
an action, fact**ŭm**, -**ī** (n.); *base actions* turpĭ**ă**, -**ŭm** (n. pl.)
active life, res agendae (f. pl.)
actually, omnīnō
adapted, apt**ŭs**, -**ă**, -**ŭm**; accommŏdāt**ŭs**, -**ă**, -**ŭm**
to add, add**ō**, -**ĕrĕ**, add**ĭdī**, add**ĭtŭm**
to adjust, accommŏd**ō**, -**ārĕ**
admirably, mīrĭfĭcē
admiration, admīrātĭ**ō**, -**ōnĭs** (f.)
to admire, admīr**ŏr**, -**ārī**; *to be admired*, adspĭcĭend**ŭs**, -**ă**, -**ŭm**
to admonish, admŏn**ĕō**, -**ērĕ**
to adorn, orn**ō**, -**ārĕ**
advantage, fruct**ŭs**, -**ūs** (m.)

advantageous, ūtĭlĭs, -ĕ
adversity, rēs adversae (f. pl.)
advice, consĭlĭŭm, -ī (n.)
to advise, mŏnĕō, -ērĕ
the Aeduans, Aedŭī, -ōrŭm (m. pl.)
Aeneas, Aenēās, -ae (m.)
an affair, rēs, rĕī (f.); nĕgōtĭŭm, -ī (n.)
affection, cārĭtās, -ātĭs (f.)
to afford, praebĕō, -ērĕ
to be afraid, tĭmĕō, -ērĕ, -ŭī, (no sup.)
Africa, Afrĭcă, -ae (f.)
Africanus, Afrĭcānŭs, -ī (m.)
after, prep. pŏst (w. acc.); conjunct., postquăm
afternoon, postmĕrĭdĭānŭs, -ă, -ŭm
afterwards, postĕā
again and again, ĭtĕrŭm atquĕ ĭtĕrŭm
against, adversŭs, contrā, ĭn (w. acc.)
an age, aetās, -ātĭs (f.); *old age*, sĕnectŭs, -ūtĭs (f.); *of the same age*, aequālĭs, -ĕ
Agesilaus, Ăgēsĭlāŭs, -ī (m.)
ago, abhinc
to agree, congrŭō, -ĕrĕ, -ī, (no sup.)
agreeable, dulcĭs, -ĕ
it is agreed, constat, convĕnĭt
agriculture, agrĭcultūră, -ae (f.)
aid, auxĭlĭŭm, -ī (n.); *by the aid*, ŏpĕ
the air, āēr, āĕrĭs (m.)
Alcibiades, Alcĭbĭădēs, -ĭs (m.)
Alexander, Ălexandĕr, -rī (m.)
Alexandria, Ălexandrĭă, -ae (f.)
to alight, consīdō, -ĕrĕ, consēdī, consessŭm
alive, vīvŭs, -ă, -ŭm
all, omnĭs, -ĕ; *at all*, prorsŭs; *all one's property*, omnĭă sŭă; *all right*, bĕnĕ hăbĕt
of Allia, Allĭensĭs, -ĕ
allied, foedĕrātŭs, -ă, -ŭm
it is allowed, lĭcĕt
almost, fĕrē
alone, sōlŭs, -ă, -ŭm
along with, ūnā cŭm
the Alps, Alpēs, -ĭŭm (f. pl.)
also, ĕtĭăm, quŏquĕ
alternation, vĭcissĭtūdō, -ĭnĭs (f.)
although, ĕtĭamsī, etsī, quamquăm, quamvīs
always, sempĕr
an ambassador, lēgātŭs, -ī (m.)
ambition, ambĭtĭō, -ōnĭs (f.)
America, Amĕrĭcă, -ae (f.)
amiable manners, hūmānĭtās, -ātĭs (f.)
amid, intĕr (w. acc.)
among, intĕr, ăpŭd (w. acc.)
amount, vīs, - (f.)
Amulius, Ămūlĭŭs, -ī (m.)
amusement, lūsŭs, -ūs (m.)
Anaxagoras, Anāxăgŏrās, -ae (m.)
the ancestors, mājōrēs, -ŭm (m. pl.)
ancient, vĕtŭs, pristĭnŭs, -ă, -ŭm; antīquŭs, -ă, -ŭm
anciently, antīquĭtŭs
and, ĕt, ăc, atquĕ, -quĕ (appended); *and not*, nĕc, nĕquĕ
anew, dēnŭō
anger, īră, -ae (f.)
an angler, piscātŏr, -ōrĭs (m.)
angry, īrātŭs, -ă, -ŭm; *to be angry*, īrascŏr, -ī, īrātŭs sŭm
an animal, ănĭmăl, -ālĭs (n.)
to announce, annuntĭō, -ārĕ
to be annoyed, mŏlestē ferrĕ (tŭlī, lātŭm)
to answer, respondĕō, -ērĕ, respondī, responsŭm
an ant, formīcă, -ae (f.)
Anthony, Antōnĭŭs, -ī (m.)
Antioch, Antĭochīă, -ae (f.)
Antiochus, Antĭochŭs, -ī (m.)
antiquity, antīquĭtās, -ātĭs (f.)
Antoninus Pius, Antōnīnŭs Pĭŭs (-ī, -ī) m.
to be anxious, stŭdĕō, -ērĕ, -ŭī, (no sup.)
any, ullŭs, -ă, -ŭm; *any one*, ălĭquĭs, quispĭăm, quisquăm; *any thing*, ălĭquĭd, quidquăm
Apelles, Apellēs, -ĭs (m.)
the Apennines, Apennīnī montēs (m. pl.)
Apollo, Ăpollō, -ĭnĭs (m.)
an apostle, ăpostŏlŭs, -ī (m.)
to appear, appārĕō, -ērĕ; vĭdĕŏr, -ērī, vīsŭs sŭm
appearance, spĕcĭēs, -ēī (f.)
an appellation, appellātĭō, -ōnĭs (f.)

an appetizer, condīmentŭm, -ī (n.)
Appian, Appĭŭs, -ă, -ŭm; *the Appian way*, vĭă Appĭa
Appius, Appĭŭs, -ī (m.)
to apply, adhĭbĕō, -ērĕ
to appoint, dēsignō, -ārĕ; constĭtŭō, -ĕrĕ, constĭtŭī, constĭtūtŭm
to approach, apprŏpinquō, -ārĕ; advĕnĭō, -īrĕ, advēnī, adventŭm
to approve, prŏbō, -ārĕ
an Arabian, Ărabs, -ăbĭs (m.)
Archias, Archĭās, -ae (m.)
Archimedes, Archĭmēdēs, -ĭs (m.)
ardent, ăcerrĭmŭs, -ă, -ŭm
ardently, ardentĕr
Arganthonius, Arganthōnĭŭs, -ī (m.)
the Argonauts, Argŏnautae, -ārŭm (m. pl.)
Arion, Arīōn, -ŏnĭs (m.)
Ariovistus, Arĭŏvistŭs, -ī (m.)
to arise, ŏrĭŏr, -īrī, ortŭs sŭm
Aristippus, Ăristippŭs, -ī (m.)
Aristotle, Ărīstŏtĕlēs, -ĭs (m.)
an armed man, armātŭs, -ī (m.)
arms, armă, -ōrŭm (n. pl.)
an army, exercĭtŭs, -ūs (m.)
around, circum (w. acc.)
to arouse, excĭtō, -ārĕ
arrangement, compŏsĭtĭō, -ōnĭs (f.)
to arrest, dēprehendō, -ĕrĕ, dēprĕhendī, dēprĕhensŭm
to arrive, pervĕnĭō, -īrĕ, pervēnī, perventŭm
an art, ars, -tĭs (f.)
Artaxerxes, Artaxerxēs, -ĭs, (m.)
artificial, artĭfĭcĭōsŭs, -ă, -ŭm
as, tamquăm, ŭt; *as if*, quăsĭ; *as it were*, quăsĭ; *as long as*, dŭm, dōnĕc; *as much as*, aequē ăc; *as. so*, ŭt..sīc; *as soon as*, ŭbĭ, ŭbĭ prīmŭm, sĭmŭlăc
to ascend, ascendō, -ĕrĕ, ascendī, ascensŭm
to be ashamed, pŭdērĕ, -ŭit
Asia, Ăsĭă, -ae (f.)
to ask, ōrō, -ārĕ; rŏgō, -ārĕ; interrŏgō, -ārĕ
to assemble, congrĕgŏr, -ārī
an assembly, concĭō, -ōnĭs (f.)
to assert, dŏcĕō, -ērĕ, -ŭī, doctŭm
to assist, subvĕnĭō, -īrĕ, subvēnī, subventŭm
assistance, auxĭlĭŭm, -ī (n.)
to assuage, mollĭō, -īrĕ; lēnĭō, -īrĕ
to assume, sustĭnĕō, -ērĕ, sustĭnŭī, sustentŭm
to be astonished, obstŭpescō, -ĕrĕ, obstŭpŭī, (no sup.)
an asylum, ăsȳlŭm, -ī (n.)
an Athenian, Athēnĭensĭs, - (m.)
Athens, Athēnae, -ārŭm (f. pl.)
Atlantic, Atlantĭcŭs, -ă, -ŭm
Atlas, Atlās, -antĭs (m.)
to attack, ăddŏrĭŏr, -īrī, ădortŭs sŭm; pĕtō, -ĕrĕ, -īvī, -ītŭm
to attain, consĕquŏr, -ī, consĕcūtŭs sŭm
Attalus, Attălŭs, -ī (m.)
to attend, ŏpĕrăm dăre (dō, dĕdī, dătŭm); *to attend to*, cūrō, -ārĕ
an attendant, sătellēs, -ĭtĭs (m.)
attention, cūră, -ae (f.)
Atticus, Attĭcŭs, -ī (m.)
Attius, Attĭŭs, -ī (m.)
to attract, attrăhō, -ĕrĕ, attraxī, attractŭm
an augur, augŭr, -ĭs (m.)
Augustus, Augustŭs, -ī (m.)
authority, auctōrĭtās, -ātĭs (f.)
autumn, autumnŭs, -ī (m.)
to avail, vălĕō, -ērĕ; *to be of little avail*, părŭm vălērĕ
avarice, ăvārĭtĭă, -ae (f.)
to avoid, fŭgĭō, -ĕrĕ, fūgī, (no sup.); vĭtō, -ārĕ
to awake, expergiscŏr, -ī, experrectŭs sŭm
to be aware of, sentĭō, -īrĕ, sensī, sensŭm
an axis, axĭs, - (f.)

B.

Babylon, Băbȳlōn, -ĭs (f.)
the back, tergŭm, -ī (n.)
bad, mălŭs, -ă, -ŭm
badness, mălŭm, -ī (n.)
a bait, escă, -ae (f.)
to bake, coquō, -ĕrĕ, coxī, coctŭm
baldness, calvĭtĭŭm, -ī (n.)
Balearic, Bălĕărĭs, -ĕ

a ball (for playing), pĭlă, -ae (f.)
to banish, dēpellō, -ĕrĕ, dēpŭlī, dēpulsŭm; aquā et ignī interdīcĕrĕ (interdixī, interdictŭm)
a banquet, ĕpŭlŭm, -ī (n.)
a barbarian, barbărŭs, -ī (m.)
a barber, tonsŏr, -ōrĭs (m.)
the bark, cortex, -ĭcĭs (m.)
base, turpĭs, -ĕ; of metals, ignōbĭlĭs, -ĕ; *base actions*, turpĭă, -ŭm (n.pl.)
a bat, vespertĭlĭō, -ōnĭs (f.)
a battle, proelĭŭm, -ī (n.)
to be, essĕ, sŭm, fŭī
a bear, ursŭs, -ī (m.)
to bear, fĕrō, -rĕ, tŭlī, lātŭm; pătĭor, -ī, passŭs sŭm
a beast, bestĭă, -ae (f.); *a beast of prey*, ănĭmăl răpax (n.)
beautiful, pulchĕr, -ră, -rŭm
beauty, pulchrĭtūdō, -ĭnĭs (f.)
because, quŏd, quĭă
to become, fīō, -ĕrī, factŭs sŭm; ēvādō, -ĕrĕ, ēvāsī, ēvāsŭm
it becomes, dĕcĕt, dĕcŭĭt, dĕcērĕ
a bee, ăpĭs, - (f.)
before, antĕ (w. acc.); prae (w. abl.); *before that*, antĕă
to begin, coepi, coepissĕ
a beginning, ĭnĭtĭŭm, -ī (n.); princĭpĭŭm, -ī (n.); *in the beginning of spring*, prīmō vērĕ
the Belgians, Belgae, -ārŭm (m.pl.)
belief, fĭdēs, -ĕī (f.)
to believe, crēdō, -ĕrĕ, -ĭdī, -ĭtŭm; existĭmō, -ārĕ; pŭtō, -ārĕ
to belong, pertĭnĕō, -ērĕ
beloved ones, sŭī, -ōrŭm (m. pl.)
to bend, tendō, -ĕrĕ, tĕtendī, tensŭm; rĕflectō, -ĕrĕ, rĕflexī, reflexŭm
beneath, subtĕr, infrā (w. acc.)
beneficence, bĕnĕficentĭă, -ae (f.)
beneficial, sălūtārĭs, -ĕ
a benefit, bĕnĕfĭcĭŭm, -ī (n.)
to benefit, prōsŭm, prōdessĕ, prōfŭī
to beseech, ōrō, -āre; obsĕcrō, -ārĕ; pĕtō, -ĕrĕ, -īvī, -ītŭm; *I beseech*, quaesō
to besiege, obsĭdĕō, -ērĕ, obsēdī, obsessŭm; oppugnō, -ārĕ
best, optĭmŭs, -ă, -ŭm
to bestow (attention) pōnō, -ĕrĕ, pŏsŭī, pŏsĭtŭm; (praise) confĕrō, -rĕ, contŭlī, collātŭm
to betray, trādō, -ĕrĕ, -ĭdī, -ĭtŭm
better, mĕlĭŏr, -ŭs; *the better classes*, bŏnī
between, intĕr (w. acc.)
to beware, căvĕō, -ērĕ, cāvī, cautŭm
beyond, trans, ultrā (w. acc.)
Bias, Bĭās, -antĭs (m.)
to bid, jŭbĕō, -ērĕ, jussī, jussŭm
a bill, rostrŭm, -ī (n.)
a bird, ăvĭs, - (f.)
a birthday, dĭēs nātālĭs (m.)
a bit, frēnă, -ōrŭm (n. pl.)
bitter, ăcerbŭs, -ă, -ŭm; ăcĕr, -rĭs -rĕ
black, nĭgĕr, -ră, -rŭm; *the Black Sea*, Pontŭs Euxīnŭs (m.)
to blame, vĭtŭpĕrō, -ārĕ; reprĕhendō, -ĕrĕ, rĕprĕhendī, rĕprĕhensŭm
to bless, bĕnĕdīcō, -ĕrĕ, bĕnĕdixī, bĕnĕdictŭm
blessed, bĕātŭs, -ă, -ŭm
blind, caecŭs, -ă, -ŭm
blood, sangŭĭs, -ĭnĭs (m.)
blotting paper, chartă bĭbŭlă (f.)
to boast, glōrĭŏr, -ārī
a body, corpŭs, -ŏrĭs (n.); *bodies of soldiers*, cōpĭae, -ārŭm (f. pl.)
a bond, vincŭlŭm, -ī (n.)
a book, lĭbĕr, -rī (m.); *a little book*, lĭbellŭs, -ī (m.)
to be born, nascŏr, -ī, nātŭs sŭm
both, ambō, ŭterquĕ; *both..and*, ĕt..ĕt
a bow, arcŭs, -ūs (m.)
a boy, pŭĕr, -ī (m.)
boyhood, pŭĕrĭtĭă, -ae (f.)
brass, aes, aerĭs (n.); *of brass*, aenĕŭs, -ă, -ŭm
brave, fortĭs, -ĕ
bravery, fortĭtūdō, -ĭnĭs (f.)
to break, frangō, -ĕrĕ, frēgī, fractŭm; *to break out*, ērumpō, -ĕrĕ, ērūpī, ēruptŭm; *of war*, exardescō -ĕrĕ, exarsī, exarsŭm
break of day, prīmă lux (f.)
breakfast, jentācŭlŭm, -ī (n.)

the breast, pectŭs, -ŏrĭs (n.)
a breeze, aurā̆, -ae (f.)
to bribe, pĕcūnĭā corrumpĕrĕ (corrūpī, corruptŭm)
a bridle, frēnŭm, -ī (n.)
bright, clārŭs, -ă, -ŭm; lūcŭlentŭs, -ă, -ŭm; *to be bright*, splendĕō, -ērĕ, (no perf. & sup.)
brilliancy, splendŏr, -ōrĭs (m.)
to bring, fĕrō, -rĕ, tŭlī, lātŭm; dūcō, -ĕrĕ, duxī, ductŭm; affĕrō, -rĕ, attŭlī, allātŭm; *to bring about*, concĭlĭō, -ārĕ; *to bring across*, transfĕrō, -rĕ, transtŭlī, translātŭm; transdūcō, -ĕrĕ, transduxī, transductŭm; *to bring great disgrace*, magnō dedecŏri essĕ; *to bring forth*, părĭō, -ĕrĕ, pĕpĕrī, partŭm; gignō, -ĕrĕ, gĕnŭī, gĕnĭtŭm; *to bring up*, ēdŭcō, -ārĕ; *to bring upon*, consciscō, -ĕrĕ, conscīvī, conscītŭm; *to bring into danger*, in pericŭlŭm mittĕrĕ (mīsī, missŭm); *to bring destruction upon*, interĭtum părārĕ; *to bring word*, nuntĭārĕ, rĕnuntĭārĕ; *to bring into*, indūcō, -ĕrĕ, induxī, inductŭm
(Great) Britain, Brĭtannĭă, -ae (f.)
broad, lātŭs, -ă, -ŭm
a brother, frātĕr, -rĭs (m.)
Brundisium, Brundĭsĭŭm, -ī (n.)
Brutus, Brūtŭs, -ī (m.)
to build, aedĭfĭcō, -ārĕ; exstrŭō, -ĕrĕ, exstruxī, exstructŭm
a bull, taurŭs, -ī (m.)
a burden, ŏnŭs, -ĕrĭs (n.)
burdensome, grăvĭs, -ĕ
a burial, sĕpultūră, -ae (f.)
to burn, ardĕō, -ērĕ, arsī, arsŭm; incendō, -ĕrĕ, incendī, incensŭm
but, sĕd, autĕm, ăt
to butcher, trŭcīdō, -ārĕ
to buy, ĕmō, -ĕrĕ, ēmī, emptŭm
by, ā, ăb (w. abl.)

C.

Cadmus, Cadmŭs, -ī (m.)
Caesar, Caesăr, -ĭs (m.)
calamity, călămĭtās, -ātĭs (f.)
California, Călĭfornĭă, -ae (f.)
Caligula, Călĭgŭlă, -ae (m.)
to call, appellō, -ārĕ; vŏcō, -ārĕ; nōmĭnō, -ārĕ; dīcō, -ĕrĕ, dixī, dictŭm; *to call in*, accĭō, -īrĕ, -īvī, -ītŭm
a calumniator, mălĕdĭcŭs, -ī (m.)
a camel, cămēlŭs, -ī (m.)
Camillus, Cămillŭs, -ī (m.)
a camp, castră, -ōrŭm (n. pl.)
a Campanian, Campānŭs, -ī (m.)
can, possŭm, possĕ, pŏtŭī
Caninius, Cănīnĭŭs, -ī (m.)
Cannae, Cannae, -ārŭm (f. pl.); *of Cannae*, Cannensĭs, -ĕ
capital charge, căpŭt, -ĭtĭs (n.)
the Capitol, Căpĭtōlĭŭm, -ī (n.)
captive, (bellō) captŭs, -ă, -ŭm
to capture, expugnō, -ārĕ
care, cūră, -ae (f.); sollĭcĭtūdō, -ĭnĭs, (f.); *to care little for*, părŭm dēsīdĕrārĕ
careless, neglĕgens, -tĭs
carelessness, neglĕgentĭă, -ae (f.)
to carp at, rodō, -ĕrĕ, rōsī, rōsŭm
to carry, fĕrō, -rĕ, tŭlī, lātŭm; portō, -ārĕ; vĕhō, -ĕrĕ, vexī, vectŭm; *to carry back*, rĕportō, -ārĕ; *to carry before*, praefĕrō, -rĕ, praetŭlī, praelātŭm; *to carry home*, dŏmŭm rĕferrĕ; *to carry on*, gĕrō, -ĕrĕ, gessī, gestŭm
Carthage, Carthāgō, -ĭnĭs (f.)
Carthaginian, Carthāgĭnĭensĭs, - (m.)
to catch, căpĭō, -ĕrĕ, cēpī, captŭm
Catiline, Catĭlīnă, -ae (m.)
a cause, causă, -ae (f.)
to cause, effĭcĭō, -ĕrĕ, effēcī, effectŭm; jŭbĕō, -ērĕ, jussī, jussŭm
cavalry, ĕquĭtātŭs, -ūs (m.); ĕquĭtēs, -ŭm (m. pl.)
a cave, spĕcŭs, -ūs (m.)
to cease, dēsĭnō, -ĕrĕ, dēsĭī, dēsĭtŭm
Cecrops, Cĕcrops, -ŏpĭs (m.)
celebrated, cĕlĕbĕr, -rĭs, -rĕ; praeclārŭs, -ă, -ŭm
a censor, censŏr, -ōrĭs (m.)
Ceres, Cĕrēs, -ĕrĭs (f.)
certain, certŭs, -ă, -ŭm; *a certain one*, quĭdam; *certainly*, certē

a chain, cătēnă, -ae (f.)
by chance, cāsū
change, mūtātĭō, -ōnĭs (f.)
to change, mūtō, -ārĕ
character, mōrēs, -ŭm (m. pl.)
capital charge, căpŭt, -ĭtĭs
to charge, accūsō, -ārĕ; in battle; prōcurrō, -ĕrĕ, prōcurrī, prōcursŭm
Charles, Cărŏlŭs, -ī (m.)
to chastise, castīgō, -ārĕ
cheaper, mĭnōrĭs
cheerful, in cheerful mood, hĭlărĭs, -ĕ
a chest, cistă, -ae (f.)
a chief, princeps, -ĭpĭs (m.)
chiefly, inprīmĭs, maxĭmē
children, lībĕrī, -ōrŭm (m. pl.)
Chilo, Chīlō, -ōnĭs (m.)
to chirrup (of the cricket), cantō, -ārĕ
to choose, ēlĭgō, -ĕrĕ, ēlēgī, ēlectŭm
Christ, Christŭs, -ī (m.); *after, before Christ*, post, ante Christum natum
a Christian, Christĭānŭs, -ī (m.)
Cicero, Cĭcĕrō, -ōnĭs (m.)
Cimon, Cīmōn, -ōnĭs (m.)
Cincinnatus, Cincinnātŭs, -ī (m.).
Cingetorix, Cingĕtŏrix, -īgĭs (m.)
Cisalpine, Cĭsalpīnŭs, -ă, -ŭm
a citadel, arx, -cĭs (f.)
a citizen, cīvĭs, - (m. & f.).
a city, urbs, -ĭs (f.)
city-manners, mōrēs urbānī (m.)
city-people, urbānī (m. pl.)
civil, cīvīlĭs, -ĕ
clamor, clāmŏr, -ōrĭs (m.)
to clank, crĕpō, -ārĕ, -ŭī, -ĭtŭm
Claudius, Claudĭŭs, -ī (m.)
clear, perspĭcŭŭs, -ă, -ŭm
Cleopatra, Clĕŏpătră, -ae (f.)
Clitus, Clītŭs, -ī (m.)
close by, proptĕr (w. acc.)
cloth (of a horse), strătŭm, -ī (n.)
to clothe, vestĭō, -īrĕ
clothing, vestēs, -ĭŭm (f. pl.)
a claud, nūbēs, -ĭs (f.)
a coast, ōră, -ae (f.)
a coat, pallĭŏlŭm, -ī (n.)
a coffer, arcă, -ae (f.)
a cohort, cŏhors, -tĭs (f.)
cold, frīgŭs, -ŏrĭs (n.)
cold, frĭgĭdŭs, -ă -ŭm
Collatinus, Collātīnŭs, -ī (m.)
to collect, collĭgō, -ĕrĕ, collēgī, collectŭm; comportō, -ārĕ
color, cŏlŏr, -ōrĭs (m.)
a coloss, cŏlossŭs, -ī (m.)
to come, vĕnĭō, -īrĕ, vēnī, ventŭm; *to come from*, prŏfĭcīscŏr, -ī, prŏfectŭs sŭm; *to come off*, exĕō, -īrĕ, -ĭī, -ĭtŭm; *to come to the throne*, ad impĕrĭŭm accēdĕrĕ (accessī, accessŭm); *to come up*, aequō, -ārĕ; *night comes on*, vespĕrascĭt
a comet, cŏmētēs, -ae (m.)
a commander, impĕrātŏr, -ōrĭs (m.)
to commingle, admiscĕō, -ērĕ, admiscŭī, admixtŭm
to commit, committō, -ĕrĕ, commīsī, commissŭm
common, commūnĭs, -ĕ; *the commons*, plēbs, -ĭs (f.)
commonly, plērumquĕ
the commonwealth, rēs publĭcă (f.)
a companion, cŏmĕs, -ĭtĭs (m.)
companionship, sŏcĭĕtās, -ātĭs (f.)
company, sŏcĭĕtās, -ātĭs (f.); coetŭs, -ūs (m.); *to keep company*, versŏr, -ārī
to compare, compărō, -ārĕ
in comparison with, prae (w. abl.)
to compel, cōgō, -ĕrĕ, cŏēgī, coactŭm
to complain, quĕrŏr, -ī, questŭs sŭm
to complete, confĭcĭō, -ĕrĕ, confēcī, confectŭm
complexion, cŏlŏr, -ōrĭs (m.)
to comprehend, intellĕgō, -ĕrĕ, intellexī, intellectŭm
to conceal, occultō, -ārĕ; cēlō, -ārĕ
to be concealed, lătĕō, -ērĕ, -ŭī, -ĭtŭm
concerning, dē (w. abl.)
it concerns, intĕrest, rēfert
to conclude, confĭcĭō, -ĕrĕ, confēcī, confectŭm
to condemn, condemnō, -ārĕ; *to condemn to death*, capĭtis damnārĕ
condemning, damnātĭō, -ōnĭs (f.)
a condition, condĭcĭō, -ōnĭs (f.); lŏcŭs, -ī (m.).

to conduct, gĕrō, -ĕrĕ, gessī, gestŭm

to confer on, trĭbŭō, -ĕrĕ, trĭbŭī, trĭbūtŭm; dēfĕrō, -rĕ, dētŭlī, dēlātŭm; *to confer benefits*, beneficĭa conferrĕ (contŭlī, collātŭm)

to confide, fīdō,-ĕrĕ, fīsŭs sŭm; confīdō, -ĕrĕ, confīsŭs sŭm

to congratulate, grātŭlŏr, -ārī

to conquer, vincō,-ĕrĕ,vīcī,victŭm; sŭpĕrō, -ārĕ

a conqueror, victŏr, -ōrĭs (m.); victrix, -īcĭs (f.)

conscience, conscĭentĭă, -ae (f.)

to consider, jūdĭcō, -ārĕ; hăbĕō, -ērĕ; pŭtō, -ārĕ: = *to reflect*, consīdĕrō, -ārĕ; *to be considered*, hăbĕŏr, -ērī; *with consideration*, consīdĕrātē

to consist, constō,-ārĕ,-ĭtī,(no sup.); essĕ w. gen.; contĭnērī w. abl.

a consolation, sōlātĭŭm, -ī (n.)

a conspiracy, conjūrātĭŏ, -ōnĭs (f.)

constant, perpĕtŭŭs, -ă, -ŭm

a consul, consŭl, -ĭs (m.)

consulship, consŭlātŭs, -ūs (m.)

to consult (some one), consŭlĕrĕ ălĭquĕm (consŭlŭī, consultŭm; *to consult the interest of some one*, consŭlĕrĕ ălĭcuī

to contemn, contemnō,-ĕrĕ, contempsī, contemptŭm

contempt, contemptŭs, -ūs (m.)

to contend, contendō, -ĕrĕ, contendī, contentŭm

content, contented, contentŭs,-ă,-ŭm

a contest, certāmĕn, -ĭnĭs (n.)

to continue, permănĕō, -ērĕ, -sī, -sŭm

continuous, contĭnŭŭs, -ă, -ŭm

to contract, contrăhō, -ĕrĕ, contraxī, contractŭm (morbum sibi contrahĕre, *to contract disease*)

contrary, contrārĭŭs, -ă, -ŭm

convenient, accommŏdātŭs, -ă, -ŭm

conveniently, commŏdē

to converse, collŏquŏr, -ī, collŏcūtus sŭm

to convict, convincō, -ĕrĕ, convīcī, convictŭm

to convince, persuādĕō, -ērĕ, persuāsī, persuāsŭm

to be copied, dēscrībendŭs, -ă, -ŭm

copper, cuprŭm, -ī (n.)

Corinth, Cŏrinthŭs, -ī (f.)

a Corinthian, Cŏrinthĭŭs, -ī (m.)

corn, frūmentŭm, -ī (n.)

Cornelia, Cornēlĭă, -ae (f.)

to correct, corrĭgō, -ĕrĕ, correxī, correctŭm

to corrupt, corrumpō, -ĕrĕ, corrūpī, corruptŭm

to cost, essĕ; stō,-ārĕ,stĕtī,stătŭm; constō, -ārĕ, constĭtī, (no sup.)

a council, counsel, consĭlĭŭm, -ī (n.)

to count it a praise, laudī dūcĕrĕ (duxī, ductŭm)

countless, innŭmĕrābĭlĭs, -ĕ

a country, terră, -ae (f.); rĕgĭŏ, -ōnĭs (f.); *one's own country*, pătrĭă, -ae (f.); *the country*, rūs, rūrĭs (n.)

a country house, villă, -ae (f.)

a country man, rustĭcŭs, -ī (m.)

a course, cursŭs, -ūs (m.)

to cover, tĕgō, -ĕrĕ, texī, tectŭm

covered with, plēnŭs, -ă, -ŭm

coward, ignāvŭs, -ă, -ŭm

cowardice, ignāvĭă, -ae (f.)

a crash, frăgŏr, -ōrĭs (m.)

Crassus, Crassŭs, -ī (m.)

craving for more, cŭpīdŏ, -ĭnĭs (f.)

credible, crēdĭbĭlĭs, -ĕ

credit, fĭdēs, -ĕī (f.)

credulity, crēdŭlĭtās, -ātĭs (f.)

to creep, rēpō, -ĕrĕ, repsī, reptŭm; *to creep into*, irrēpĕrĕ

Crete, Crētă, -ae (f.)

a cricket, cīcādă, -ae (f.)

a crime, crīmĕn, -ĭnĭs (n.)

a crocodile, crŏcŏdīlŭs, -ī (m.)

Croesus, Croesŭs, -ī (m.)

crooked, flexŭōsŭs, -ă, -ŭm

a crop, sĕgĕs, -ĕtĭs (f.)

cross, mōrōsŭs, -ă, -ŭm

to cross, transĕō, -īrĕ, -ĭī, -ĭtŭm trājĭcĭō, -ĕrĕ, trājēcī, trājectŭm

the crowd, multĭtūdŏ, -ĭnĭs (f.)

to crowd, convĕnĭō, -īrĕ, convēnī, conventŭm

crowded, frĕquens, -tis
a crown, cŏrōnă, -ae (f.)
cruel, atrox, -ōcis
cruelty, crūdēlĭtās, -ātis (f.)
to crush, opprĭmō, -ĕrĕ, oppressī, oppressŭm
to cry, plōrō, -ārĕ; *to cry out*, clāmō, -ārĕ
a cubit, cŭbĭtŭm, -ī (n.)
a cuckoo, cŭcūlŭs, -ī (m.)
to cull, ēlĭgō, -ĕrĕ, -ēlēgī, ēlectŭm
to cultivate, exercĕō, -ērĕ; cŏlō, -ĕrĕ, cŏlŭī, cultŭm
cultivation, hūmānĭtās, -ātis (f.); cultūră, -ae (f.)
Cumae, Cūmae, -ārŭm (f. pl.)
a cup, pōcŭlŭm, -ī (n.)
a cure, cūrātĭŏ, -ōnis (f.)
to cure, mĕdĕŏr, -ērī, (no perf. & sup.)
Curius, Cŭrĭŭs, -ī (m.)
to curse, mălĕdīcō, -ĕrĕ, mălĕdixī, mălĕdictŭm
custom, mōs, mōrĭs (m.)
Cyrus, Cȳrŭs, -ī (m.)

D.

daily, cŏtīdĭē, quŏtīdĭē
to dance, saltō, -ārĕ
danger, pĕrīcŭlŭm, -ī (n.)
dangerous, pĕrīcŭlōsŭs, -ă, -ŭm
Dareus, Dărēŭs, -ī (m.)
daring, audax, -ācis
a dart, tēlŭm, -ī (n.)
a daughter, fīlĭă, -ae (f.)
David, Dāvīdēs, -is (m.)
a day, dĭēs, -ēī (m. & f.); *every day*, cotīdĭē; *from day to day*, in dĭēs; *the other day*, nūpĕr; *day breaks*, lūcescĭt
daybreak, prima lux
dead, mortŭŭs, -ă, -ŭm; *the dead*, dēfunctī (m. pl.)
dear, cārŭs, -ă, -ŭm; *dearer*, plūrĭs
death, mors, -tis (f.); *violent death*, nex, nĕcĭs (f.); *to condemn to death*, căpĭtĭs damnārĕ
to declare, dēclārō, -ārĕ
to decline, vergō, -ĕrĕ, (no perf. & sup.)
a decoration, ornāmentŭm, -ī (n.)
to decrease, dēcrescō, -ĕrĕ, dēcrēvī, dēcrētŭm
to decree, stătŭō, -ĕrĕ, stătŭī, stătūtŭm
to dedicate, consĕcrō, -ārĕ
a deed, actĭŏ, -ōnis (f.), factŭm, -ī (n.)
deep, altŭs, -ă, -ŭm
to defeat, vincō, -ĕrĕ, vīcī, victŭm
a defect, vĭtĭŭm, -ī (n.)
to defend, dēfendō, -ĕrĕ, dēfendī, dēfensŭm
a defendant, rĕŭs, -ī (m.)
a defender, dēfensŏr, -ōrĭs (m.)
delay, dīlātĭŏ, -ōnis (f.)
to delay, tardō, -ārĕ
to deliberate, dēlībĕrō, -ārĕ
deliberation, dēlībĕrātĭŏ, -ōnis (f.)
to delight, dēlectō, -ārĕ
to deliver, trādō, -ĕrĕ, -ĭdī, -ĭtŭm; lībĕrō, -ārĕ; *to deliver from*, ērĭpĭō, -ĕrĕ, ērĭpŭī, ēreptŭm; *to deliver a speech*, ōrātĭōnĕm hăbērĕ
to demand, poscō, -ĕrĕ, pŏposcī, (no sup.)
to demolish, dīrŭō, -ĕrĕ, -ī, -tŭm; vastō, -ārĕ
demolition, rŭīnae, -ārŭm (f. pl.)
Demosthenes, Dēmosthĕnēs, -is (m.)
dense, densŭs, -ă, -ŭm; crassŭs -ă, -ŭm
to deny, nĕgō, ārĕ
to depart, exĕō, -īrĕ, -iī, -ĭtŭm; discēdō, -ĕrĕ, discessī, discessŭm; prŏfĭciscŏr, -ī, prŏfectŭs sŭm
to deprive, orbō, -ārĕ; prīvō, -ārĕ
to derive, căpĭō, -ĕrĕ, cēpī, captŭm
to describe, dēscrībō, -ĕrĕ, descripsī, descriptŭm
to desert, dēsĕrō, -ĕrĕ, -ŭī, -tŭm
a deserter, transfŭgă, -ae (m.)
deserts, dēsertă, -ōrŭm (n. pl.)
to deserve, mĕrĕō, -ērĕ; mĕrĕŏr, -ērī; *not to deserve*, non satis dignum esse
deserved, deserving, mĕrĭtŭs, -ă, -ŭm
deservedly, mĕrĭtō
a design, consĭlĭŭm, -ī (n.)

desirable, optābĭlĭs, -ĕ; expĕtendŭs, -ă, -ŭm
desire, cŭpĭdĭtās, -ātĭs (f.); cŭpīdŏ, -ĭnĭs (f.)
to desire, optō, -ārĕ; dēsīdĕrō, -ārĕ
desirous, cŭpĭdŭs, -ă, -ŭm
to despair, dēspērō, -ārĕ
to despise, contemnō, -ĕrĕ; contempsī, contemptŭm
destiny, fātŭm, -ī (n.)
to destroy, dēlĕō, -ērĕ, -ēvī; -ētŭm; dīrŭō, -ĕrĕ, -ī, -tŭm; ēvertō, -ĕrĕ, -ēvertī, -ēversŭm; *to destroy by fire*, incendĭo absūmĕrĕ (absumpsī, absumptŭm)
destruction, excĭdĭŭm, -ī (n.)
to detain, rĕtĭnĕō, -ērĕ, rĕtĭnŭī, rĕtentŭm
to detect, dētĕgō, -ĕrĕ, dētexī, detectŭm
to deter, dēterrĕō, -ērĕ
to determine, dēcernō, -ĕrĕ, dēcrēvī, dēcrētŭm; constĭtŭō, -ĕrĕ, constĭtŭī, constĭtūtŭm; stătŭō, -ĕrĕ, stătŭī, statūtŭm
to devastate, pŏpŭlŏr, -ārī
to devise, invĕnĭō, -īrĕ, invēnī, inventŭm
to devote one's self, stŭdĕō, -ērĕ, -ŭī, (no sup.)
to devour, dēvŏrō, -ārĕ
to dictate, dictō, -ārĕ
a dictator, dictātŏr, -ōrĭs (m.)
a die, ālĕă, -ae (f.); tessĕră, -ae (f.)
to die, mŏrĭŏr, -ī, mortŭŭs sŭm
to differ, abhorrĕō, -ērĕ, -ŭī, (no sup.)
it makes no difference, nihil intĕrest
different, dīversŭs, -ă, -ŭm
difficult, diffĭcĭlĭs, -ĕ
to diffuse, diffundō, -ĕrĕ, diffūdī, diffūsŭm
to dig, fŏdĭō, -ĕrĕ, fōdī, fossŭm
dignity, dignĭtās, -ātĭs (f.)
diligence, dīlĭgentĭă, -ae (f.)
diligent, dīlĭgens, -tĭs
to diminish, dīmĭnŭō, -ĕrĕ, dīmĭnŭī, dīmĭnūtŭm
dinner, cēnă, -ae (f.)
Diogenes, Dĭŏgĕnēs, -ĭs (m.)
Diomedon, Dĭŏmĕdōn, -ontĭs (m.)
Dionysius, Dĭŏnȳsĭŭs, -ī (m.)
a disaster, incommŏdŭm, -ī (n.); călămĭtās, -ātĭs (f.)
to disband, dīmittō, -ĕrĕ, dīmīsī, dīmissŭm
to discern, cernō, -ĕrĕ (crēvī, crētŭm)
to discharge, sătisfăcĭō, -ĕrĕ, sătisfēcī, sătisfactŭm (pass. sătisfĭĕrī)
a disciple, discĭpŭlŭs, -ī (m.)
a discipline, disciplīnă, -ae (f.)
to discourse, dissĕrō, -ĕrĕ, -ŭī, -tŭm
to discover, dētĕgō, -ĕrĕ, dētexī, dētectŭm
a disease, morbŭs, -ī (m.)
diseased, aegrōtans, -tĭs
a disgrace, dēdĕcŭs, -ŏrĭs (n.); ignōmĭnĭă, -ae (f.); *to bring great disgrace*, magno dedecōri esse
disgraceful, turpĭs, -ĕ
it disgusts, pĭgĕt, -ērĕ, -ŭĭt
to be disheartened, anĭmos dīmittĕrĕ; (dīmīsī, dīmissŭm)
dishonor, infāmĭă, -ae (f.)
to dismiss, dīmittō, -ĕrĕ, dīmīsī, dīmissŭm
to dispense, cărĕō, -ērĕ, -ŭī, (no sup.)
to display, monstrō, -ārĕ
natural disposition, ingĕnĭŭm, -ī (n.)
to dispute, dispŭtō, -ārĕ
disregard, dērĕlictĭŏ, -ōnĭs (f.)
to dissuade, dissuādĕō, -ērĕ, dissuāsī, dissuāsŭm
at a distance, prŏcŭl
to be distant, ăbessĕ, absŭm, āfŭī; distō, -ārĕ, (no perf. & sup.)
distinction, discrīmĕn, -ĭnĭs (n.)
to distinguish one's self, excellō, -ĕrĕ, (no perf. & sup.)
distinguished, praestans, -tĭs; *to be distinguished*, flōrĕō, -ērĕ, -ŭī, (no sup.)
to disturb, sollĭcĭtō, -ārĕ
to divide, dīvĭdō, -ĕrĕ, dīvīsī, dīvīsŭm
divine, dīvīnŭs, -ă, -ŭm
Divitiacus, Dīvĭtĭăcŭs, -ī (m.)

to do, făcĭō, -ĕrĕ, fēcī, factŭm; *to do evil, ill*, mălĕ ăgĕrĕ (ēgī, actŭm); *to do good*, prōdessĕ, prōsŭm, prōfŭī; *to do right*, recte facĕre; *to do without*, cărĕō,-ērĕ,-ŭī, (no sup.); *nothing to do*, nĭhĭl nĕgōtĭī; *doing wrong*, injūrĭă, -ae (f.)
a doctor, mĕdĭcŭs, -ī (m.)
a dog, cănĭs, - (m.)
a dolphin, delphīnŭs, -ī (m.)
dominion, regnŭm, -ī (n.)
a donkey, ăsellŭs, -ī (m.)
a door, ostĭŭm, -ī (n.)
to double, duplĭcō, -ārĕ
a doubt, dŭbĭŭm, -ī (n.)
to doubt, dŭbĭtō, -ārĕ
doubtful, dŭbĭŭs, -ă, -ŭm
to drag, trăhō, -ĕrĕ, traxī, tractŭm; *to draw after*, ductō, -ārĕ; *to draw enmities upon one's self*, inimicitĭas sibi concĭlĭārĕ; *to draw from*, dētrăhō, -ĕrĕ, dētraxī, dētractŭm; *to draw off*, abdūcō, -ĕrĕ, abduxī, abductŭm; *to draw out*, ēlĭcĭō, -ĕrĕ, -ŭī, -ĭtŭm
a dream, somnĭŭm, -ī (n.)
to dream, somnĭō, -ārĕ
a drink, pōtĭō, -ōnĭs (f.)
to drink, bĭbō, -ĕrĕ, -ī, (no sup.)
to drive, impellō, -ĕrĕ, impŭlī, impulsŭm; *to drive from, out*, pellĕrĕ, dēpellĕrĕ; ējĭcĭō,-ĕrĕ, ējēcī, ējectŭm
a drop, guttă, -ae (f.)
the Druids, Drŭĭdēs, -ŭm (m. pl.)
a drum, tympănŭm, -ī (n.)
to dry, siccō, -ārĕ
a duck, ănăs, -ătĭs (f.)
dull, hĕbĕs, -ĕtĭs
dumb, mūtŭs, -ă, -ŭm
during, pĕr, intĕr (w. acc.)
dust, pulvĭs, -ĕrĭs (m.)
a duty, offĭcĭŭm, -ī (n.)
a dwarf, pūmĭlĭō, -ōnĭs (m. & f.)
to dwell, hăbĭtō, -ārĕ

E.

each, quisquĕ
eager, cŭpĭdŭs, -ă, -ŭm; ăvĭdŭs, -ă, -ŭm
an eagle, ăquĭlă, -ae (f.)
the ear, aurĭs, - (f.)
early in the morning, mānĕ; *right early in the morning*, bĕnĕ mānĕ
to earn, consĕquŏr, -ī, consĕcūtŭs sŭm
the earth, terră, -ae (f.)
an ear-witness, testĭs aurītŭs (m.)
of ease, ōtĭōsŭs, -ă, -ŭm
easily, făcĭlĕ
the east, ŏrĭens, -tĭs (m.)
easy, făcĭlĭs, -ĕ; *easy access*, făcĭlĭtās, ātĭs (f.)
to eat, ĕdō, -ĕrĕ, ēdī, ēsŭm; vescŏr, -ī, (no sup.)
Ebro, Ĭbērŭs, -ī (m.)
an eclipse, dēfectĭō, -ōnĭs (f.); eclipsĭs, - (f)
to eclipse, obscūrō, -ārĕ
to make an edict, ēdīcō, -ĕrĕ, edixī, ēdictŭm
to educate, ēdŭcō, -ārĕ
education, ēdŭcātĭō, -ōnĭs (f.), doctrīnă, -ae (f.)
effeminacy of temper, mollĭtĭēs, -ēī (f.)
effeminate, mollĭs, -ĕ
an egg, ōvŭm, -ī (n.)
Egypt, Aegyptŭs, -ī (f.)
eighty, octōgintā
either..or, aut..aut, vĕl..vĕl
elder, mājŏr nātū: *the elder Cato*, Căto mājŏr
elegance, ēlĕgantĭă, -ae (f.)
the elements of education, ĕlĕmentă (n. pl.) littĕrārum
an elephant, ĕlĕphantŭs, -ī (m.)
eloquence, ēlŏquentĭă, -ae (f.)
eloquent, ēlŏquens, -tĭs: dĭsertŭs, -ă, -ŭm; *eloquently*, ēlŏquentĕr
else, ălĭŭs, -ă, -ŭd: *elsewhere*, ălĭbī
to embalm, condĭō, -īrĕ
to embark, in nāvēs impōnĕrĕ (impŏsŭī, impŏsĭtŭm)
an embassy, lēgātĭō, -ōnĭs (f.)
an emperor, impĕrātŏr, -ōrĭs (m.)
an empire, impĕrĭŭm, -ī (n.)
to employ, adhĭbĕō, -ērĕ: ūtŏr, -ī, ūsŭs sŭm
empty, vădŭs, -ă, -ŭm

to emulate, aemŭlŏr, -āri
an end, fīnĭs, - (m.); *at the end of*, ultĭmŭs, -ă, -ŭm; *to put an end*, fīnĭŏ, -īrĕ
to endeavor, cōnŏr, -āri
endowed with, praedĭtŭs, -ă, -ŭm; partĭceps, -ĭpĭs
to endure, fĕrŏ, -rĕ, tŭlī, lātŭm
enemy, adversārĭŭs, -ī (m.); hostĭs - (m.)
energy, vīrēs, -ĭŭm (f. pl.)
English, Anglĭcŭs, -ă, -ŭm
to engrave, incīdŏ, -ĕrĕ, incīdī, incīsŭm
to enjoy, frŭŏr, -ī, (frŭĭtŭs sŭm)
enjoyment, jūcundĭtās, -ātĭs (f.)
to enlarge, amplĭfĭcŏ, -ārĕ
enmity, ĭnĭmīcĭtĭă, -ae (f.)
enormous, ingens, -tĭs
enough, sătĭs
to enter, intrŏ, -ārĕ
entire, omnĭs, -ĕ
to entreat, pĕtŏ, -ĕrĕ, -īvī, -ītŭm
to enumerate, ēnŭmĕrŏ, -ārĕ
an envoy, ōrātŏr, -ōrĭs (m.)
envy, invĭdĭă, -ae (f.)
to envy, invĭdĕŏ, -ērĕ, invīdī, invīsŭm
Epaminondas, Ĕpămīnondās, -ae (m.)
Ephesus, Ĕphĕsŭs, -ī (f.)
Ephesian, Ĕphĕsĭŭs, -ă, -ŭm
an Epicurean, Ĕpĭcūrēŭs, -ī
equal, păr, părĭs; aequālĭs, -ĕ
equally, aequālĭtĕr, aequē
to eradicate, exstirpŏ, -ārĕ
to erect monuments, monumenta pōnĕrĕ (pŏsŭī, pŏsĭtŭm)
to err, errŏ, -ārĕ
to escape, fŭgĭŏ, -ĕrĕ, fūgī, (no sup.); effŭgĕrĕ
especially, inprīmĭs, maxĭmē, praecĭpŭē
to establish, confirmŏ, -ārĕ *(peace)*; instĭtŭŏ, -ĕrĕ, instĭtŭī, instĭtūtŭm *(laws)*
an estate, praedĭŭm, -ī (n.)
to esteem, aestĭmŏ, -ārĕ; *to esteem lightly*, parvī pendĕrĕ (pĕpendī, pensŭm); *to esteem of more value*, plūrĭs aestĭmārĕ
to estimate, aestĭmŏ, -ārĕ

eternal, aeternŭs, -ă, -ŭm; sempĭternŭs, -ă, -ŭm
eternity, aeternĭtās, -ātĭs (f.)
Euphrates, Euphrātēs, -ĭs (m.)
Europe, Eurōpă, -ae (f.)

F.

far, *by far*, multō, longē; *very far*, longissĭmē; *far away from*, prŏcŭl ā
a farmer, ăgrĭcŏlă, -ae (m.)
fat, pinguĭs, -ĕ
a father, pătĕr, -rĭs (m.)
a fault, culpă, -ae (f.); vĭtĭŭm, -ī (n.)
Faustulus, Faustŭlŭs, -ī (m.)
a favor, făvŏr, -ōrĭs (m.)
to favor, făvĕŏ, -ērĕ, fāvī, fautŭm; indulgĕŏ, -ērĕ, indulsī, indultŭm
fear, mĕtŭs, -ūs (m.); tĭmŏr, -ōrĭs (m.)
a feast, convīvĭŭm, -ī (n.)
a feather, plūmă, -ae (f.)
feeble, imbĕcillŭs, -ă, -ŭm
to feel, sentĭŏ, -īrĕ, sensī, sensŭm
the feelings, ănĭmŭs, -ī (m.)
to feign, sĭmŭlŏ, -ārĕ
a fellow-citizen, cīvĭs, - (m.)
a fellow-soldier, commīlĭtŏ, -ōnĭs (m.)
fertility, fertĭlĭtās, -ātĭs (f.)
fetters, vincŭlă, -ōrŭm (n. pl.)
few, *a few*, paucī, -ae, -ă
fidelity, fĭdēs, -ĕī (f.)
a field, ăgĕr, -rī (m.); rūs, rūrĭs (n.)
the fifth, quintŭs, -ă, -ŭm
a fight, pugnă, -ae (f.)
to fight, dīmĭcŏ, -ārĕ; pugnŏ, -ārĕ; *to fight a battle*, pugnam committĕrĕ (commīsī, commissŭm)
figure, formă, -ae (f.)
to fill up, complĕŏ, -ērĕ, -ēvī, -ētŭm
filled, rĕfertŭs, -ă, -ŭm
to find, rĕpĕrĭŏ, -īrĕ, reppĕrī, rĕpertŭm; *to find (out)*, invĕnĭŏ, -īrĕ, invēnī, inventŭm; investīgŏ, -ārĕ; *to find fault with*, rĕprĕhendŏ, -ĕrĕ, rĕprĕhendī, rĕprĕhensŭm
fine, pulchĕr, -ră, -rŭm

a finger, dĭgĭtŭs, -ī (m.)
to finish, fīnĭō, -īrĕ; perfĭcĭō, -ĕrĕ, perfēcī, perfectŭm; confĭcĭō, -ĕrĕ, confēcī, confectŭm (bellum)
fire, ignĭs, - (m.)
firm, firmŭs, -ă, -ŭm
first, prīmŭs, -ă, -ŭm; *at first*, prīmō, prīmŭm
a fish, piscĭs, - (m.)
to fish, piscŏr, -ārī
fit, ĭdōnĕŭs, -ă, -ŭm
fitted, fitting, aptŭs, -ă, -ŭm
five, quinquĕ
fixed, fixŭs, -ă, -ŭm
a flash of lightning, fulgŭr, -ĭs (n.)
a flatterer, ădūlātŏr, -ōrĭs (m.)
flattering, blandŭs, -ă, -ŭm
a fleece, vellŭs, -ĕrĭs (n.)
a fleet, classĭs, - (f.)
a flight, fŭgă, -ae (f.)
a flock, grex, grĕgĭs (m.)
to flock, conflŭō, -ĕrĕ, confluxī, confluxŭm
to flog, verbĕrō, -ārĕ
to flourish, flōrĕō, -ērĕ, -ŭī, (no sup.)
to flow, flŭō, -ĕrĕ, fluxī, fluxŭm
a flower, flōs, flōrĭs (m.)
a fly, muscă, -ae (f.)
to fly, vŏlō, -ārĕ; *to fly off, away*, āvŏlō, -ārĕ; *to fly = to flee*, fŭgĭō, -ĕrĕ, fūgī, (no sup.)
a foe, hostĭs, - (m.)
one's folks, sŭī, -ōrŭm (m. pl.)
to follow, sĕquŏr, -ī, sĕcūtŭs sŭm; subsĕquŏr, -ī, subsĕcūtŭs sŭm
one's followers, sŭī, -ōrŭm (m. pl.)
following, postĕrŭs, -ă, -ŭm
folly, stultĭtĭă, -ae (f.)
fond, ămans, -tĭs
food, cĭbŭs, -ī (m.)
a fool, stultŭs, -ī (m.)
a foot, pēs, pĕdĭs (m.)
a foot-soldier, pĕdĕs, -ĭtĭs (m.)
a footstep, vestīgĭŭm, -ī (n.)
for, prep. prō (w. abl.); conjunct., nām, ĕnĭm
to forbid, vĕtō, -ārĕ, -ŭī, -ĭtŭm; interdīcō, -ĕrĕ, interdixī, interdictŭm
forces, cōpĭae, -ārŭm (f. pl.)
the forehead, frons, -tĭs (f.)
foreign, ălĭēnŭs, -ă, -ŭm; *a foreigner*, pĕrĕgrīnŭs, -ī (m.)
forever, sempĕr
to forget, oblīviscŏr, -ī; oblītŭs sŭm
to forgive, ignoscō, -ĕrĕ, ignōvī, (no sup.)
to form, effĭcĭō, -ĕrĕ, effēcī, effectŭm
former, prĭŏr, -ŭs; pristĭnŭs, -ă, -ŭm; *in former times*, ōlĭm; *the former victory*, vetus victorĭa
formerly, ōlĭm, quondăm, antĕā
to forsake, dēsĭŭm, dēessĕ, dēfŭī; dēsĕrō, -ĕrĕ, -ŭī, -tŭm
a fort, castellŭm, -ī (n.)
fortified walls, moenĭă, -ŭm (n. pl.)
to fortify, mūnĭō, -īrĕ
fortune, fortūnă, -ae; *good fortune*, fēlīcĭtās, -ātĭs (f.)
to found, condō, -ĕrĕ, -ĭdī, -ĭtŭm
a foundation, fundāmĕntŭm, -ī (n.)
a fountain, fons, -tĭs (m,)
four, quattŭor
frail, cădūcŭs, -ă, -ŭm; frăgĭlĭs, -ĕ
frailty, frăgĭlĭtās, -ātĭs (f.)
a fraud, fraus, -dĭs (f.)
free, lībĕr, -ă, -ŭm; *free from*, văcŭŭs, -ă, -ŭm; *to be free from*, văcārĕ
to free, lībĕrō, -ārĕ
freedom, lībertās, -ātĭs (f.)
to freeze, gĕlascō, -ĕrĕ, (no perf. & sup.)
frequent, crēbĕr, -ră, -rŭm; frĕquens, -tĭs
frequently, crebrō, saepĕ
a friend, ămīcŭs, -ī (m.)
friendship, ămīcĭtĭă, -ae (f.)
a frog, rānă, -ae (f.)
from, ā, ăb, abs (w. abl.); ē, ex, (w. abl.)
frugality, frūgālĭtās, -ātĭs (f.) parsĭmōnĭă, -ae (f.)
fruit, fructŭs, -ūs (m.)
fruitless, irrĭtŭs, -ă, -ŭm
a fugitive, fŭgĭens, -tĭs (m.)
full, plēnŭs, -ă, -ŭm
a funeral pile, rŏgŭs, -ī (m.)
furiously, vĕhĕmentĕr
future, fŭtūrŭs, -ă, -ŭm

G.

gain, lucrŭm, -ī (n.)
to gain, ădĭpiscŏr, -ī, ădeptŭs sŭm; consĕquŏr, -ī, consĕcūtŭs sŭm; *to gain advantage*, fructum capĕrĕ
Gallic, Gallĭcŭs, -ă, -ŭm
a game, lūdŭs, -ī (m.)
gaming, lūsŭs, -ūs (m.)
a garrison, praesĭdĭŭm, -ī (n.)
a gate, portă, -ae (f.)
a Gaul, Gallŭs. -ī (m.)
a gem, gemmă, -ae (f.)
a general, impĕrātŏr, -ōrĭs (m.)
a generation, saecŭlŭm, -ī (n.)
a German, Germānŭs, -ī (m.)
Germany, Germānĭă, -ae (f.)
to get, nanciscŏr, -ī, nactŭs sŭm; *to get one's self*, sibi părārĕ; *to get up*, surgō, -ĕrĕ, surrexī, surrectŭm; *to get ready for war*, bellum părārĕ
a gift, dōs, dōtĭs (f.)
a girl, pŭellă, -ae (f.); virgŏ, -ĭnĭs (f.)
to give, dō, dărĕ, dĕdī, dătŭm; *to give one's self up to*, sē dărĕ (*to work*, labōri); *to give notice*, signĭfĭcō, -ārĕ; *to give as a present*, dōnō dărĕ; *to give up (life)* prōfundō, -ĕrĕ, prōfūdī, prōfūsŭm; *to give orders*, impĕrā ĕ; *to give the command*, praefĭcĭō, -ĕrĕ, praefēcī, praefectŭm; *to give in marriage*, In matrimonĭum dărĕ
of glass, vĭtrĕŭs, -ă, -ŭm
to glide away, cēdō, -ĕrĕ, cessī, cessŭm
a globe, glŏbŭs, -ī (m.)
glorious, dĕcōrŭs, -ă, -ŭm; magnĭfĭcŭs, -ă, -ŭm; *most glorious*, pulcherrĭmŭs, -ă, -ŭm
glory, glōrĭă, -ae (f.)
a gnat, cŭlex, -ĭcĭs (f.)
to go, ĕō, īrĕ, īvī, ĭtŭm: *to go away* ăbĕō, -īrĕ, -iī, -ĭtŭm; *to go* (to war), prŏfĭciscŏr, -ī, prŏfectŭs sŭm: *to go* (to battle), ēgrĕdĭŏr, -ī, ēgressŭs sŭm; *to go to sleep*, obdormiscō,-ĕrĕ, obdormīvī, obdormītŭm
God, dĕŭs, -ī (m.)
a goddess, dĕă, -ae (f.)
gold, aurŭm, -ī (n.)
good, bŏnŭs, -ă, -ŭm; prospĕr, -ă, -ŭm; *very good*, perbŏnŭs; *a good*, bŏnŭm, -ī (n.); *to do good*, prōdessĕ; *good health*, prospĕra valetūdo; *good will*, vŏluntās, -ātĭs (f.), *good qualities*, bŏnă, -ōrŭm (n. pl.)
goodness, bĕnignĭtās, -ātĭs (f.); sanctĭtās, -ātĭs (f.)
a goose, ansĕr, -ĭs (m.)
a goosequill, pennā ansĕrīnā
to govern, impĕrō, -ārĕ; rĕgō, -ĕrĕ, rexī, rectŭm
government, regnŭm, -ī (n.); impĕrĭŭm, -ī (n.), admĭnistrātĭŏ, -ōnĭs (of the world) (f.)
a governor, praesĕs, -ĭdĭs (m.)
Gracchus, Gracchŭs, -ī (m.)
a grain, grānŭm, -ī (n.)
a grandson, nĕpōs, -ōtĭs (m.)
a grandfather, ăvŭs, -ī (m.)
to grant, dō, dărĕ, dĕdī, dătŭm
granted that, ŭt; *granted that not*, nē
a grape, ūvă, -ae (f.)
grateful, grātŭs, -ă, -ŭm
a grave, sĕpulcrŭm, -ī (n.)
great, magnŭs, -ă, -ŭm; *so great*, tantŭs, -ă, -ŭm; *greatest*, summŭs, -ă, -ŭm
Great Britain, Brĭtannĭă, -ae (f.)
greatly, magnŏpĕrĕ
greatness, magnĭtūdŏ, -ĭnĭs (f.)
Greece, Graecĭă, -ae (f.)
greed, cŭpĭdŏ, -ĭnĭs (f.)
Greek, Graecŭs, -ă, -ŭm
grief, dŏlŏr, -ōrĭs (m.), luctŭs, -ūs (m.)
to grieve, dŏlĕō, -ērĕ, -ŭī, ĭtŭm; maerĕō, -ĕrĕ, (no perf. & sup.); *to be grieved*, aegrē pătī (pătĭŏr, passus sŭm); *it grieves*, pĭgĕt, -ērĕ, -ŭĭt
grievous, mĭsĕr, -ă, -ŭm
the ground, terră, -ae (f); lŏcŭs, -ī (m.); hŭmŭs, -ī (f.): *to dig the ground*, rus fŏdĕrĕ
to grow, crescō, -ĕrĕ, crēvī, crētŭm; *to grow old*, sĕnescō, -ĕrĕ; sĕnŭī, (no sup.)

a guard, praesĭdĭŭm, -ī (n.); *to be on one's guard*, căvĕō, -ērĕ, cāvī, cautŭm
a guide, dux, -cĭs (m.)
guilty, noxĭŭs, -ă, -ŭm; sons, -tĭs; *a guilty person*, nŏcens, -tĭs

H.

hail, grandŏ, -ĭnĭs (f.)
it hails, grandĭnat
a hair, căpillŭs, -ī (m.)
the half, dīmĭdĭŭm, -ī (n.)
the hand, mănŭs, -ūs (f.); *at hand*, praestō; *in the hands of*, pĕnĕs (w. acc.); *hand to hand*, commĭnŭs
to hand down, trādō, -ĕrĕ, -ĭdī, -ĭtŭm
a handful, mănŭs, -ūs (f.)
handsome, pulchĕr, -ră, -rŭm
Hannibal, Hannĭbal, -ĭs (m.)
it happens, fit, fĭĕrī, factŭm est; ēvĕnĭt, -īrĕ, ēvēnĭt; contingĭt, -ĕrĕ, contĭgit
happily, fēlīcĭtĕr
happiness, fēlīcĭtās, -ātĭs (f.)
happy, bĕātŭs, -ă, -ŭm; fēlix, -īcĭs
hard, dūrŭs, -ă, -ŭm; *(times)* ardŭŭs, -ă, -ŭm
hard by, juxtā (w. acc.)
hardly, vix; *hardly any*, nullus fere
hardship, lăbŏr, -ōrĭs (m.)
a hare, lĕpŭs, -ŏrĭs
to do harm, nocĕō, -ērĕ
harmless, innoxĭŭs, -ă, -ŭm
Harpagus, Harpăgŭs, -ī (m.)
Hasdrubal, Hasdrŭbăl, -ĭs (m.)
to hasten, prŏpĕrō, -ārĕ
to hatch, exclūdō, -ĕrĕ, exclūsī, exclūsŭm
to hate, ōdī, ōdissĕ
hateful, ŏdĭōsŭs, -ă, -ŭm
hatred, ŏdĭŭm, -ī (n.)
haughtiness, arrŏgantĭă, -ae (f.)
to have, hăbĕō, -ērĕ; *to have to do with*, versŏr, -ārī
he, she, it, ĭs, ĕă, ĭd
the head, căpŭt, -ĭtĭs (n.)
to heal, cūrō, -ārĕ; sānō, -ārĕ
health, vălētūdō, -ĭnĭs (f.); *to be in good health*, vălĕō, -ērĕ

a heap, ăcervŭs, -ī (m.)
to hear, audĭō, -īrĕ
the heart, cŏr, cordĭs (n.); ănĭmŭs, -ī (m.); *a pure heart*, pura mens; *the heart of Germany*, intĭma Germanĭa
heat, călŏr, -ōrĭs (m.)
heaven, caelŭm, -ī (n.)
heavenly, caelestĭs, -ĕ
heavy, grăvĭs, -ĕ
a Hebrew, Hebraeŭs, -ī (m.)
Hector, Hectŏr, -ŏrĭs (m.)
a hedge, saepēs, -ĭs (f.)
an heir, hērēs, -ēdĭs (m.)
help, auxĭlĭŭm, -ī (n.)
to help, adjŭvō, -ārĕ, adjūvī, adjūtŭm; prōdessĕ, prōsŭm, prōfŭī
a Helvetian, Helvētĭŭs, -ī (m.)
a hen, gallīnă, -ae (f.)
hence, indĕ
an herb, herbă, -ae (f.)
hereafter, mox
a hero, hērŏs, -ōĭs (m.)
Herodotus, Hērŏdŏtŭs, -ī (m.)
to hesitate, dŭbĭtō, -ārĕ
hewn, quadrātŭs, -ă, -ŭm
to hide, abscondō, -ĕrĕ, -ĭdī, -ĭtŭm
high, altŭs, -ă, -ŭm; *higher*, supĕrĭŏr, -ŭs
himself, herself, itself, ipsĕ
to hinder, impĕdĭō, -īrĕ; offĭcĭō, -ĕrĕ, offēcī, offectŭm
to hire, condūcō, -ĕrĕ, conduxī, conductŭm
his, her, its, sŭŭs, -ă, -ŭm
a historian, histŏrĭcŭs, -ī (m.)
history, histŏrĭă, -ae (f.)
a hive, alvĕŭs, -ī (m.)
to hold, hăbĕō, -ērĕ; tĕnĕō, -ērĕ, ŭī, tentŭm
a hole, căvernă, -ae (f.)
a holiday, dies festus; *holidays*, fērĭae, -ārŭm (f. pl.)
hollow, concăvŭs, -ă, -ŭm
to (make) hollow, căvō, -ārĕ
a home, dŏmĭcĭlĭŭm, -ī (n.); *at home*, dŏmī; *from home*, dŏmō; *home*, dŏmŭm
Homer, Hŏmērŭs, -ī (m.)
honest, hŏnestŭs, -ă, -ŭm; *honestly*, hŏnestē

honesty, hŏnestās, -ātĭs (f.); hŏnestŭm, -ī (n.)
honey, mel, mellĭs (n.)
an honor, hŏnŏr, -ōrĭs (m.)
to honor, cŏlō, -ĕrĕ, cŏlŭī, cultŭm
honorable, hŏnestŭs, -ă, -ŭm
a hook, hāmŭs, -ī (m.)
a hoop, trŏchŭs, -ī (m.)
hope, spēs, spĕī (f.)
to hope for, spērō, -ārĕ
Horace, Hŏrātĭŭs, -ī (m.)
a horn, cornū, -ūs (n.)
horny, cornĕŭs, -ă, -ŭm
a horse, ĕquŭs, -ī (m.); *horse*, ĕquĭtēs, -ŭm (m. pl.)
on horseback, ĕquĭtans, -tĭs
Hortensius, Hortensĭŭs, -ī (m.)
an hour, hōră, -ae (f.)
a house, dŏmŭs, -ūs (f.); *a noble house*, nōbĭlĭs lŏcŭs
a household thing, rēs dŏmestĭcă
how great, quantŭs, -ă, -ŭm; *how long?* quamdĭū? *how many?* quŏt? *how much?* quantŭm?
however, ăt, tămĕn, vērō; *however much*, quamvīs
huge, ingens, -tĭs
human, hūmānŭs, -a, -ŭm
humanity, hūmānĭtās, -ātĭs (f.)
a hundred, centŭm
hunger, fămēs, -ĭs (f.)
hungry, fămēlĭcŭs, -ă, -ŭm
to be hungry, ēsŭrĭō, -īrĕ, (no perf. & sup.)
to hunt, vēnŏr, -ārī
to hurt, nŏcĕō, -ērĕ; laedō, -ĕrĕ, laesī, laesŭm
hurtful, noxĭŭs, -ă, -ŭm
a husband, mărītŭs, -ī (m.)

I.

I, ĕgŏ, ĕgŏmĕt
ibis, ībĭs, - (f.)
an idea, nōtĭŏ, -ōnĭs (f.)
idle, ignāvŭs, -ă, -ŭm; *idle (hope)*, ĭnānĭs, -ĕ
if, sī
ignorant, ignārŭs, -ă, -ŭm; inscĭŭs, -ă, -ŭm; impĕrītŭs, -ă, -ŭm; *to be ignorant*, ignōrō, -ārĕ
ill, aegrōtŭs, -ă, -ŭm; *to be ill*, aegrōtō, -ārĕ
to illuminate, illustrō, -ārĕ
illustrious, clārŭs, -ă, -ŭm
an image, ĭmāgŏ, -ĭnĭs (f.)
to imitate, ĭmĭtŏr, -ārī
imitation, ĭmĭtātĭŏ, -ōnĭs (f.)
immediately, stătĭm; *immediately after*, sĕcundŭm (w. acc.)
immense, ingens, -tĭs; innŭmĕrābĭlĭs, -ĕ
immortal, immortālĭs, -ĕ
immortality, immortālĭtās, -ātĭs (f.)
impenetrable, impĕnĕtrābĭlĭs, -ĕ
impious, impĭŭs, -ă, -ŭm
to implore, implōrō, -ārĕ
important, grăvĭs, -ĕ
to improve, angĕō, -ērĕ, auxī, auctŭm
incapable of enduring, impătĭens, -tĭs
incited, commōtŭs, -ă, -ŭm
inclined, prōpensŭs, -ă, -ŭm
income, vectīgal, -ālĭs (n.); census, -ūs (m.)
inconsiderately, inconsultō
inconstant, inconstans, -tĭs
to increase, augĕō, -ērĕ, auxī, auctŭm; crescō, -ĕrĕ, crēvī, crētŭm
incredible, incrēdĭbĭlĭs, -ĕ
indeed, quĭdĕm, sānē, prŏfectō
India, Indĭă, -ae (f.)
to indicate, signĭfĭcō, -ārĕ; indĭcō, -ārĕ
indolence, ignāvĭă, -ae; pigrĭtĭă, -ae (f.)
industry, industrĭă, -ae (f.)
to be inflamed, exardescō, -ĕrĕ, exarsī, exarsŭm
to inform, certiōrem făcĕrĕ (fēcī, factŭm)
infrequency, rārĭtās, -ātĭs (f.)
to inhabit, incŏlō, -ĕrĕ, incŏlŭī, incultŭm
an inhabitant, incŏlă, -ae (m.)
to injure, nŏcĕō, -ērĕ; vĭŏlō, -ārĕ (*to violate*)
an injury, injūrĭă, -ae (f.)
injustice, injustĭtĭă, -ae (f.)
inmost, intĭmŭs, -ă, -ŭm

innocence, innŏcentĭă, -ae (f.)
innocent, innŏcens, -tĭs
innumerable, innŭmĕrābĭlĭs, -ĕ
to inquire, quaerō, -ĕrĕ, quaesīvī, quaesītŭm; *to inquire into*, spectō, -ārĕ; rĕquīrō, -ĕrĕ, rĕquīsīvī, rĕquīsītŭm
an inscription, tĭtŭlŭs, -ī (m.)
inspite, nōlens, -tĭs
instance, exemplŭm, -ī (n.); *for instance*, ŭt
to instruct, ērŭdĭō, -īrĕ
an insult, injūrĭă, -ae (f.)
integrity, integrĭtās, -ātĭs (f.)
intercourse, consuētūdŏ, -ĭnĭs (f.)
interest, ūsūră, -ae (f.)
it interests, is the interest, intĕrest
to interpolate, intercălō, -ārĕ
an interpreter, interprĕs, -ĕtĭs (m.)
to intervene, obstō, -ārĕ, obstĭtī, (no sup.)
the intestines, intestīnă, -ōrŭm (n.pl.)
intimacy, fămĭlĭārĭtās, -ātĭs (f.); *in the greatest intimacy*, fămĭlĭārissĭmē
on intimate terms, fămĭlĭārĭtĕr
into, ĭn (w. acc.)
intolerable, intŏlĕrābĭlĭs, -ĕ
to introduce, indūcō, -ĕrĕ, induxī, inductŭm
to invent, invĕnĭō, -īrĕ, invēnī, inventŭm
to invite, invītō, -ārĕ
the Ionians, Iōnĕs, -ŭm (m. pl.)
Ireland, Hĭbernĭă, -ae (f.)
irksome, mŏlestŭs, -ă, -ŭm
iron, ferrŭm, -ī (n.)
an island, insŭlă, -ae (f.); *the Islands of the Blessed*, insŭlae fortunātae
Isocrates, Isŏcrătēs, -ĭs (m.)
an Italian, Itălŭs, -ī (m.)
Italy, Itălĭă, -ae (f.)

J.

a javelin, jăcŭlŭm, -ī (n.)
Jerusalem, Hĭĕrŏsŏlȳmă, -ōrŭm (n. pl.)
a jest, jŏcŭs, -ī (m.); *in jest*, jŏcō
to be joined, adhaerĕō, -ērĕ, adhaesī, adhaesŭm
a journey, itĕr, -ĭnĕrĭs (n.)
joy, gaudĭŭm, -ī (n.)
a judge, jūdex, -ĭcĭs (m.); *a better judge*, pĕrītĭŏr
to judge, jūdĭcō, -ārĕ; *to judge of*, prŏbō, -ārĕ
judgment, jūdĭcĭŭm, -ī (n.); *severe judgment*, sĕvērĭtās, -ātĭs (f.); *according to my judgment*, jūdĭcĭō
Jugurtha, Jŭgurthă, ae (m.)
Julius, Jūlĭŭs, -ī (m.)
Jupiter, Jupitĕr, Jovis (m.)
the jury, jūdĭcēs, -ŭm (m. pl.)
just, justŭs, -ă, -ŭm; *just*, ipsĕ
justice, justĭtĭă, -ae (f.)
justly, mĕrĭtō

K.

to keep, hăbĕō, -ērĕ; rĕtĭnĕō, -ērĕ, -ŭī, rĕtentŭm; *(of animals)* ălō, -ĕrĕ, -ŭī, -ĭtŭm; *to keep one's hands from*, abstĭnērĕ mănŭs; *to keep (a treaty)* servārĕ; *to keep out*, dēpellō, -ĕrĕ, dēpŭlī, dēpulsŭm; *to keep up*, tĕnĕō, -ērĕ, tĕnŭī, tentŭm
a keeper, custōs, -ōdĭs (m.); *to be a keeper*, pascō, -ĕrĕ, pāvī, pastŭm
to kill, interfĭcĭō, -ĕrĕ, interfēcī, interfectŭm
kind, bĕnĕvŏlŭs, -ă, -ŭm
a kind, gĕnŭs, -ĕrĭs (n.); *a kind of*, quīdam
kindness, bĕnĕfĭcĭŭm, -ī (n.)
a king, rex, rēgĭs (m.)
kingly, rēgĭŭs, -ă, -ŭm
a kinsman, prŏpinquŭs, -ī (m.)
a kite, mĭlŭŭs, -ī (m.)
a knight, ĕquĕs, -ĭtĭs (m.)
to know, cognoscō, -ĕrĕ, cognōvī, cognĭtŭm; nōvī, nōvissĕ; *not to know*, ignōrō, -ārĕ; nescĭō, -īrĕ; *one who does not know*, ignārŭs, -ă, -ŭm
knowledge, scĭentĭă, -ae (f.)
known, nōtŭs, -ă, -ŭm

L.

labor, lăbŏr, -ōrĭs (m.)
to labor, lăbōrō, -ārĕ
a Lacedaemonian, Lăcĕdaemŏnĭŭs, -ī (m.)

laden, ŏnustŭs, -ă, -ŭm
lame, claudŭs, -ă, -ŭm
the land, terră, -ae (f.); *in the land of*, ăpŭd (w. acc.); *by land and sea*, terrā marīque; *by land*, pĕdĭbŭs
a land animal, anĭmal terrestre
the language, lingŭă, -ae (f.); vox, vōcĭs (f.)
large, magnŭs, -ă, -ŭm; *at large*, ŭnĭversŭs, -ă, -ŭm
a lark, ălaudă, -ae (f.)
last, ultĭmŭs, -ă, -ŭm; postrēmŭs, -ă, -ŭm; proxĭmŭs, -ă, -ŭm
to last, dūrō, -ārĕ
too late, sērŭs, -ă, -ŭm
lately, nūpĕr
Latin, Lătīnŭs, -ă, -ŭm
the latter, hīc, illă
to laugh, rīdĕō, -ērĕ, rīsī, rīsŭm
law, jūs, jūrĭs (n.); lex, lēgĭs (f.); *civil law*, jūs cīvīlĕ
it is lawful, lĭcĕt, -ŭĭt, -ērĕ
to lay down, pōnō, -ĕrĕ, pŏsŭī, pŏsĭtŭm; *(an office)* sē abdĭcārĕ; *to lay (a way)*, aedĭfĭcārĕ
lazy, pĭgĕr, -ră, -rŭm
lead, plumbŭm, -ī
to lead, dūcō, -ĕrĕ; duxī, ductŭm; *to lead forth, across*, transdūcĕrĕ; *to lead out*, ēdūcĕrĕ; *it would lead to far*, longŭm est; *to lead a life*, vitam ăgĕrĕ (ēgī, -actŭm)
a leader, dux, dŭcĭs (m.)
a leaf, fŏlĭŭm, -ī (n.)
to leap across, transĭlĭō, -īrĕ, -ŭī, (no sup.)
to learn, discō, -ĕrĕ, dĭdĭcī, (no sup.)
learned, doctŭs, -ă, -ŭm; *a learned man*, doctŭs, -ī (m.)
learning, doctrīnă, -ae (f.)
least, mĭnĭmŭs, -ă, -ŭm
to leave (behind), rĕlinquō, -ĕrĕ, rĕlīquī, rĕlictŭm
led on, inductŭs, -ă, -ŭm
left, sinistĕr, -ră, -rŭm
the leg, crūs, crūrĭs (n.)
a legion, lĕgĭō, -ōnĭs (f.)
to lend, commŏdō, -ārĕ
length, longinquĭtās, -ātĭs (f.); *at length*, tandĕm

Lentulus, Lentŭlŭs, -ī (m.)
less, mĭnŏr, -ŭs; adv. mĭnŭs
to lessen, lĕvō, -ārĕ
to let (a house), lŏcō, -ārĕ; *to let slip*, praetermittō, -ĕrĕ, praetermīsī, praetermissŭm
a letter, ĕpĭstŭlă, -ae (f.); littĕrae, -ārŭm (f. pl.); *letters*, littĕrae, -ārŭm (f. pl.)
of Leuctra, Leuctrĭcŭs, -ă, -ŭm
a liar, hŏmŏ mendax (-ĭnĭs -ācĭs)
liberal, lībĕrālĭs, -ĕ
liberality, lībĕrālĭtās, -ātĭs (f.)
a library, biblĭŏthēcă, -ae (f.)
a lictor, lictŏr, -ōrĭs (m.)
a lie, mendācĭŭm, -ī (n.)
to lie, tell a lie, mentĭŏr, -īrī
to lie, jăcĕō, -ērĕ
life, vītă, -ae (f.)
lifeless, exănĭmĭs, -ĕ
light, lux, lūcĭs (f.)
light (not heavy), lĕvĭs, -ĕ
lightning, fulgŭr, -ĭs (n.); *a lightning, (that strikes)*, fulmĕn, -ĭnĭs (n.)
like (adj.), sĭmĭlĭs, -ĕ; instăr; (conjunct.), ŭt, sīcŭt
to like, ămō, -ārĕ; lĭbĕt, -ērĕ
liked, grātĭōsŭs, -ă, -ŭm
a likeness, ĭmāgŏ, -ĭnĭs (f.); effĭgĭēs, -ēī (f.)
likewise, ĭtĕm
a limit, mŏdŭs, -ī (m.)
to limp, clandĭcō, -ārĕ
a line, līnĕă, -ae (f.); *a line of life*, gĕnŭs vītae; *a line of battle*, ăcĭēs, -ēī (f.)
a lion, lĕŏ, -ōnĭs (m.)
Liscus, Liscŭs, -ī (m.)
literary studies, stŭdĭŭm littĕrārŭm
a litter, lectīcă, -ae (f.)
little, paucae res; *a little one*, parvŭlŭs, -ī (m.)
to live, vīvō, -ĕrĕ, vixī, victŭm
living, vīvŭs, -ă, -ŭm; *a living being* ănĭmans, -tĭs (m., f. & n.)
to lodge, hăbĭtō, -ārĕ
lofty, celsŭs, -ă, -ŭm; excelsŭs, -ă, -ŭm
London, Londĭnŭm, -ī (n.)

long, longŭs, -ă, -ŭm; *long = for a long time*, diū
to long for, exoptō, -ārĕ
to look, spectō, -ārĕ; *to look at, to look upon*, intŭĕŏr, -ērī, intŭĭtŭs sŭm; *to look for*, pĕtō, -ĕrĕ, -īvī, -ītŭm; exspectō, -ārĕ; *to look into*, inspĭcĭō, -ĕrĕ, inspexī, inspectŭm; *to look out for*, quaerō, -ĕrĕ, quaesīvī, quaesītŭm; *to look into the future*, fŭtūră prōspĭcĕrĕ
loquacity, lŏquācĭtās, -ātĭs (f.)
to lose, āmittō, -ĕrĕ, āmīsī, āmissŭm
a loss, damnŭm, -ī; jactūră, -ae (f.); intĕrĭtŭs, -ūs (m.)
a lot, sors, -tĭs (f.); *a hard lot*, aspĕră fortūna
lovable, ămābĭlĭs, -ĕ
love, ămŏr, -ōrĭs (m.); *love of letters*, stŭdĭŭm litterārum
to love, ămō, -ārĕ; dīlĭgō, -ĕrĕ, dīlexī, dīlectŭm
a lover (of truth), dīlĭgens, -tĭs
lower, infĕrĭŏr, -ŭs; *lowest*, infĭmŭs, -ă, -ŭm; *low stature*, brĕvĭtās, -ātĭs (f.)
loyalty, fĭdēs, -ĕī (f.)
Lucania, Lūcānĭă, -ae (f.)
Lucanian, Lūcanŭs, -ă, -ŭm
Lucilius, Lūcīlĭŭs, -ī
a lung, pulmŏ, -ōnĭs (m.)
to lure, allĭcĭō, -ĕrĕ, allexī, allectŭm
a lurking place, lătĕbră, -ae (f.)
lust, lĭbīdŏ, -ĭnĭs (f.)
luxury, luxŭrĭă, -ae (f.)
Lycurgus, Lycurgŭs, -ī (m.)
Lydia, Lydĭă, -ae (f.)
a Lydian, Lydŭs, -ī (m.)
lying, mendācĭŭm, -ī (n.)

M.

mad, răbĭōsŭs, -ă, -ŭm
madness, ămentĭă, -ae (f.)
Maecenas, Maecēnās, -ātĭs (m.)
a magistrate, măgistrātŭs, -ūs (m.)
a magnet, magnēs, -ētĭs (m.)
magnetic, magnētĭcŭs, -ă, -ŭm
magnificence, splendŏr, -ōrĭs (m.)
magnificent, magnĭfĭcŭs, -ă, -ŭm
magnitude, magnĭtūdŏ, -ĭnĭs (f.)
to maintain, servō, -ārĕ; hăbĕō, -ērĕ
to make, făcĭō, -ĕrĕ, fēcī, factŭm; effĭcĭō, -ĕrĕ, effēcī, effectŭm; reddō, -ĕrĕ, -ĭdī, -ĭtŭm; *to make of very little account*, mĭnĭmī făcĕrĕ; *to make the acquaintance*, cognoscō, -ĕrĕ, cognōvī, cognĭtŭm; *to make friends*, amīcos compărārĕ; *to make for Italy*, Italĭam petĕrĕ (-īvī, -ītŭm); *to make one's self master of*, pŏtĭŏr, -īrī; *to make bad use*, ăbūtŏr, -ī, abūsŭs sŭm; *to make a present*, dono dărĕ (dĕdī, dătŭm); *to make an edict*, ēdīcō, -ĕrĕ, ēdixī, ēdictŭm; *to make war upon*, bellum inferrĕ (intŭlī, inlātŭm) alicŭi
a maker, architectŭs, -ī (m.)
man, a man, hŏmŏ, -ĭnĭs (m.); vĭr, -ī (m.); *one's men*, sŭī, -ōrŭm (m. pl.)
Manlius, Manlĭŭs, -ī (m.)
manner, mŏdŭs, -ī (m.); *after the manner*, rītū; *amiable manners*, hūmānĭtās, -ātĭs (f.); *in no manner*, nullō mŏdō
many, multŭs, -ă, -ŭm; *as many as possible*, quam plurĭmi
marble, marmŏr, -ĭs (n.)
Marcus, Marcŭs, -ī (m.)
Marius, Mărĭŭs, -ī (m.)
to mark off, descrībō, -ĕrĕ, descripsī, dēscriptŭm
a market, mercātŭs, -ūs (m.)
a marriage, mātrĭmōnĭŭm, -ī (n.)
to marry (of the woman), nūbō, -ĕrĕ, nupsī, nuptŭm
Marseilles, Massĭlĭă, -ae (f.)
a marsh, pălūs, -ūdĭs (f.)
a mass (of gold), vīs, - (f.)
a Massilian, Massĭliensĭs, - (m.)
a master (teacher), măgistĕr, -trī; rectŏr, -ōrĭs; *to make one's self master of*, pŏtĭŏr, -īrī; *master of*, compŏs, -ŏtĭs
material, mātĕrĭēs, -ēī (f.)

it is no matter, nĭhil intĕrest
it matters, intĕrest, rĕfert
a meadow, prātŭm, -ī (n.)
mean, sordĭdŭs, -ă, -ŭm
means, făcultās, -ātĭs (f.); ŏpēs, -ŭm (f. pl.); *by no means*, mĭnĭmē; *by means of*, pĕr (w. acc.)
meanwhile, intĕrĭm
measure, mŏdŭs,-ī(m.); *in a measure*, quodammŏdō
to measure, mētĭŏr, -īrī, mensŭs [sŭm
meat, cărŏ, -nĭs (f.)
Media, Mēdĭă, -ae (f.)
a medicine, mĕdĭcīnă, -ae (f.)
mediocrity, mĕdĭŏcrĭtās, -ātĭs
a meeting, conventŭs, -ūs (m.)
to melt, solvī, sŏlūtŭs sŭm
memory, mĕmŏrĭă, -ae (f.)
mention, mentĭŏ, -ōnĭs (f.)
a merchant, mercātŏr, -ōrĭs (m.)
a merit, virtūs, -ūtĭs (f.)
a metal, mĕtallŭm, -ī (n.)
Metellus, Mĕtellŭs, -ī (m.)
to migrate, mĭgrō, -ārĕ
mild, mītĭs, -ĕ
mildness, mansuētūdŏ, -ĭnĭs (f.)
a mile, milĭārĭŭm, -ī (n.); millĕ passŭum
military service, mīlĭtĭă, -ae (f.)
of Miletus, Mīlēsĭŭs, -ă, -ŭm
milk, lac, lactĭs (n.)
the mind, mens, -tĭs (f.); ănĭmŭs, -ī (m.)
to mind, attendō, -ĕrĕ, attendī, attentŭm; cūrō, -ārĕ
mindful, mĕmŏr, -ĭs
Minos, Mīnōs, -ōĭs (m.)
a mirror, spĕcŭlŭm, -ī (n.)
a miser, ăvārŭs, -ī (m.)
miserable, mĭsĕr, -ă, -ŭm
misery, mĭsĕrĭă, -ae (f.)
misfortune, mălŭm, -ī; călămĭtās, -ātĭs (f.)
to be mistaken, errō, -ārĕ; fallŏr, -ī, falsŭs sŭm
Mithridates, Mithrĭdātēs, -ĭs (m.)
mockery, lūdĭbrĭŭm, -ī (n.)
moderation, abstĭnentĭă, -ae (f.)
modest, mŏdestŭs, -ă, -ŭm; vĕrēcundŭs, -ă, -ŭm
modesty, mŏdestĭă, -ae (f.)
a moment, mōmentŭm, -ī (n.)
money, pĕcūnĭă, -ae (f.)
a month, mensĭs, - (m.)
a monument, mŏnŭmentŭm, -ī (n.)
the moon, lūnă, -ae (f.)
morals, mōrēs, -ŭm (n. pl.)
more, plūs, măgĭs, amplĭŭs; *more or less*, alĭquid
morning (adj.), mātūtĭnŭs, -ă, -ŭm; (subst.), tempus matutĭnum
the morning-star, Lūcĭfĕr, -ī (m.)
the morrow, dĭēs crastĭnus
mortal, mortālĭs, -ĕ
most, plūrĭmŭs, -ă, -ŭm; plērīquĕ, plēraequĕ, plērăquĕ; (adverb), maxĭmē, plūrĭmŭm
a mother, mātĕr, -rĭs (f.); gĕnĕtrīx, -īcĭs (f.)
motion, mōtŭs, -ūs (m.)
a mound, aggĕr, -ĭs (m.)
a mount, *mountain*, mons, -tĭs (m.)
to mourn, lugĕō, -ērĕ, luxī, luctŭm; maerĕō, -ērĕ, (no perf. & sup.)
a mouse, mūs, mūrĭs (m.)
the mouth, ōs, -ōrĭs (n.); *(of a river)*, ostĭă, -ae (f.)
to move, mŏvĕō, -ērĕ, mōvī, mōtŭm; commŏvĕō, -ērĕ, commōvī, commōtŭm; *to move out*, ēgrĕdĭŏr, -ī, ēgressŭs sŭm
much, multŭs, -ă, -ŭm, *very much*, plūrĭmŭs, -ă, -ŭm; permultŭs, -ă, -ŭm; (adv.), valdē; *too much*, nĭmĭs, nĭmĭŭm; *so much as*, tăm.. quăm
to mulct, mulctō, -ārĕ
a multitude, multĭtūdō, -ĭnĭs (f.)
Mummius, Mummĭŭs, -ī (m.)
a murder, caedēs, -ĭs (f.); nex, nĕcĭs (f.)
to murder, occīdō, -ĕrĕ, occīdī, occīsŭm
music, mūsĭcē, -ēs (f.)
mute, mūtŭs, -ă, -ŭm
mutual, mūtŭŭs, -ă, -ŭm
my, mĕŭs, -ă, -ŭm
Myndus, Myndŭs, -ī (f.)
myself, ipsĕ

N.

naked, nūdŭs, -ă, -ŭm
a name, nōmĕn, -ĭnĭs (n.)
to name, nōmĭnō, -ārĕ
Naples, Nĕāpŏlĭs, - (f.)
Narbo, Narbŏ, -ōnĭs (m.)
to narrate, narrŏ, -ārĕ
a narrative, narrātiŏ, -ōnis (f.)
a narrator, scriptŏr, -ōrĭs (m.)
narrow, angustŭs, -ă, -ŭm
a nation, nātĭŏ, -ōnĭs (f.); pŏpŭlŭs, -ī (m.); gens, -tĭs (f.)
natural, nātūrālĭs, -ĕ; *natural disposition*, ingĕnĭŭm, -ī (n.)
nature, nātūră, -ae (f.)
naval, nāvālĭs, -ĕ
nay, immō
near, prŏpinquŭs, -ă, -ŭm; *nearer*, prŏpĭŏr, -ŭs; *nearest*, proxĭmŭs, -ă, -ŭm
near (prepos.), prŏpĕ, proptĕr, juxtā (w. acc.)
nearly, paenē
necessary, nĕcessārĭŭs, -ă, -ŭm; *it is necessary*, ŏpŭs est
necessity, nĕcessĭtās, -ātĭs (f.)
the neck, cervix, -īcĭs (f.); collŭm, -ī (n.)
to be in need, ĕgĕō, -ērĕ, -ŭī, (no sup.)
there is need, ŏpus est, ŏportĕt
needless, sŭpervăcŭŭs, -ă, -ŭm
to neglect, neglĕgō, -ĕrĕ, neglexī, neglectŭm
to neigh to, adhinnĭō, -īrĕ
neighing, hinnītŭs, -ūs (m.)
a neighbor, vīcīnŭs, -ī
neither (of the two), neutĕr, -ră, -rŭm
neither..nor, nequĕ..nequĕ; nĕc..nĕc
Neoptolemus, Nĕoptŏlĕmŭs, -ī (m.)
Nepos, Nĕpōs, -ōtĭs (m.)
Neptune, Neptūnŭs, -ī (m.)
a nerve, nervŭs, -ī (m.)
a nest, nīdŭs, -ī (m.)
Nestor, Nestŏr, -ŏrĭs (m.)
a net, rētĕ, -ĭs (n.)
never, numquăm
nevertheless, tămĕn
new, nŏvŭs, -ă, -ŭm
New York, Ebŏrăcŭm Nŏvŭm (-ī, -ī)
next, proxĭmŭs, -ă, -ŭm; *next to*, (prepos.) sĕcundŭm (w. acc.)
the night, nox, -ctĭs (f.)
a nightingale, luscĭnĭă, -ae (f.)
night-time, tempŭs nocturnŭm
the (river) Nile, Nīlŭs, -ī (m.)
nine, nŏvĕm
ninety, nōnāgintā
the ninth, nōnŭs, -ă, -ŭm
no, no one, nullŭs, -ă, -ŭm; nēmŏ, -ĭnĭs
nobility, nōbĭlĭtās, -ātĭs (f.)
noble, nōbĭlĭs, -ĕ; *the nobles*, vĭrī nōbĭlēs
nobody, nēmŏ, -ĭnĭs
none, nullŭs, -ă, -ŭm
noon, mĕrīdĭēs, -ēī (m.)
nor, nec
the northwind, bŏrĕās, -ae (m.)
the nose, nāsŭs, -ī (m.)
not, nōn; *not only..but also*, nōn sōlŭm ..sĕd ĕtĭăm
nothing, nĭhĭl, nullă res; *nothing to do*, nĭhĭl nĕgōtĭī
to give notice, signĭfĭcō, -ārĕ
to nourish, ălō, -ĕrĕ, ălŭī, ălĭtŭm
noxious, noxĭŭs, -ă, -ŭm
Numa Pompilius, Nŭmă Pompĭlĭŭs (-ae, -ī)
Numantia, Nŭmantĭă, -ae (f.)
a number, nŭmĕrŭs, -ī (m.)
to number, nŭmĕrō, -ārĕ
numberless, innŭmĕrābĭlĭs, -ĕ; innŭmĕrŭs, -ă, -ŭm
Numidia, Nŭmĭdĭă, -ae (f.)
Numitor, Nŭmĭtŏr, -ōrĭs (m.)

O.

an oath, rĕlĭgĭŏ, -ōnĭs (f.)
to obey, pārĕō, -ērĕ; *to obey the laws*, legĭbus ūtī (ūsŭs sŭm)
under obligation, alĭcuī restrictŭs, -ă, -ŭm
obliging, dulcĭs, -ĕ
to obscure, obscūrō, -ārĕ
to observe = to utter, dīcō, -ĕrĕ, dixī, dictŭm; *to observe justice*, justitĭam servārĕ; *to observe a limit*, modum tĕnērĕ (tĕnŭī, tentŭm)

to obtain, părō, -ārĕ; ădĭpiscŏr, -ī, ădeptŭs sŭm
an occupation, nĕgōtĭŭm, -ī (n.)
to occupy, occŭpō, -ārĕ
the ocean, ōcĕănŭs, -ī (m.)
Octavia, Octāvĭă, -ae (m.)
odd, impār, impărĭs
of, ē, ex, dē (w. abl.)
to offer, offĕrō, -rĕ, obtŭlī, oblātŭm; prōpōnō, -ĕrĕ, prōpŏsŭī, prōpŏsĭtŭm: *to offer one's self*, se praebērĕ; *to offer resistance*, rĕsistō, -ĕrĕ, restĭtī, (no sup.)
the office of praetor, praetūrā, -ae (f.)
often, saepĕ
old, vĕtŭs, -ĕrĭs, (to denote the age) nātŭs. -ă, -ŭm; *older*, mājŏr nātū; *old age*, sĕnectŭs, -ūtĭs (f.)
an olive, ŏlĕă, -ae (f.)
Olympia, Olympĭă, -ae (f.)
on, ĭn, dē, sŭpĕr (w. abl.)
once, sĕmĕl; quondăm
one, ūnŭs, -ă, -ŭm; *one..another*, ălĭŭs..ălĭŭs; *the one..the other*, altĕr ..altĕr; *one of two*, altĕr
one-eyed, mŏnŏcŭlŭs, -ă, -ŭm
only, tantŭm
onslaught, impĕtŭs, -ūs (m.)
open, ăpertŭs, -ă, -ŭm
to open, pătĕfăcĭō, -ĕrĕ, pătĕfēcī, pătĕfactŭm (pass. pătĕfĭĕrī); ăpĕrĭō, -īrĕ, -ŭī, ăpertŭm
openly, pălăm
an opinion, opīnĭō, -ōnĭs (f.); sententĭă, -ae (f.)
an opponent, adversārĭŭs, -ī (m.)
an opportunity, occāsĭō, -ōnĭs (f.)
to oppose, oppōnō, -ĕrĕ, oppŏsŭī, oppŏsĭtŭm; rĕluctŏr, -ārī
opposite to, contrā (w. acc.)
to oppress, grăvō, -ārĕ
opulent, ŏpŭlentŭs, -ă, -ŭm
or, aut, sīvĕ, -vĕ (appended), vĕl; *or not*, annōn, necnĕ: *either..or*, aut..aut; vĕl..vĕl; *whether..or*, sīvĕ..sīvĕ
an oracle, ōrācŭlŭm, -ī (n.)
an orator, ōrātŏr, -ōrĭs (m.)
an orchard, pōmārĭŭm, -ī (n.)
to ordain, instĭtŭō, -ĕrĕ, instĭtŭī, instĭtūtŭm
order, ordō, -ĭnĭs (m.); *by order*, jussū; *contrary to orders*, contra imperĭum; *to give orders*, impĕrārĕ
to order, jŭbĕō, -ērĕ, jussī, jussŭm; mandō, ārĕ
the organ of hearing, audītŭs, -ūs (m.)
Orgetorix, Orgĕtŏrix, -īgĭs (m.)
origin, orīgō, -ĭnĭs (f.)
an ornament, dĕcŭs, -ŏrĭs (n.)
Orpheus, Orpheus, Orphĕī (m.)
other, ălĭŭs, -ă, -ŭd; (of two) altĕr, -ă, -ŭm
otherwise, ălĭtĕr, sĕcŭs
I ought, dēbĕō, -ērĕ; *it ought*, ŏportĕt, -ērĕ, -ŭit
our, nostĕr, -ră, -rŭm
out of, ē, ex (w. abl.); extrā (w. acc.)
an outrage, injūrĭă, -ae (f.)
over, sŭpĕr, suprā, trans (w. acc.); *over against*, contrā (w. acc.)
overbearing, sŭperbŭs, -ă, -ŭm
to overcome, prĕmō, -ĕrĕ, pressī, pressŭm; vincō, -ĕrĕ, vīcī, victŭm
overflow, ăbundantĭă, -ae (f.)
to overtake, dēprĕhendō, -ĕrĕ, dēprĕhendī, dēprĕhensŭm; opprĭmō, -ĕrĕ, oppressī, oppressŭm
to overthrow, ēvertō, -ĕrĕ, ēvertī, ēversŭm
to owe, dēbĕō, -ērĕ
an owl, noctŭă, -ae (f.), ŭlŭlă, -ae, (f.)
his, her, its own, sŭŭs, -ă, -ŭm
owner, dŏmĭnŭs, -ī (m.)
an ox, bōs, bŏvĭs (m.)

P.

a page, pāgĭnă, -ae (f.)
pain, dŏlŏr, -ōrĭs (m.)
to paint, pingō, -ĕrĕ, pinxī, pictŭm
a painter, pictŏr, -ōrĭs (m.)
Palatine, Pălātīnŭs, -ă, -ŭm
a parent, părens, -tĭs (m. & f.)
parricide, parrĭcīdĭŭm, -ī (n.)
a part, pars, -tĭs (f.)
partaker, partĭceps, -ĭpĭs
a Parthian, Parthŭs, -ī (m.)

partiality, studĭŭm, -ī (n.)
particular, certŭs, -ă, -ŭm; *most particularly*, maxĭmŏpĕrĕ
to pass away, transĕō, -īrĕ, -iī, -ĭtŭm; intĕrĕō, -īrĕ, -iī, -ĭtŭm; *to pass by* or *on*, praetĕrĕō, -īrĕ, -iī, -ĭtŭm; *to pass into heaven*, pervĕnīrĕ in caelum; *to pass one's life*, vītăm ăgĕrĕ (ēgī, actŭm); *to pass over*, transcendō, -ĕrĕ, transcendī, transcensŭm; transĕō, -īrĕ, -iī, -ĭtŭm; *to pass through*, transmittō, -ĕrĕ, transmīsī, transmissŭm
a passage, ĭtĕr, -ĭnĕrĭs (n.); transĭtŭs, -ūs (m.)
passion, cŭpĭdĭtās, -ātĭs (f.)
past, praetĕrĭtŭs, -ă, -ŭm
a pasture, pascŭŭm, -ī (n.)
paternal, paternŭs, -ă, -ŭm
patience, pătĭentĭă, -ae (f.)
patiently, pătĭentĕr
a patrician, patrĭcĭŭs, -ī (m.)
a patron, patrōnŭs, -ī (m.)
Paul, Paulŭs, -ī (m.)
to pay, pendō, -ĕrĕ, pĕpendī, pensŭm; *to pay one's respects*, sălūtō, -ārĕ
peace, pax, pācĭs (f.); *peace and quiet*, bona pax
a peacock, pāvŏ, -ōnĭs (m.)
a pear, pĭrŭm, -ī (n.)
a peck, mŏdĭŭs, -ī (m.)
peculiar, proprĭŭs, -ă, -ŭm
Pelopidas, Pĕlŏpĭdās, -ae (m.)
Peloponnesian, Pĕlŏponnēsĭăcŭs, -ă, -ŭm
to penetrate, pĕnĕtrō, -ārĕ
a people, pŏpŭlŭs, -ī (m.); *people*, hŏmĭnēs; *other people's*, ălĭēnŭs, -ă, -ŭm; *all people*, cunctī, -ae, -ă
to perceive, sentĭō, -īrĕ, sensī, sensŭm
perchance, fortĕ
perched, sĕdens, -tĭs
perfect, perfectŭs, -ă, -ŭm; *perfectly*, plānē
a Pergamean, Pergamēnŭs, -ī (m.)
Pergamum, Pergămŭm, -ī (n.)
perhaps, forsĭtăn, fortassĕ

Pericles, Pĕrĭclēs, -ĭs (m.)
a period, tempŭs, -ŏrĭs (n.)
to perish, intĕrĕō, -īrĕ, -iī, -ĭtŭm; pĕrĕō, -īrĕ, -iī, -ĭtŭm
a perjury, perjūrĭŭm, -ī (n.)
permission, concessŭs, -ūs (m.)
pernicious, pernĭcĭōsŭs, -ă, -ŭm; *a most pernicious evil*, res perniciosissĭma
a Persian, Persă, -ae (m.)
a person, hŏmŏ, -ĭnĭs (m.); *a guilty person*, nŏcens, -tĭs
perspiration, sūdŏr, -ōrĭs (m.)
to persuade, suādĕō, -ērĕ, suāsī, suāsŭm; persuādĕō, -ērĕ, persuāsī, persuāsŭm
a perusal, lectĭŏ; -ōnĭs (f.)
Philip, Phĭlippŭs, -ī (m.)
a philosopher, phĭlŏsŏphŭs, -ī (m.)
Phoenicia, Phoenīcĭă, -ae (f.)
a physician, mĕdĭcŭs, -ī (m.)
a piece of land, fundŭs, -ī (m.)
to pierce, confŏdĭō, -ĕrĕ, confōdī, confossŭm
piety, pĭĕtās, -ātĭs
a funeral pile, rŏgŭs, -ī (m.)
a pillow, pulvīnŭs, -ī (m.)
a pilot, gŭbernātŏr, -ōrĭs (m.)
a pint, sextārĭŭs, -ī (m.)
pious, pĭŭs, -ă, -ŭm
a pirate, pīrātă, -ae (m.)
to pitch (a camp); pōnō, -ĕrĕ, pŏsŭī, pŏsĭtŭm
a pitchfork, furcă, -ae (f.)
pity, mĭsĕrĭcordĭă, -ae (f.)
a place, lŏcŭs, -ī (m.); *in place of*, lŏcō ălĭcŭjus
to place on, impōnō, -ĕrĕ, impŏsŭī, impŏsĭtŭm
a plague, pestĭs, - (f.)
a plain, campŭs, -ī (m.)
plain, perspĭcŭŭs, -ă, -ŭm
a plan, consĭlĭŭm, -ī (n.)
to plan, mōlĭŏr, -īrī
a planet, plănētă, -ae (f.); *the planet Saturn*, *Venus*, stella Saturni, Venĕris
to plant, sĕrō, -ĕrĕ, sēvī, sătŭm
planted, consĭtŭs, -ă, -ŭm
a Plataean, Plătaeensĭs, - (m.)
a play, lūdŭs, -ī (m.)

to play, lūdō, -ĕrĕ, lūsī, -sŭm
pleasant, jūcundŭs, -ă, -ŭm
pleasing, grātŭs, -ă, -ŭm
pleasure, vŏluptās; -ātĭs (f.); *at pleasure*, ad nutum
plenty, affātĭm
Pliny, Plīnĭŭs, -ī (m.)
a plow, ărātrŭm, -ī (n.)
to plow, ărō, -ārĕ
to pluck, carpō, -ĕrĕ, carpsī, carptŭm; *to pluck out*, ēvellō, -ĕrĕ, ēvellī, ēvulsŭm
plunder, răpīnae, -ārŭm (f. pl.)
to plunder, spŏlĭō, -ārĕ; dīrĭpĭō, -ĕrĕ, dīrĭpŭī, dīreptŭm
to plunge, sē prōjĭcĕrĕ (prōjēcī, projectŭm)
Pluto, Plūtō, -ōnĭs (m.)
a poet, pŏētă, -ae (m.)
a poison, vĕnēnŭm, -ī (n.)
Pompey, Pompējŭs, -ī (n.)
Pontic, Pontĭcŭs, -ă, -ŭm
poor, paupĕr, -ĭs
the populace, plēbs, -ĭs (f.)
a portion of time, tempŭs, -ŏrĭs
a position, lŏcŭs, -ī (m.)
to possess, possĭdĕō, -ērĕ, possēdī, possessŭm
a possession, rēs, -rēī (f.); bŏnŭm, -ī (n.); possessĭō, -ōnĭs (f.)
a post, lŏcŭs, -ī (m.)
poverty, paupertās, -ātĭs (f.)
power, pŏtentĭă, -ae (f.); pŏtestās, -ātĭs (f.); vīs, - (f.); *desire for power*, cŭpĭdĭtās regnī
powerful, pŏtens, -tĭs
powerless to control, impŏtens, -tĭs
a practice, ūsŭs, -ūs (m.); exercĭtātĭō, -ōnĭs (f.)
to practice, exercĕō, -ērĕ; *to practice justice*, virtūtem, justĭtĭam colĕre
praise, laus, -dĭs (f.)
to praise, laudō, -ārĕ
praiseworthy, laude dignŭs, -ă, -ŭm
pray, -năm, tandĕm
to pray, ōrō, -ārĕ
to precede, antĕgrĕdĭŏr, -ī, antĕgressŭs sŭm; antĕcedō, -ĕrĕ, antĕcessī, antĕcessŭm; praecurrō, -ĕrĕ, praecurrī, praecursŭm
a precept, praeceptŭm, -ī (n.)
precious, nōbĭlĭs, -ĕ
a precursor, praenuntĭŭs, -ī (m.)
to predict, praedīcō, -ĕrĕ, praedixī, praedictŭm
to prefer, antĕpōnō, -ĕrĕ, antĕpŏsŭī, anteposĭtŭm
in preference, prae (w. abl.)
premature, immātūrŭs, -ă, -ŭm
in presence of, cŏrăm (w. abl.)
a present, dōnŭm, -ī (n.); *to give as a present*, dōnō dărĕ; dōnārĕ
to present with, dōnō, -ārĕ
to press sorely, urgĕō, -ērĕ, ursī, (no sup.)
pressing, urgens, -tĭs
to prevent, impĕdĭō, -īrĕ; rĕpellō, -ĕrĕ, rĕpŭlī, rĕpulsŭm
of prey, răpax, -ācĭs
Priam, Prĭămŭs, -ī (m.)
a price, prĕtĭŭm, -ī (n.); *at a very high price*, plūrĭmō (pretĭo), *at a low price*, parvō; *at a very low price*, mĭnĭmō; *at the same price*, tantĭdĕm
pride, superbĭă, -ae (f.)
to pride one's self, sŭperbĭō, -īrĕ, (no perf. & sup.)
a priest, săcerdōs, -ōtĭs (m.)
a prince, princeps, -ĭpĭs (m.)
principally, maxĭmē, praecĭpŭē
of printing, tўpŏgrăphĭcŭs, -ă, -ŭm
a prison, carcĕr, -ĭs (m.)
privately, sēcrētō
probable, vērī sĭmĭlĭs, -ĕ
probity, prŏbĭtās, -ātĭs (f.)
to proceed, contendō, -ĕrĕ, contendī, contentŭm
a procession, pompă, -ae (f.)
to proclaim, narrō, -ārĕ
to produce, prōcrĕō, -ārĕ
projecting, prōcērŭs, -ă, -ŭm
prominent, excellens, -tĭs; *to be prominent*, ēmĭnĕō, -ērĕ, -ŭī, (no sup.)
to promise, pollĭcĕŏr, -ērī; prōmittō, -ĕrĕ, prōmīsī, prōmissŭm
prone, prōnŭs, -ă, -ŭm
proper, ĭdōnĕŭs, -ă, -ŭm
property, possessĭō, -ōnĭs (f.); *our property*, nostră, -ōrŭm (n. pl.)

the property of others, ălĭēnă, -ōrŭm, (n. pl.); *one's property*, sŭă, -ōrŭm
Proserpine, Prōserpĭnă, -ae (f.)
prosperity, rēs sĕcundae (f. pl.)
to protect, tŭĕŏr, -ērī
a protector, pătrōnŭs, -ī (m.); pătrōnă, -ae (f.); custōs, -ōdĭs (m.& f.)
proud, sŭperbŭs, -ă, -ŭm
a proverb, prōverbĭŭm, -ī (n.)
to provide, compărō, -ārĕ
provided, dŭm, dummŏdŏ, sī mŏdŏ
providence, prōvĭdentĭă, -ae (f.)
a province, prōvincĭă, -ae (f.)
to provoke, lăcessō, -ĕrĕ, -īvī, -ītŭm
prudence, prūdentĭă, -ae (f.)
prudent, prūdens, -tĭs
Prusias, Prūsĭās, -ae (m.)
public opinion, fāmă, -ae (f.)
Publius, Publĭŭs, -ī (m.)
Punic, Pūnĭcŭs, -ă, -ŭm
to punish, mulctō, -ārĕ
punishment, poenă, -ae (f.); supplĭcĭŭm, -ī (n.)
a pupil, discĭpŭlŭs, -ī (m.)
to purchase, ĕmō, -ĕrĕ, -ēmī, emptŭm
pure, pūrŭs, -ă, -ŭm
on purpose, de industrĭa, consultō
a pursuit, stŭdĭă, -ōrŭm (n. pl.)
to put, pōnō, -ĕrĕ, pŏsŭī, pŏsĭtŭm; *to put to flight*, in fugam vertĕrĕ (vertī, versŭm); *to put an end to*, fīnĭō, -īre; *to put off*, diffĕrō, -rĕ, distŭlī, dīlātŭm; *to put under*, suppōnō, -ĕrĕ, suppŏsŭī, suppŏsĭtŭm
a pyramid, pȳrămĭs, -ĭdĭs (f.)
Pyrrhus, Pyrrhŭs, -ī (m.)
Pythagoras, Pȳthăgŏrās, -ae (m.)
a Pythagorean, Pȳthăgŏrēŭs, -ī (m.)
Pythian, Pȳthĭŭs, -ă, -ŭm

Q.

a quadruped, quădrŭpēs, -ĕdĭs (m.)
a quaestor, quaestŏr, -ōrĭs (m.)
a quail, cŏturnix, -īcĭs (f.)
good qualities, bŏnă, -ōrŭm (n. pl.)
a great quantity, vīs, – (m.)
quarrelsome, jurgĭōsŭs, -ă, -ŭm
from every quarter, undĭquĕ
the question is, quaerĭtur
to question, interrŏgō, -ārĕ
quickly, cĕlĕrĭtĕr
quicksilver, argentŭm vīvŭm (n.)
quite, plānē

R.

a rabbit, cŭnīcŭlŭs, -ī (m.)
a race, gĕnŭs, -ĕrĭs (n.); *the human race at large*, homĭnum genus universum
a race (course), stădĭŭm, -ī (n.)
to rack, vexō, -ārĕ
rain, plŭvĭă, -ae (f.)
a rainbow, arcŭs caelestĭs (-ūs, -)
to raise (an army), compărō, -ārĕ
a rampart, vallŭm, -ī (n.)
rank, ordŏ, -ĭnĭs (m.)
rarely, rārō
rather, pŏtĭŭs, măgĭs
a raven, corvŭs, -ī (m.)
a ray, rădĭŭs, -ī (m.)
to reach, pervĕnĭō, -īrĕ, pervēnī, perventŭm
to read, lĕgō, -ĕrĕ, lēgī, lectŭm
readily, făcĭlĕ
ready, părātŭs, -ă, -ŭm
real, vērŭs, -ă, -ŭm
reality, res vēră
reason, rătĭŏ, -ōnĭs (f.); *for the reason*, īdēō; *for this very reason*, propter id ipsum; *for no other reason*, nulla alĭa de causa
a rebuke, admŏnĭtĭŏ, -ōnĭs (f.)
to recall, rĕvŏcō, -ārĕ
to receive, accĭpĭō, -ĕrĕ, accēpī, acceptŭm
to reckon, nŭmĕrō, -ārĕ
to recognize, cognoscō, -ĕrĕ, cognōvī, cognĭtŭm; (Deum) anĭmadvertō, -ĕrĕ, ănĭmadvertī, ănĭmadversŭm
to recollect, rĕmĭniscŏr, -ī, (no perf.)
recollection, rĕcordātĭŏ, -ōnĭs (f.)
to recommend, commendō, -ārĕ; suādĕō, -ērĕ, suāsī, suāsŭm
a recommendation, commendātĭŏ, -ōnĭs (f.)
a recompense, mercēs, -ēdĭs (f.)

to recover, rĕcŭpĕrō, -ārĕ; (*from disease*) convălescō, -ĕrĕ, convălŭī, convălĭtŭm
recovery, sānĭtās, -ātĭs (f.)
recreation, rĕcrĕātĭō, -ōnĭs (f.)
red, rŭbĕr, -ră, -rŭm
to redeem, rĕdĭmō, -ĕrĕ, rĕdēmī, rĕdemptŭm
a reed-pen, călămŭs, -ī (m.)
to reflect (*an image*), reddō, -ĕrĕ, -ĭdī, -ĭtŭm
reflection, rătĭō, -ōnĭs (f.)
a refuge, rĕfŭgĭŭm, -ī (n.)
to refuse, rĕcūsō, -ārĕ
regard, cūră, -ae (f.)
to regard, existĭmō, -ārĕ
a region, rĕgĭō, -ōnĭs (f.)
to regulate, mŏdĕrŏr, -ārī
to rehearse, commĕmŏrō, -ārĕ
to reign, regnō, -ārĕ
to rejoice, gaudĕō, -ērĕ, gāvīsŭs sŭm; laetŏr, -ārī
to relate, narrō, -ārĕ
a relative, prŏpinquŭs, -ī (m.)
to release, lībĕrō, -ārĕ
religion, rĕlĭgĭō, -ōnĭs (f.)
relying, frētŭs, -ă, -ŭm
to remain, mănĕō,-ērĕ, mansī, mansŭm
a remedy, rĕmĕdĭŭm, -ī (n.)
to remember, rĕcordŏr, -ārī; remĭniscŏr,-ī,(no perf.): mĕmĭnī,-īsse
remembrance, mĕmŏrĭă, -ae (f.); rĕcordātĭō, -ōnĭs (f.)
to remind, mŏnĕō,-ērĕ; commŏnĕō, -ērĕ; admŏnĕō, -ērĕ; commŏnĕfăcĭō, -ĕrĕ, -fēcī, -factŭm
to remove, mĭgrō, -ārĕ
Remus, Rĕmŭs, -ī (m.)
to render service, munus afferrĕ (attŭlī, allātŭm)
renowned, praeclārŭs, -ă, -ŭm
to repair, rĕfĭcĭō, -ĕrĕ, rĕfēcī, rĕfectŭm
it repents, paenĭtĕt, -ērĕ, -ŭĭt
to reply, respondĕō, -ērĕ, responsī, responsŭm
a reproach, opprŏbrĭŭm, -ī (n.)
a repulse, dēpulsĭō, -ōnĭs (f.)
reputation and credit, fāmă et fĭdēs

to request, rŏgō, -ārĕ
at the request, rŏgātū
to require, dēsīdĕrō, -ārĕ; postŭlō, -ārĕ; indĭgĕō, -ērĕ, -ŭī, (no sup.)
resemblance, sĭmĭlĭtūdō, -ĭnĭs (f.)
respect, vĕnĕrātĭō, -ōnĭs (f.); *to pay one's respects*, sălūtō, -ārĕ; *mutual respect*, vĕrēcundĭă, -ae (f.)
to respect, cŏlō, -ĕrĕ, cŏlŭī, cultŭm
respecting, dē (w. abl.)
the rest, cētĕrī, -ae, -ă
to rest, quĭescō, -ĕrĕ, -quĭēvī, quĭētŭm; *to rest on*, nītŏr,-ī, nixŭs sŭm
to restore, rĕpărō,-ārĕ; reddō,-ĕrĕ, -ĭdī, -ĭtŭm: restĭtŭō, -ĕrĕ, restĭtŭī, restĭtūtŭm; rĕfĭcĭō,-ĕrĕ, rĕfēcī, rĕfectŭm
to restrain, arcĕō, -ērĕ; cŏhĭbĕō, -ērĕ; prŏhĭbĕō, -ērĕ
to retain, servō, -ārĕ
to retreat, sē rĕcĭpĭō, -ĕrĕ, rĕcēpī, rĕceptŭm
to return, revertŏr,-ī, revertī (active); rĕdĕō, -īrĕ, -ĭī, -ĭtŭm; rĕcurrō, -ĕrĕ, rĕcurrī, rĕcursŭm; reddō, -ĕrĕ, -ĭdī, -ĭtŭm; *to return thanks*, grātĭās ăgĕrĕ (ēgī, actŭm)
to reveal, indĭcō, -ārĕ; *to reveal one's self*, dētĕgī, detectŭs sŭm
to reverence, rĕvĕrĕŏr, -ērī
a revolution, res novae (f. pl.); *of heavenly bodies*) mōtŭs, -ūs
to revolve, sē convertĕrĕ (convertī, conversŭm)
a reward, mercēs, -ēdĭs (f.); praemĭŭm, -ī (n.)
the Rhine, Rhēnŭs, -ī (m.)
a rhinoceros, rhīnŏcĕrōs, -ōtĭs (m.)
the Rhone, Rhŏdănŭs, -ī (m.)
rich, dīvĕs,-ĭtĭs
riches, dīvĭtĭae, -ārŭm (f. pl.)
to ride, ĕquĭtō, -ārĕ; *to ride a horse*, equo vehī (vectŭs sum)
right (subst.), fās (indecl.); jūs, jūrĭs (n.); *it is right*, fās est

right (adject.), *opposite to left*, dextĕr, -ră, -rŭm; (adverb), rectē; *to do right*, rectē făcĕrĕ; *at the right time*, suo tempŏre
rightly, jūrĕ, rectē
to ripen, mātūrescō, -ĕrĕ, mātūrŭī, (no sup.)
to rise, surgō, -ĕrĕ, surrexī, surrectŭm; ŏrĭŏr, -īrī, ortŭs sŭm
a risk, pĕrīcŭlŭm, -ī (n.)
a river, flūmĕn, -ĭnĭs (n.); flŭvĭŭs, -ī (m.); amnĭs, - (m.)
a road, vĭă, -ae (f.)
to roar, rŭgĭō, -īrĕ
to rob, spŏlĭō, -ārĕ
a rock, rūpēs, -ĭs (f.); saxŭm, -ī (n.)
a rod, virgă, -ae (f.)
Roman, Rōmānŭs, -ă, -ŭm
Rome, Rōmă, -ae (f.)
Romulus, Rōmŭlŭs, -ī (m.)
a roof, tectŭm, -ī (n.)
roomy, amplŭs, -ă, -ŭm
a root, rādix, -īcĭs (f.); stirps, -ĭs (f.)
Roscius, Roscĭŭs, -ī (m.)
a rose, rŏsă, -ae (f.)
round (of the earth), glŏbōsŭs, -ă, -ŭm
to rout, fundō, -ĕrĕ, fūdī, fūsŭm
a route, vĭă, -ae (f.)
to rove about, errō, -ārĕ
ruin, pernĭcĭēs, -ēī (f.)
to ruin, perdō, -ĕrĕ, -ĭdī, -ĭtŭm
rule, impĕrĭŭm, -ī (n.); *rules for acting*, praeceptă ăgendī
to rule, rĕgō, -ĕrĕ, rexī, rectŭm
rumor, fāmă, -ae (f.)
to run, currō, -ĕrĕ, cŭcurrī, cursŭm; *to run away*, aufŭgĭō, -ĕrĕ, aufūgī, (no sup.)
to rush, irrŭō, -ĕrĕ, -ī, (no sup.)

S.

Sabine, Săbīnŭs, -ă, -ŭm
sacred, săcĕr, -ră, -rŭm; sanctŭs, -ă, -ŭm
a sacrifice, săcrĭfĭcĭŭm, -ī (n.)
sad, tristĭs, -ĕ
safe, tūtŭs, -ă, -ŭm; salvŭs, -ă, -ŭm
safety, sălūs, -ūtĭs (f.)
sagacious, săgax, -ācĭs
Saguntine, Săguntīnŭs, -ă, -ŭm
Saguntum, Săguntŭm, -ī (n.)
a sail, vēlŭm, -ī (n.); nāvĭs, - (f.)
to sail, nāvĭgō, -ārĕ
a sailing, nāvĭgātĭō, -ōnĭs (f.)
for the sake of, causā, grātĭā (w. gen.)
Salamis, Sălămĭs, -īnĭs (f.)
salubrious, sălūbĕr, -rĭs, -rĕ
salutary, sălūtārĭs, -ĕ
to salute, sălūtō, -ārĕ
the same, īdĕm, ĕădĕm, ĭdĕm
to sanction, sancĭō, -īrĕ, sanxī, sancītŭm
a Sardini in, Sardŭs, -ī (m.)
to satisfy, sătĭō, -ārĕ
Saturn, Sāturnŭs, -ī (m.); *the planet Saturn*, Sāturni stellă
to save, servō, -ārĕ; lībĕrō, -ārĕ
to say, dīcō, -ĕrĕ, dixī, dictŭm
a saying, dictŭm, -ī (n.)
the scale (of a fish), squāmă, -ae (f.)
scanty, exĭgŭŭs, -ă, -ŭm
a scar, cĭcātrix, -īcĭs (f.)
scarcely, vix
scarceness, rārĭtās, -ātĭs (f.)
scarcity, pēnūrĭă, -ae (f.)
a scholar, discĭpŭlŭs, -ī (m.)
a school, schŏlă, -ae
Scipio, Scīpĭō, -ōnĭs (m.)
a scourge, flăgellŭm, -ī (n.)
to scourge, flăgellīs caedĕrĕ (cĕcīdī, caesŭm)
to scrape together, corrādō, -ĕrĕ, corrāsī, corrāsŭm
a Scythian, Scy̆thă, -ae (m.)
the sea, mărĕ, -ĭs (n.); *over the sea*, mărĭtĭmŭs, -ă, -ŭm
the season, tempŭs anni
the second, sĕcundŭs, -ă, -ŭm; altĕr, -ă, -ŭm; *a second time*, ĭtĕrŭm
secret, occultŭs, -ă, -ŭm
secure, tūtŭs, -ă, -ŭm
to secure, effĭcĭō, -ĕrĕ, effēcī, effectŭm
sedition, sēdĭtĭō, -ōnĭs (f.)
to see, vĭdĕō, -ērĕ, vīdī, vīsŭm
to seek, pĕtō, -ĕrĕ, -īvī, -ītŭm; appĕtō, -ĕrĕ, -īvī, -ītŭm

to seem, vĭdĕŏr, -ērī, vīsŭs sŭm
to seize, căpĭō, -ĕrĕ, cēpī, captŭm
seldom, rārō
to sell, vendō, -ĕrĕ, -ĭdī, -ĭtŭm
Semiramis, Sĕmīrămĭs, -ĭdĭs (f.)
the senate, sĕnātŭs, -ūs (m.)
to send, mittō, -ĕrĕ, mīsī, missŭm; *to send back*, rĕmittō, -ĕrĕ, rĕmīsī, rĕmissŭm
a sense, sensŭs, -ūs (m.)
sensible, prūdens, -tĭs
a sentence, sententĭă, -ae (f.)
to separate, sēpărō, -ārĕ; dīvĭdō, -ĕrĕ, dīvīsī, dīvīsŭm
serene, sĕrēnŭs, -ă, -ŭm
serious, sērĭŭs, -ă, -ŭm
seriously, grăvĭtĕr
a serpent, serpens, -tĭs (m.)
a servant, servŭs, -ī (m.)
a service, ūtĭlĭtās, -ātĭs (f.); *to submit to the service*, ūtĭlĭtātī pārērĕ; mūnŭs, -ĕrĭs (n.); *to render service*, mūnŭs afferrĕ
to set (of the sun) occĭdō, -ĕrĕ, occĭdī, occāsŭm: *to set out*, prŏfĭciscŏr, -ī, prŏfectŭs sŭm
a settlement, sēdēs, -ĭs (f.)
seven, septĕm
several, plūrēs, -ă
severe, sĕvērŭs, -ă, -ŭm; grăvĭs, -ĕ
Severus, Sĕvērŭs, -ī (m.)
shabby, sordĭdŭs, -ă, -ŭm
a shade, *a shadow*, umbră, -ae
shame, dĕdĕcŭs, -ŏrĭs (n.)
shameful, turpĭs, -ĕ; *a shameful deed*, flāgĭtĭŭm, -ī (n.)
a share, portĭŏ, -ōnĭs (f.)
to share, partĭŏr, -īrī
sharp, ācĕr, -rĭs, -rĕ
to sharpen, ăcŭō, -ĕrĕ, ăcŭī, ăcūtŭm
to shave, tondĕō, -ērĕ, tŏtondī, tonsŭm
to shear, tondĕō, -ērĕ, tŏtondī, tonsŭm
to shed, prŏfundō, -ĕrĕ, prŏfūdī, prŏfūsŭm
a sheep, ŏvĭs, - (f.)
to shelter, tĕgō, -ĕrĕ, texī, tectŭm
a shepherd, pastŏr, -ōrĭs (m.)
a shield, clĭpĕŭs, -ī (m.)
to shine, lūcĕō, -ērĕ, luxī, (no sup.)
a ship, nāvĭs, - (f.)
a shore, lītŭs, -ŏrĭs (n.); ōră, -ae (f.)
short, brĕvĭs, -ĕ
a show, spĕcĭēs, -ēī (f.)
to show, monstrō, -ārĕ; ostendō, -ĕrĕ, ostendī, ostensŭm; *to show one's self*, se praebērĕ; se praestārĕ (praestĭtī, no sup.)
to shudder at, horrĕō, -ērĕ, -ŭī, no sup.
to shun, fŭgĭō, -ĕrĕ, fūgī, no sup.
to shut, claudō, -ĕrĕ, clausī, clausŭm
sick, aegĕr, -ră, rŭm; *a sick person*, hŏmō aeger
sickness, morbŭs, -ī (m.)
a side (of a pyramid), lătŭs, -ĕrĭs (n.), pars, -tĭs (f.); *on the other side of*, ultrā (w. acc.); *on this side*, cĭs, citrā (w. acc.)
sight, conspectŭs, -ūs (m.)
a signal, signŭm, -ī (n.)
to be silent, tăcĕō, -ērĕ
silly, rĭdĭcŭlŭs, -ă, -ŭm
silver, argentŭm, -ī (n.)
similar, sĭmĭlĭs, -ĕ
simple, simplex, -ĭcĭs
to sin, peccō, -ārĕ
since, cŭm, quŏnĭăm, quandŏquĭdĕm
sincere, sincērŭs, -ă, -ŭm
to sing, cantō, -ārĕ; cănō, -ĕrĕ, cĕcĭnī, cantŭm
single, singŭlī, -ae, -ă
a sister, sŏrŏr, -ōrĭs (f.)
to sit, sĕdĕō, -ērĕ, sēdī, sessŭm
situate, *situated*, sĭtŭs, -ă, -ŭm; collŏcātŭs, -ă, -ŭm
situation, sĭtŭs, -ūs (m.)
sixty, sexāgintā
size, magnĭtūdŏ, -ĭnĭs (f.)
skill, sōlertĭă, -ae (f.)
skilled, pĕrītŭs, -ă, -ŭm
skillful, pĕrītŭs, -ă, -ŭm
a skin, pellĭs, - (f.)
to skin, dēglūbō, -ĕrĕ, dēglupsī, dēgluptŭm
the sky, *the open sky*, caelŭm, -ī (n.)

a slave, servŭs, -ī (m.); *to be a slave*, serviō, -īrĕ
slavery, servĭtŭs, -ūtĭs (f.)
to slay, trŭcīdō, -ārĕ; nĕcō, -ārĕ; occīdō, -ĕrĕ, occīdī, occīsŭm
sleep, somnŭs, -ī (m.)
to sleep, dormiō, -īrĕ
slender, tĕnuĭs, -ĕ
to slip, ēlābŏr, -ī, ēlapsŭs sŭm
small, parvŭs, -ă, -ŭm; *smaller*, mĭnŏr, -ŭs
smart, callĭdŭs, -ă, -ŭm
smell, ŏdŏr, -ōrĭs (m.)
smoke, fūmŭs, -ī (m.)
snake, anguĭs, - (m.)
to snatch away, ērĭpiō, -ĕrĕ, ērĭpŭī, ēreptŭm
snow, nix, nĭvĭs (f.)
so, tăm, ĭtă, sīc; *so much*, ădĕŏ; *so much as*, tăm..quăm
sober, sobrĭŭs -ă, -ŭm
Socrates, Sōcrătēs, -ĭs (m.)
soft, mollĭs, -ĕ
the soil, sŏlŭm, -ī (n.)
a soldier, mīlĕs, -ĭtĭs (m.); *a foot-soldier*, pĕdĕs, -ĭtĭs (m.); *a horse-soldier*, ĕquĕs, -ĭtĭs (m.)
solitude, sōlĭtūdō, -ĭnĭs (f.)
Solomon, Sălŏmōn, -ōnĭs (m.)
Solon, Sŏlōn, -ōnĭs (m.)
some, nonnullī, -ae -ă,; ălĭquŏt; *some ..others*, ălĭī..ălĭī; *at some time*, ălĭquandō
something, quiddăm
sometime, ălĭquandō
sometimes, nonnumquăm, interdŭm
somewhere else, ălĭcŭbī
a son, fīlĭŭs, -ī (m.)
a song, cantŭs, -ūs (m.)
Sophocles, Sŏphoclēs, -ĭs (m.)
sorrow, dŏlŏr, -ōrĭs (m.); *it causes sorrow*, paenĭtĕt, -ērĕ, -ŭĭt
to be sorry, paenĭtĕt, -ērĕ, -ŭĭt
of what sort, quālĭs, -ĕ
the soul, ănĭmŭs, -ī (m.)
sound, sānŭs, -ă, -ŭm
a source, fons, -tĭs (m.); ŏrīgō, -ĭnĭs (f.)
space, spătĭŭm, -ī (n.)
Spain, Hispānĭă, -ae (f.)
a Spaniard, Spanish, Hispānŭs, -ŭm
to spare, parcō, -ĕrĕ, pĕpercī, (no sup.); tempĕrō, -ārĕ (alĭcui)
a Spartan, Spartānŭs, -ī (m.)
to speak, lŏquŏr, -ī, lŏcūtŭs sŭm; dīcō, -ĕrĕ, dixī, dictŭm
a speech, ōrātĭō, -ōnĭs (f.); vōcēs, -ŭm (f. pl.)
to spend (winter, summer), ăgō, -ĕrĕ, ēgī, actŭm
a spider, ărānĕă, -ae (f.)
the spirit, ănĭmŭs, -ī (m.)
splendid, splendĭdŭs, -ă, -ŭm; magnĭfĭcŭs, -ă, -ŭm
splendor, splendŏr, -ōrĭs (m.)
to spread abroad, dīvulgō, -ārĕ
spring, vēr, -ĭs (n.)
to spring, ŏrĭŏr, -īrī, ortŭs sŭm
to spur on, incĭtō, -ārĕ
to stab, transfīgō, -ĕrĕ, transfixī transfixŭm
stability, stăbĭlĭtās, -ātĭs (f.)
a stage-player, scēnĭcŭs, -ī (m.)
to stain, imbŭō, -ĕrĕ, imbŭī, imbūtŭm
to stamp, imprĭmō, -ĕrĕ, impressī, impressŭm .
to stand, stō, -ārĕ, stĕtī, stătŭm; consistō, -ĕrĕ, constĭtī, (no sup.); *to stand around*, circumstō, -ārĕ, circumstĕtī, (no sup.)
a star, stellă, -ae (f.)
a starling, sturnŭs, -ī (m.)
a state, rēs publĭcă (-ĕī -ae); cīvĭtās, -ātĭs (f.)
to state (one's opinion), dīcō, -ĕrĕ, dixī, dictŭm
stature, stătūră, -ae (f.); *low stature*, brĕvĭtās, -ātĭs (f.)
to stay, mănĕō, -ērĕ, mansī, -sŭm
to steal, fūrŏr, -ārī
a steed, ĕquŭs, -ī (m.)
stiff, rĭgĭdŭs, -ă, -ŭm
still, tămĕn, adhūc, (before a comparat.) ĕtĭăm
a stilus, stĭlŭs, -ī (m.)
to sting, pungō, -ĕrĕ, pŭpŭgī, punctŭm
stock, cōpĭă, -ae (f.)

the stomach, stŏmăchŭs, -ī (m.)
a stone, lăpĭs, -ĭdĭs; *hewn stone*, saxŭm quadrātum
a stork, cicōnĭă, -ae (f.)
a storm, tempestās, -ātĭs (f.)
to storm, vī expugnō, -ārĕ
stormy weather, tempestās, -ātĭs (f.)
a story, histŏrĭă, -ae (f.); *there is a story*, fāmă est
stout, rōbustŭs, -ă, -ŭm
straight, rectŭs, -ă, -ŭm
strength, vīrēs,-ĭŭm (f. pl.); rōbŭr, -ŏrĭs (n.)
stricken in, confectŭs, -ă, -ŭm
to strike (*by lightning*) tangō, -ĕrĕ, tĕtĭgī, tactŭm; *to strike into*, injĭcĭō, -ĕrĕ, injēcī, injectŭm
to strip, nūdō, -ārĕ; spŏlĭō, -ārĕ
to strive, contendō, -ĕrĕ, contendī, contentŭm [tŭm
to strive for, pĕtō, -ĕrĕ, -īvī, -ī-
a stroke, ictŭs, -ūs (m.)
strong, vălĭdŭs, -ă, -ŭm; (*desire*) magnŭs, -ă, -ŭm; *so strong*, tantŭs, -ă, -ŭm
to study, stŭdĕō, -ēre, -ŭī, (no sup.)
stuffed, rĕfertŭs, -ă, -ŭm
to style, appellō, -ārĕ
to subdue, sŭbĭgō, -ĕrĕ, sŭbēgī, sŭbactŭm; sŭpĕrō, -ārĕ; *to subdue in war*, bello dŏmārĕ (-ŭī, -ĭtŭm)
subject, obnoxĭŭs, -ă, -ŭm
to subject, subjĭcĭō, -ĕrĕ, subjēcī, subjectŭm
to subjugate, dŏmō, -ārĕ, -ŭī, -ĭtŭm
to submit (*to the service*), pārĕō,-ērĕ
a successor, successŏr, -ōrĭs (m.)
such, tantŭs, -ă, -ŭm
to suck, sūgō, -ĕrĕ, suxī, suctŭm
to sue (for peace), pĕtō, -ĕrĕ, -īvī, -ītŭm (pācĕm)
the Suebi, Suēbī, -ōrŭm (m. pl.)
to suffer, pătĭŏr, -ī, passŭs sŭm; sĭnō, -ĕrĕ, sīvī, sĭtŭm; *to suffer patiently*, perpĕtĭŏr, -ī, perpessŭs sŭm
not to be sufficient, dĕfĭcĭō, -ĕrĕ, dēfēcī, defectŭm
sufficiently, săt, sătĭs
suitable, opportūnŭs, -ă, -ŭm
suited, aptŭs, -ă, -ŭm; ĭdōnĕŭs, -ă, -ŭm
Sulla, Sullă, -ae (m.)
a sum of money, pĕcūnĭă, -ae (f.)
the summer, aestās, -ātĭs (f.)
summer time, tempus aestīvŭm
to summon, arcessō, -ĕrĕ, -īvī, ītŭm
sumptuous, lautŭs, -ă, -ŭm
superior, sŭpĕrĭŏr, -ŭs
superstition, sŭperstĭtĭŏ, -ōnĭs (f.)
sure, certŭs, -ă, -ŭm
a surname, cognōmĕn, -ĭnĭs (n.)
to surname, cognomĭne appellārĕ
to surrender, trādō, -ĕrĕ, -ĭdī, -ĭtŭm
to surround, circumdō, -ărĕ, -ĕdī, ătŭm
Susa, Sūsă, -ōrŭm (n. pl.)
suspected, suspectŭs, -ă, -ŭm
a swallow, hĭrundŏ, -ĭnĭs (f.)
a swan, cygnŭs, -ī (m.)
sweet, dulcĭs, -ĕ
to swell, intŭmescō, -ĕrĕ, intŭmŭī, no sup.
swiftness, cĕlĕrĭtās, -ātĭs (f.)
to swim, nătō, -ārĕ
a swine, sūs, sŭĭs (f.)
a sword, glădĭŭs, -ī (m.); ferrŭm, -ī; *with fire and sword*, ferro ignīque
Syracuse, Sўrăcūsae, -ārŭm (f.)
Syria, Sўrĭă, -ae (f.)

T.

a table, tăbŭlă, -ae (f.)
Tacitus, Tăcĭtŭs, -ī (m.)
a tail, caudă, -ae (f.)
to take, căpĭō, -ĕrĕ, cēpī, captŭm; *to take from*, abdūcō, -ĕrĕ, abduxī, abductŭm; *to take away*, tollō, -ĕrĕ, sustŭlī, sublātŭm; ērĭpĭō, -ĕrĕ, ērĭpŭī, ēreptŭm; ădĭmō, -ĕrĕ,-ădēmī, ădemptŭm; *to take care*, cūrō, -ārĕ; *to take too little pains*, părŭm lăbōrō, -ārĕ; *to take in marriage*, in mātrĭmōnĭŭm dūcĕrĕ (duxī, ductŭm); *to take prisoner*, căpĭō, -ĕrĕ, cēpī, cap-

tŭm; *to take in sail*, vēlă contrăhĕrĕ (contraxī, contractŭm); *to take the side of*, partēs sĕquī (sĕcūtŭs sŭm); *to take a walk*, ambŭlō, -ārĕ
talent, ingĕnĭŭm, -ī (n.)
a talk, sermō, -ōnĭs (m.)
tall, altŭs, -ă, -ŭm; excelsŭs, -ă, -ŭm; prōcērŭs, -ă, -ŭm
to tame, dŏmō, -ārĕ, -ŭī, -ĭtŭm
Tarquin, Tarquĭnĭŭs, -ī (m.)
Tarraco, Tarrăcō, -ōnĭs (f.)
Tarsus, Tarsŭs, -ī (f.)
to taste, gustō, -ārĕ
to teach, dŏcĕō, -ērĕ, dŏcŭī, doctŭm
a teacher, măgistĕr, -rī (m.)
a tear, lăcrĭmă, -ae (f.)
tedious, longŭs, -ă, -ŭm
tedium, taedĭŭm, -ī (n.)
to tell, narrō, -ārĕ; dīcō, -ĕrĕ, dixī, dictŭm; *to tell a lie*, mentĭŏr, -īrī
a temple, templŭm, -ī (n.)
the temples, tempŏră, -ŭm (n. pl.)
ten, dĕcĕm
tender, tĕnĕr, -ă, -ŭm
the tenth, dĕcĭmŭs, -ă, -ŭm
a territory, fīnēs, -ĭŭm (n. pl.)
terror, terrŏr, -ōrĭs (m.)
to testify, testŏr, -ārī
testimony, testĭmōnĭŭm, -ī (n.)
than, quăm
thankful, grātŭs, -ă, -ŭm
thanks, grātĭae, -ārŭm (f. p.)
that (demonstr.) ĭs, ĕă, ĭd; *that* (conjunct.) ŭt, quō, quŏd; *that not*, nē, quīn, quōmĭnŭs
a thatched roof, culmŭs, -ī (m.)
the..the, quō..ĕō; quantō..tantō
a Theban, Thēbānŭs, -ī (m.)
Thebes, Thēbae, -ārŭm (f. pl.)
Themistocles, Thĕmistŏclēs, -ĭs (m.)
thence, indĕ
there, ĭbī; *there is*, est
therefore, idcircō, ĭgĭtŭr, ĭtăquĕ
Thermopylae, Thermŏpȳlae, -ārŭm, (f. pl.)
thick, crassŭs, -ă, -ŭm
a thief, fūr, -ĭs (m.)
thin, tĕnŭĭs, -ĕ
a thing, rēs, reī (f.)
to think, cōgĭtō, -ārĕ; ŏpīnŏr, -ārī; *to think nothing of*, nĭhĭlī dūcĕrĕ (duxī, ductŭm)
thirst, sĭtĭs, - (f.)
to thirst for, sĭtĭō, -īrĕ
thirsty, sĭtiens, -tĭs; *to be thirsty*, sĭtĭō, -īrĕ
thirty, trīgintā
this, hīc, haec, hŏc
though, ŭt, lĭcĕt, cŭm, etsī
a thousand, millĕ (n.); *a thousand times*, millĭēs
to threaten, mĭnŏr, -ārī
three, trēs; *three hundred*, trēcentī, -ae, -a; *a space of three years*, trĭennĭŭm, -ī
a threshold, līmĕn, -ĭnĭs (n.)
to thrive, prōvĕnĭō, -īrĕ, prōvēnī, prōventŭm; vĭgĕō, -ērĕ, no perf. & sup.
the throat, faux, -cĭs (f.)
a throne, regnŭm, -ī (n.)
through, pĕr (w. acc.)
to throw (into prison), conjĭcĭō, -ĕrĕ, conjēcī, conjectŭm
thunder, tŏnĭtrŭ, -ūs (n.)
to thunder, tŏnō, -ārĕ, -ŭī, -ĭtŭm
Tiberius, Tĭbĕrĭŭs, -ī (m.)
a tiger, tigrĭs, - (f.)
to till (the field), cŏlō, -ĕrĕ, colŭī, cultŭm
time, tempŭs, -ŏrĭs (n.); *in former times*, ōlĭm; *a second time*, ĭtĕrŭm; *in our fathers' time*, apud majōres nostrōs; *at the time when*, tŭm cŭm; *I have no time*, ōtĭŭm non est
timid, tĭmĭdŭs, -ă, -ŭm
Timoleon, Tĭmŏlĕōn, -ontĭs (m.)
it tires, taedĕt, -ērĕ, pertaesŭm est
Titus, Tĭtŭs, -ī (m.)
to, ăd, ĭn (w. acc.)
to-day, hŏdĭē
together, sĭmŭl
toil, lăbŏr, -ōrĭs (m.)
a tomb, sĕpulcrŭm, -ī (n.)
the tongue, linguă, -ae (f.)
too, quŏquĕ, ĕtĭăm; *too* (*great* or *much*), nĭmĭs

the top of a mountain, summŭs mons
torture, crŭcĭātŭs, -ūs (m.)
to torture, crŭcĭō, -ārĕ
toward, ergā, ĭn (w. acc.); *toward the east*, orientem versŭs; *toward winter*, sŭb hĭĕmĕm
a town, oppĭdŭm, -ī (n.)
a townsman, oppĭdānŭs, -ī (m.)
the trade-winds, ĕtēsĭae, -ārŭm (f. pl.)
Trajan, Trājānŭs, -ī (m.)
tranquil, tranquillŭs, -ă, -ŭm
to transact, ăgō, -ĕrĕ, ēgī, actŭm
Transalpine, Transalpīnŭs, -ă, -ŭm
to travel, prŏfĭciscŏr, -ī, prŏfectŭs sŭm
traveling, ĭtĭnĕră, -ŭm (n. pl.)
treachery, prōdĭtĭŏ, -ōnĭs (f.); insĭdĭae, -ārŭm (f. pl.)
a treasury, thēsaurŭs, -ī (m.)
to treat, tractō, -ārĕ; = *to heal*, mĕdĕŏr, -ērī, no perf.
a treaty, foedŭs, -ĕrĭs (n.)
a tree, arbŏr, -ŏrĭs (f.)
a trench, fossă, -ae (f.)
a trial for life, jūdĭcĭŭm căpĭtis
a tribe, gens, -tĭs (f.)
a tribune, trĭbūnŭs, -ī (m.)
tried, expertŭs, -ă, -ŭm
a triumph, trĭumphŭs, -ī (m.)
to triumph, trĭumphō, -ārĕ
Trojan, Trōjānŭs, -ă, -ŭm
trouble, mŏlestĭă, -ae (f.); incommŏdŭm, -ī (n.)
troublesome, mŏlestŭs, -ă, -ŭm
Troy, Trōjă, -ae (f.)
true, vērŭs, -ă, -ŭm
truly, vērē, vērō
a trumpet, tŭbă, -ae (f.)
the trunk (*of a tree*), truncŭs, -ī (m.); (*of an elephant*), prŏboscĭs, -ĭdĭs (f.)
to trust, fīdō, -ĕrĕ, fīsŭs sŭm; confīdō, -ĕrĕ, confīsŭs sŭm; committō, -ĕrĕ, commīsī, commissŭm
truth, vērĭtās, -ātĭs (f.)
to try, cōnŏr, -ārī; expĕrĭŏr, -īrī, expertŭs sŭm; *to try* (*one's luck*) pĕrīclĭtŏr, -ārī
Tullus Hostilius, Tullŭs Hostīlĭŭs (-ī -ī) (m.)
to turn out, ēvādō, -ĕrĕ, ēvāsī, ēvāsŭm
a Tusculan farm, Tuscŭlānŭm, -ī (n.)
a tusk, dens, -tĭs (m.)
twenty, vīgintī
twice, bĭs
a tyrant, tyrannŭs, -ī (m.)

U.

unable to control, impŏtens, -tĭs
unaccustomed, insŏlĭtŭs, -ă, -ŭm
unanimous, ūnănĭmŭs, -ă, -ŭm; *the unanimous decision of the judges*, omnĭum judĭcum sententĭa
it is unbecoming, dēdĕcĕt, -ērĕ, dēdĕcŭit
uncertain, incertŭs, -ă, -ŭm
an uncle, ăvuncŭlŭs, -ī (m.)
uncommon, ĭnūsĭtātŭs, -ă, -ŭm
under, infrā (w. acc.); sŭbtĕr (w. acc.); sŭb (w. acc. or abl.)
to undergo, sŭbĕō, -īrĕ, -ĭī, -ĭtŭm
to understand, intellĕgō, -ĕrĕ, intellexī, intellectŭm; *one who does not understand*, impĕrĭtŭs, -ă, -ŭm
to undertake, suscĭpĭō, -ĕrĕ, suscēpī, susceptŭm
unfavorable, adversŭs, -ă, -ŭm
unfortunate, infēlix, -īcĭs
ungrateful, ingrātŭs, -ă, -ŭm
unhappy, infēlix, īcĭs
a unicorn, mŏnŏcĕrōs, -ōtĭs (m.)
to unite, conjungō, -ĕrĕ, conjunxī, conjunctŭm
the universe, mundŭs, -ī (m.)
unjust, injustŭs, -ă, -ŭm
unjustly, immĕrĭtō, injūrĭā
unless, nĭsĭ
unlike, dissĭmĭlĭs, -ĕ
unquestionably, făcĭlĕ
unsatisfied, ĭnīquŭs, -ă, -ŭm
unshaved, intonsŭs, ă, -ŭm
unto, ergā (w. acc.)
unworthy, indignŭs, -ă, -ŭm
up to, tĕnŭs (w. abl.); usquĕ ăd (w. acc.)

upon, in (w. acc. or abl.); sŭpĕr (w. acc.)
upper, sŭpĕrĭŏr, -ŭs
upright, prŏbŭs, -ă, -ŭm
use, ūsŭs, -ūs (m.); ūtĭlĭtās, -ātĭs (f.)
to use, ūtŏr, -ī, ūsŭs sŭm; = *to be wont* sŏlĕō, -ērĕ, sŏlĭtŭs sŭm; *to use care*, curam adhĭbērĕ
useful, ūtĭlĭs, -ĕ; *to be useful*, prōsŭm, prōdessĕ, prōfŭī
usually, to be translated by sŏlĕō, -ērĕ, sŏlĭtŭs sum, *I am wont*
Utica, Utĭcă, -ae (f.)
utility, ūtĭlĭtās, -ātĭs (f.)
utmost, summŭs, -ă, -ŭm
utterly, pessĭmē

V.

in vain, vainly, frustrā
Valerius, Vălĕrĭŭs, -ī (m.)
valor, virtŭs, -ūtĭs (f.)
to value, aestĭmō, -ārĕ; *highly*, magnī; *very highly*, plūrĭmī
to vanquish, vincō, -ĕrĕ, vīcī, victŭm
vapor, văpŏr, -ōrĭs (m.)
variety, vărĭĕtās, -ātĭs (f.)
various, vărĭŭs, -ă, -ŭm
to vary, vărĭō, -ārĕ
vast, ingens, -tĭs
Veii, Vēiī, -ōrŭm (m. pl.); *the people of Veii*, Vēientēs, -ĭŭm (m. pl.)
Venice, Vĕnĕtĭae, -ārŭm (f. pl.)
Venus, Vĕnŭs, -ĕrĭs (f.)
Verres, Verrēs, -ĭs (m.)
a verse, versŭs, -ūs (m.)
very, valdē; ipsĕ, -ă, -ŭm; *not very*, părŭm
Vespasian, Vespăsĭānŭs, -ī (m.)
a vessel, văs, -ĭs (n.), pl. vāsă, -ōrŭm
Vesuvius, Vĕsŭvĭŭs, -ī (m.)
a vice, vĭtĭŭm, -ī (n.)
victorious, victŏr, -ōrĭs (m.); victrix, -īcĭs (f.)
a victory, victōrĭă, -ae (f.)
to view, spectō, -ārĕ
vigilance, vĭgilantĭa, -ae (f.)
a village, vīcŭs, -ī (m.)
a vine, vītĭs, - (f.)
to violate, vĭŏlō, -ārĕ; laedō, -ĕrĕ, laesī, laesŭm
violence, vīs, - (f.)
violent, vĕhĕmens, -tĭs; *violent death*, nex, -cĭs (f.)
Virgil, Vergĭlĭŭs, -ī (m.)
virtue, virtŭs, -ūtĭs (f.)
virtuous, prŏbŭs, -ă, -ŭm; *virtuously*, cum virtūte
to visit, vīsĭtō, -ārĕ
a voice, vox, vōcĭs (f.)
void, ĭnānĭs, -ĕ; văcŭŭs, -ă, -ŭm; *to be void of*, văcō, -ārĕ
Vulcan, Vulcānŭs, -ī (m.)

W.

a wagon, plaustrŭm, -ī (n.)
to wait for, exspectō, -ārĕ
a waiting-maid, pĕdĭsĕquă, -ae (f.)
to wake, vĭgĭlō, -ārĕ
wakefulness, vĭgĭlantĭă, -ae (f.)
to (take a) walk, ambŭlō, -ārĕ
a walk, ambŭlātĭŏ, -ōnĭs (f.)
a wall, mūrŭs, -ī (n.)
to wander over, pĕrăgrō, -ārĕ
wandering, errans, -tĭs
want, ĭnŏpĭă, -ae (f.)
to want, vŏlō, vellĕ, vŏlŭī; dēsīdĕrō, -ārĕ
war, bellŭm, -ī (n.)
to ward off, rĕpellō, -ĕrĕ, rĕpŭlī, rĕpulsŭm
ware, merx, -cĭs (f.)
warfare, bellŭm, -ī (n.)
warlike, bellĭcōsŭs, -ă, -ŭm; fĕrox, -ōcĭs
warm, călĭdŭs, -ă, -ŭm
to warn, mŏnĕō, -ērĕ
a warning, admŏnĭtĭŏ, -ōnĭs (f.)
to watch, custōdĭō, -īrĕ
a watchman, custōs, -ōdĭs (m.); spĕcŭlātŏr, -ōrĭs (m.)
water, aquă, -ae (f.)
a way, mŏdŭs, -ī (m.); *in every way*, omni ratĭōne; *in the same way*, eādem viā
weak, dēbĭlĭs, -ĕ
wealth, ŏpēs, -ŭm (f. pl.)
wealthy, ŏpŭlentŭs, -ă, -ŭm

weapons, armă, -ōrŭm (n. pl.)
to wear (skins), ūtŏr, -ī, ūsŭs sŭm (pellĭbus)
it wearies, taedēt, -ērĕ, pertaesŭm est
weary, fessŭs, -ă, -ŭm
to weave, texō, -ĕrĕ, -ŭī, -tŭm
a weed, herbă, -ae (f.)
weight, pondŭs, -ĕrĭs (n.); mōlēs, -ĭs (f.)
welcome, jūcundŭs, -ă, -ŭm
welfare, sălūs, -ūtĭs (f.)
a well, pŭtĕŭs, -ī (m.)
well, bĕnĕ; *to be well*, vălĕō, -ērĕ
the west, occĭdens, -tĭs; occāsŭs, -ūs (m.)
whatever, quidquĭd
when, sī, cŭm, quandō
where, ŭbĭ
whether, -nĕ, nŭm, ŭtrŭm; *whether..or*, ŭtrŭm..ăn; sīvĕ..sīvĕ
which, quī, quae, quŏd
while, whilst, dŭm
white, albŭs, -ă, -ŭm
who, quī, quae, quŏd; quĭs, quĭd
whole, tōtŭs, -ă, -ŭm; *the whole world*, orbĭs terrārum
wholesome, sălūbĕr, -rĭs, -rĕ; sălūtārĭs, -ĕ
wholly, prorsŭs
why? cūr, quārĕ, quĭd ?
wicked, imprŏbŭs, -ă, -ŭm; prāvŭs, -ă, -ŭm
a wife, conjux, -ŭgĭs; uxŏr, -ōrĭs (f.)
the will, good will, vŏluntās, -ātĭs (f.); *against one's will*, invītŭs, -ă, -ŭm; *a will*, testāmentŭm, -ī (n.)
willing(ly), lĭbens, lĭbentĕr
to be willing, vŏlō, vellĕ, vŏlŭī; *to be more willing*, mālō, mallĕ, mālŭī
wily, cautŭs, -ă, -ŭm
to win, sibī concĭlĭō, -ārĕ; *to win upon*, blandĭŏr, -īrī
a window, fĕnestră, -ae (f.)
wine, vīnŭm, -ī (n.)
a wing, ālă, -ae (f.); *wings*, pennae, -ārŭm (f. pl.)
winter, hĭems, -ĭs (f.)
wisdom, săpĭentĭă, -ae (f.)
wise, săpĭens, -tĭs
wisely, săpĭentĕr
a wish, vŏluntās, -ātĭs (f.)
to wish for, vŏlō, vellĕ, vŏlŭī
wit, ingĕnĭŭm, -ī (n.)
with, cŭm (w. abl.), ăpŭd (w. acc.),
within, intrā (w. acc.)
without, sĭnĕ (w. abl.); extrā (w. acc.); *to be or do without*, cărĕō, -ērĕ
a witness, testĭs, - (m. & f.)
a wolf, lŭpŭs, -ī (m.)
a woman, mŭlĭĕr, -ĭs (f.); fēmĭnă, -ae (f.)
to wonder at, mīrŏr, -ārī; admīrŏr, -ārī
wonderful, mīrābĭlĭs, -ĕ
to be wont, sŏlĕō, -ērĕ, sŏlĭtŭs sŭm; consŭēvī, -issĕ
a wood, silvă, -ae (f.); *woods*, saltŭs, -ūs (m.)
a word, verbŭm, -ī (n.)
to work, lăbōrō, -ārĕ
the world, mundŭs, -ī (m.); *where in the world*, ubi terrārum
a worm, vermĭs, - (m.)
worse, dētĕrĭŏr, -ŭs
to worship (God), cŏlō, -ĕrĕ, cŏlŭī, cultŭm
worst, dēterrĭmŭs, -ă, -ŭm
to be worth, vălĕō, -ērĕ; *to be worth more*, plūris essĕ
worthy, dignŭs, -ă, -ŭm
a wound, vulnŭs, -ĕrĭs (n.)
wretched, mĭser, -ă, -ŭm
to write, scrībō, -ĕrĕ, scripsī, scriptŭm; *to write on*, inscrībō, -ĕrĕ, inscripsī, inscriptŭm
a writer, scriptŏr, -ōrĭs (m.); auctŏr, -ōrĭs
a wrong, injūrĭă, -ae (f.)

X.

Xanthippe, Xanthippē, -ēs (f.)
Xenocrates, Xĕnŏcrătēs, -ĭs (m.)
Xerxes, Xerxēs, -ĭs (m.)

Y.

to yawn, oscĭtō, -ārĕ
a year, annŭs, -ī (m.)

yes, ĭtă; ĭtă est; ĕtĭăm
yesterday, hĕrī
to yield up, concēdō, -ĕrĕ, concessī, concessŭm
York, Ebŏrăcŭm, -ī (n.)
you, tū, vōs
a young (*of animals*), pullŭs, -ī (m.); *a young man*, ădŭlescens, -tĭs (m.)
your, tŭŭs, -ă, -ŭm; vestĕr, -ră, -rŭm
youth, ădŭlescens, -tĭs (m.); jŭvĕnĭs, - (m.)

Z.

Zama, Zămă, -ae (f.)
zeal, stŭdĭŭm, -ī (n.)
Zopyrus, Zōpȳrŭs, -ī (m.)

www.ingramcontent.com/pod-product-compliance
Lightning Source LLC
Chambersburg PA
CBHW032014010726
47493CB00007B/2402
* 9 7 8 3 3 3 7 3 7 1 1 8 0 *